"Thatch is super shy about PDA," Lyric said. Her laugh was about as authentic as the plastic ficus in the corner.

"I'm not shy." Thatch whirled back to her. And if he *was* with someone like Lyric, he wouldn't be shy at all about showing her some love in front of anyone and everyone.

Her eyes widened, and her lips formed the most perfect O.

Lyric wanted everyone to think they were dating? Fine.

Thatch scooped his arms around her waist and drew her to him, those exotic eyes growing larger with each inch. Before she could respond, he laid one on her—pressing his lips against hers. He wasn't anticipating how soft they would be. Or how the subtle strawberry taste of her lip gloss would hit him. Against his will, he lingered there, holding her, inhaling her, letting his lips lull hers into a rhythm. She didn't push him away. In fact—

Her hands gripped his arms tight,
as if trying to hold him there.

PRAISE FOR SARA RICHARDSON

"With wit and warmth, Sara Richardson creates heartfelt stories you can't put down."

—Lori Foster, *New York Times* bestselling author

"Sara Richardson writes unputdownable, unforgettable stories from the heart."

—Jill Shalvis, *New York Times* bestselling author

"Sara [Richardson] brings real feelings to every scene she writes."

—Carolyn Brown, *New York Times* bestselling author

Betting on a Good Luck Cowboy

"A must-read for cowboy romance fans."

—*Publishers Weekly*

The Summer Sisters

"This is sure to win readers' hearts."

—*Publishers Weekly*

One Night with a Cowboy

"Richardson has a gift for creating empathetic characters and charming small-town settings, and her taut plotting and sparkling prose keep the pages turning. This appealing love story is sure to please." —*Publishers Weekly*

Home for the Holidays

"Fill your favorite mug with hot chocolate and whipped cream as you savor this wonderful holiday story of family reunited and dreams finally fulfilled. I loved it!"
—Sherryl Woods, #1 *New York Times* bestselling author

"You'll want to stay home for the holidays with this satisfying Christmas read."
—Sheila Roberts, *USA Today* bestselling author

First Kiss with a Cowboy

"The pace is fast, the setting's charming, and the love scenes are delicious. Fans of cowboy romance are sure to be captivated." —*Publishers Weekly*, Starred Review

A Cowboy for Christmas

"Tight plotting and a sweet surprise ending make for a delightful Christmas treat. Readers will be sad to see the series end." —*Publishers Weekly*

COUNTING *on a*
COWBOY

COUNTING *on a*
COWBOY

SARA
RICHARDSON

A STAR VALLEY NOVEL

FOREVER
New York Boston

Forever
Hachette Book Group
1290 Avenue of the Americas, New York, NY 10104
read-forever.com
twitter.com/readforeverpub

First Edition: February 2024

Forever is an imprint of Grand Central Publishing. The Forever name and logo are trademarks of Hachette Book Group, Inc.

The publisher is not responsible for websites (or their content) that are not owned by the publisher.

The Hachette Speakers Bureau provides a wide range of authors for speaking events. To find out more, go to hachettespeakersbureau.com or email HachetteSpeakers@hbgusa.com.

Forever books may be purchased in bulk for business, educational, or promotional use. For information, please contact your local bookseller or the Hachette Book Group Special Markets Department at special.markets@hbgusa.com.

ISBNs: 9781538725924 (mass market); 9781538725931 (ebook)

Printed in the United States of America

OPM

10 9 8 7 6 5 4 3 2 1

To P.J. Parker

CONTENT GUIDANCE

Hello, dear readers,

I am thrilled to share the last book in my Star Valley series with you! Lyric and Thatch's story holds a very special place in my heart as these two characters overcome so much pain to embrace hope and healing on their journey to finding love. Before you dive in, I wanted to let you know that this book deals with domestic violence, and some scenes may be difficult to read. I did my best to handle this topic with sensitivity and discretion, but I know it may be intense and triggering for some people. As Lyric deals with her past, she finds her strength through a strong community of friends who support her. In walking through my own hardships, I have come to believe that no one should ever struggle alone. We need each other. If you need to talk, reach out to a friend. Chances are, they need the support as much as you do.

Best wishes,
Sara

CHAPTER ONE

Thatch Hearst climbed up onto the fence next to the snorting bronc named Wild Bill with an adrenaline buzz that had eluded him for far too long. Back in his SEAL days, he used to get a rush almost daily, but ever since moving to Star Valley, Wyoming, a few years ago to help out on his fallen comrade's ranch, a true adrenaline rush had been harder to come by.

"All right, Hearst." Kirby Leatherman gazed up from his post next to the gate at the front of the bucking chute. Though now slightly hunched with arthritis, the old cowboy had once been a saddle bronc riding legend, and he never let anyone forget it. "You ready for this?" Amusement gleamed in his faded brown eyes, and the leathered skin around his mouth pulled into a tight smirk. Even though he was the best trainer in these parts, the man always loved watching amateur cowboys get tossed into the dirt.

"Just about ready." This might only be a training run

to prepare for the big event at the Star Valley Rodeo Days in just over a month, but Thatch had to treat it like the real deal. He'd already made good enough scores in two qualifying events, but his showing wouldn't be enough to win him the purse—or any respect. And maybe the latter was even more important, considering his family would be attending.

"Remember, hotshot—three and a half finger lengths on the bronc rein. And don't do any of that rocking you seem so fond of. You gotta stay in control to score points." Kirby always reminded him how far he had to go. He was a gruff old ass, but Thatch had waited months to get a spot in his training schedule, so he never complained about Kirby's methods. All he wanted was results.

"All right. I'm going." He wound his hand around the bronc rein and slid onto the saddle. Wild Bill thrashed beneath him, and Kirby released the gate to set him free.

Thatch's head immediately jerked back. That first jump always threw him off. But he recovered and raised his left arm. Flashes of the arena passed in front of him— the rafters above, the dirt below, the fence—

"Stop turning your toes out!" Kirby barked. "And lock it down, Hearst. You look like a rag doll out there."

He *was* trying to lock it down. Thatch gritted his teeth, attempting to move in sync with the animal, but Wild Bill jackknifed and sent him flying. He hit the ground and rolled.

"Damn it." Had he even stayed on for eight seconds? If he couldn't meet the minimum time requirement, style would mean nothing.

While one of Kirby's assistants corralled Wild Bill, Thatch scrambled to his feet and retrieved his hat from the dirt a few feet away, shaking the dust off. "I don't understand." He met his trainer by the fence. "I can't get past this." Every time he rode, it was the same thing—he'd manage to stay on the bronc's back long enough, but there was no finesse. Which meant he'd never win anything.

"You're too stiff up there," Kirby informed him for probably the fiftieth time. "The best riders know how to move with the animal. You want to score high? You have to work the spurs and make it look easy."

"I know. I've watched hours of video." But he couldn't make his body cooperate once that bronc left the chute. Instead of finding a rhythm, his body tensed all over and locked up on him. "How did you do it?" he demanded. Wasn't that why he'd hired the great Kirby Leatherman in the first place? To learn all his secrets?

"Hell, I dunno. I just figured it out." His tone always kept a sharp edge, so Thatch didn't hold it against him.

"Well, what can I do? I have a month to figure this out." He had just over a month before his entire family came to watch him ride, and he couldn't make a fool of himself. Not in front of his brother. Not after what had happened between them. This was Thatch's chance for redemption—to prove he wasn't the fool Liam had made him out to be when he'd swooped in and stolen Thatch's fiancée, Sienna, marrying her.

Kirby leaned an elbow against the fence. "Back in my day, the judges weren't as strict on form. We got away with powering through."

"That doesn't help me much." He could power through all day. He was in the best shape of his life, even compared with his past SEAL training. "I need to make my riding look more refined." And that was the one thing he didn't know how to do.

Kirby straightened and led him out through the gate, stopping at the bench that held Thatch's bag. "There're all kinds of alternative methods now. A lot of the young guys are doing yoga to make them more flexible." He snorted like one of the broncs. "You wouldn't've ever caught me pushing my ass up in the air like that, but whatever."

Thatch pulled off his gloves and tossed them into his bag. "I know a yoga instructor." He hadn't seen Lyric much lately. She'd been busy with the clinic she'd opened up with her friend Kyra in Star Valley—teaching yoga and taking holistic health clients. There was another reason he'd been avoiding her for the past few months, too, but he didn't want to think about that right now. "I guess I could sign up for a couple of sessions with her." Not that he wanted his two best friends and ex-colleagues to ever get wind of the fact he'd resorted to doing yoga. Silas and Aiden were more like brothers than friends, and they'd never let him hear the end of it.

"Maybe it wouldn't hurt to give the yoga a go," Kirby grumbled. "Other than that, I'm out of suggestions." The man walked away. "I gotta take a leak. I'll see you next time."

"Yeah. See you soon." While Kirby might not be able to help him find his inner ballerina, Thatch still needed the man's arena and training facility so he could continue to log hours on the back of a bronc before the big competition. He needed as much practice as possible to make his riding click.

He couldn't let his brother watch him fail.

After removing all his protective gear, he lugged

his bag to his truck outside and tossed it into the back before climbing into the driver's seat, where he hesitated. When he'd asked Lyric out at the Christmas party several months back, she'd made it pretty clear she didn't want to hang out with him. *I'm not dating right now*, she'd said. So he'd backed off. He knew how to read between the lines. She wasn't interested in him, and he had no desire to keep trying to win her over—been there, done that in the past, and the effort had crashed and burned when his fiancée had married Liam.

Anyway.

Heaving a sigh, he started up the engine. The fact was, he knew when to admit he needed help, and Lyric was the only one who could give him some pointers when it came to finesse. He had to ask her. He had no choice. They didn't have to get along or even like each other...

Yeah, right.

He'd tried to force the woman out of his thoughts, and that hadn't gotten him anywhere. But he needed her expertise. Now he just had to decide how to ask her for it.

He backed out of the parking spot and turned onto the rutted dirt road that wound through an aspen grove before leaving Kirby's two-hundred-acre ranch. That view of the mountains got to him every time—jagged snow-dusted peaks towering over the valley stretched out before him. The brush and grasses were still soggy from the melting snow, but the world was starting to come alive again too— a patch of green here, buds forming on the tree branches there. The scene held a wild beauty he hadn't encountered growing up in the Midwest.

After living in the mountains for the past couple of years, he knew he'd find it hard to live anywhere else. He used to think about leaving Star Valley sometimes. Ever since he'd broken up with Sienna eight years ago, restlessness had plagued him. That was what had driven him to become a SEAL in the first place. And now, after losing his best friend on the battlefield and wandering in search of a new purpose, he'd finally found something that made him feel driven again.

Thatch slowed the truck to turn onto Main Street. The town itself wasn't much of a draw—there were the typical shops, one hotel, and a few decent restaurants. But the people in this valley were gold. He'd seen the power of community after Jace's death. They'd all come together to help his widow, Tess, rallying behind her when she'd established a wild horse sanctuary on her property in Jace's memory. These people took care of one another, stood up for one another, and showed up for one another. In someone's worst and best moments. And he got to be a part of that.

As per usual, the café at the Meadowlark Hotel was hopping, though it wasn't the facade that drew people in. Like most of the other buildings on Main Street, the Meadowlark had a basic brick-and-clapboard structure, but the owners, Louie and Minnie, kept the inside cozy and friendly and warm.

He spotted a number of familiar vehicles in the parking lot, including Aiden's, Silas's, and...Lyric's. Lately, whenever he saw her car parked out front, he'd drive right on by, but today he was on a mission.

Thatch squeezed into a parking spot and climbed out of the truck with a crick in his lower back again. Somehow, the ground never got softer when he got bucked.

He walked into the restaurant, slightly hunched, and

found his friends sitting at a table together in the middle of the happy hour action.

"It's about time you showed up to have a beer with us." Silas dragged over another chair. He was sitting next to his wife, Tess. At first, Thatch hadn't known how he felt about Silas being with their late best friend's wife, but it turned out the two of them together were just right. His friend had adopted Morgan and Willow, Tess's two little girls, and now Tess was only a few months away from having another baby to add to their family.

"Yeah, how long has it been since you joined us for happy hour?" Aiden demanded. He was also sitting next to his wife, Kyra.

And they wondered why Thatch stayed away.

Lyric sat between Kyra and Tess. He couldn't let his gaze linger on her too long, or he'd give himself away. Keeping his eyes off her proved to be a challenge, though. The woman mesmerized him. She had the most expressive dark eyes, a genuine smile that literally made him hear music, and long silky black hair that he swore shimmered.

"So what've you been so busy with lately?" Tess rested a hand on her belly and shifted as though she was uncomfortable.

He could relate. "Uh. You know. This and that." He hadn't told anyone about his new pastime except for Silas, whom he'd sworn to secrecy, and Lyric, whom he'd only briefly mentioned it to in passing. Thatch didn't want anyone to know until he was ready to compete.

"You said you had a doctor's appointment this afternoon." Aiden sipped his beer. "Everything okay?"

"Great. Everything's great." He'd taken off from the rec center job site to do his training run. As a general rule, he didn't lie to Silas and Aiden, but this was a special circumstance. "How's everyone here?" Might as well get the attention off himself. "How's that baby, Tess?"

"Big," she said fondly. "And I'm pretty sure this little jumping bean is going to be a gymnast."

"You should feel the kicks," Silas mused, easing his arm around his wife.

Thatch got an internal ache every once in a while when he saw something he'd thought he would've had by now right in front of him. He was going to get married once. He and Sienna had talked about kids...

"Oh, shoot." Lyric hopped up. "I didn't realize it was so late. I have to get going." She slipped on her jacket. "See you all later."

Was she leaving because he'd come? It didn't matter. He had to put his pride aside and talk to her.

"I should get going too." Thatch stood so fast he almost knocked the chair over backward.

"But you just got here," Aiden protested.

"And you haven't even had a beer yet," Silas added.

"That'll have to wait. I forgot I have some things to take care of." He hurried away before they could ask more questions and caught up to Lyric so he could hold open the door for her.

"Oh. Thank you." Her eyes didn't quite meet his. "I haven't seen you around much."

"Yeah. I've been busy." He walked her to her car even though his truck sat on the opposite side of the parking lot.

"Still training?" she asked too politely. She was probably afraid he was going to ask her out again.

He might as well put that fear to rest right now. "Yes, and that's what I need to talk to you about." No sense in dragging out this conversation with small talk. "I need more flexibility and finesse to smooth out my rides. Kirby suggested I try yoga."

Lyric laughed and then quickly held a hand over her mouth. "Sorry. You're serious? You tried yoga once, remember?"

"How could I forget?" He'd been sore after a training run a few months back, so he'd asked Lyric for some stretches. Needless to say, he hadn't enjoyed contorting his body that way. "I need to make some major progress before the Rodeo Days, though. At this point, I'll try anything."

Her smile faded. "You're competing at Rodeo Days?"

"Planning on it. I've already qualified." He studied those eyes. She was trying to mask her concern. He could tell.

"I thought bronc riding was just a hobby for you. Why would you compete?" She shook her head. "I don't understand. You, Silas, and Aiden have a successful business. You're busy. Why do you need to spend time getting bucked off a bronc?"

"I like the challenge." He tried to scrub the defensiveness out of his tone. "The rush. And I have to put up a good showing." She didn't need to know about his rivalry with his brother. "So will you help me?"

"I don't know, Thatch." Lyric pressed her key fob to unlock her door. "I used to have a lot of connections in that world, and I don't want anything to do with it these days."

The temptation to ask what her connections had been burned in his chest. She'd never said anything before. But Lyric got into her car, and he couldn't let her go without an answer. "You don't have to be part of the rodeo world to help me. You don't even have to show up at Kirby's place for training or watch me compete or anything. I just need to work on my finesse. That can be done in your studio." He stepped back so he didn't crowd her. He didn't want to bully her into this, but he wasn't above begging. "We could make a trade. I could do work around your house or help you with a project or something. I just really need *your* help." Welp, there went all his pride again.

"I'll think about it, okay?" She latched in her seat belt and started up the engine. "I mean, I'm really busy with my classes and appointments at the clinic."

"I know." And he didn't want to add any complications to her life. "We could meet a few times a week. Whenever you have openings. I'll totally work around your schedule." Having said all he needed to, he moved aside so she could back out. "Think about it and let me know."

He wouldn't hold his breath for that phone call.

CHAPTER TWO

Lyric pulled the mats down from their stack on the shelf at the front of her studio and spaced them out evenly on the bamboo floor. This was her space—her happy place. From the leaded stained-glass windows along the west wall to the barely turquoise Calm Breeze color she'd painted on the walls, this room always brought her a centered calm.

She sat on one of the mats in lotus pose, connecting with her breath. Deep inhale. Slow methodic exhale. The pattern didn't settle her mind the way it usually did. She had Thatch to thank for that. She was still too wired from their conversation. Why had she agreed to think about doing one-on-one yoga sessions with the man?

Ever since her divorce six years ago, Lyric had managed to avoid dating. It wasn't too hard given the low population in Star Valley. Some of her clients had asked her out when she'd taught at the resorts in Jackson, but they were easy to reject because she didn't care about them. Most of the time, she never saw them again after class.

Saying no had been harder with Thatch when he'd asked her out. For a few seconds, she'd been tempted to say yes. But she'd dated a cowboy once. Then she'd married said cowboy, and that had been the biggest mistake of her life. Since then, she'd built a successful business. She'd built a life that made *her* happy all on her own.

Yet she couldn't deny her attraction to Thatch. He was laid-back and down-to-earth. Easy to be with. She'd felt some intense flutterings anytime she looked into his perceptive hazel eyes, but those flutterings were how all her troubles had started years ago too. No. She couldn't date Thatch. She liked the simplicity of her life, the ease. She had no desire to create room for anything—or anyone—else.

The door to the studio opened, and her newest clients traipsed in—a group of girls from the local high school. She'd agreed to take them on because they'd all failed gym class last term. Apparently, they preferred sitting on the bleachers to chat over doing anything physical. Since the gym teacher was a friend of hers, Lyric had said she'd help out and hopefully convince them to love a different kind of physical exercise in the process.

"Hi, everyone." She hopped up to greet them. After studying the pictures her friend had sent with info about each student, she recognized them. Elina was the one with long black hair. Actually, she was easy to remember because she reminded Lyric of herself at that age. Tallie had lighter hair and the most amazing spiked pixie cut with the tips dyed hot pink. Cheyenne was taller than the rest of them and had auburn ringlet curls, and Skye wore her blond hair in a long braid down her back.

Most of them mumbled "hey" back, but they weren't

smiling like she was. No matter. Give her a few weeks with these girls, and they'd all be smiling by the end.

Lyric turned on some music to get the class started on the right foot. As far as she was concerned, things were already going well. She'd actually remembered their names and faces! Usually, that wasn't her forte.

"Glad you all made it." They were all dressed in athletic wear too, which was a plus. In the pictures she'd received, there'd been a lot of skintight denim. "We're going to have so much fun together over the next several weeks," she assured them. Her friend had informed her that these four girls were full of potential...they just needed some direction and maybe a little mentoring along the way. And Lyric always loved a project.

"Right." Tallie shot Skye a glare. "Giving up our whole night for a school yoga class is *super* fun."

"How long is this gonna take, anyway?" Elina asked, glancing at her smartwatch. "I have to be out of here by seven."

Lyric kept her smile intact. There'd been a time back in the days of her own teenage strife when she'd had a bit of a 'tude too. "As long as we get through everything, you should be out of here in an hour." She pointed to the low floating shelves by the door. "You can take off your shoes and put them over there, and then each of you choose your mat."

The girls took their sweet time trudging to the shelves, chatting in hushed tones while they took off their shoes.

"It smells weird in here," Cheyenne said to Skye.

"That's just my essential oils diffuser," Lyric informed them brightly. "The scent is called Cheer. It inspires an energizing and positive environment." Judging from their obvious distaste for yoga, they would need all the positivity they could get. "The first thing we're going to work on today is breath," she said when they'd all found a place on their mats. "Breath is a foundational part of movement."

"We know how to breathe." Skye had certainly mastered the art of eye rolling.

"Good. Then this shouldn't be too hard." Lyric hit the volume button on the remote for her speaker, bumping it up a few notches. Maybe the instrumentals would help bring in the positivity. "Let's all stand at the center of our mats with our feet hip distance apart."

They glowered at her but assumed the stance. Keeping her smile steady, she walked them through the five golden rules for yoga breathing and then led them through forward folds.

"This is so boring," Tallie complained, standing up abruptly instead of moving her spine one vertebra at a time as Lyric had instructed.

"I kind of like it." Cheyenne took her time rolling back up to her full height and then shook out her shoulders. "At least it's not hard like that soccer unit in gym class."

"Who cares about breathing?" Skye grumbled, messing with her own smartwatch.

Okay, Lyric would have to ban the watches. She inhaled deeply, grasping at patience.

"Sometimes, it's hard to slow down your mind enough to connect with your body," she acknowledged. Maybe jumping right in with these four wasn't the best approach. She needed to build a rapport with them. Yoga had done so much for her—helping her manage anxiety, giving her an outlet to connect her body, spirit, and mind. Maybe they would find it beneficial too, but only if she helped them see the benefits. She paused the music. "Why don't we all take a seat on the mats for a few minutes?" She lowered herself and struck a butterfly pose with the soles of her feet together and her knees bent out wide.

Looking at one another hesitantly, the girls all followed suit.

"Ow." Elina straightened her legs out instead of bending her knees. "That hurts."

"That's because your muscles are tight." In fact, none of them was able to get too close to a real butterfly pose. "Yoga is all about flexibility and strength, control and finesse. And I promise, if you try what I'm asking, your bodies will all feel better by the end of our sessions."

But first they needed to start at the very beginning.

Lyric spent the next half hour walking them through some gentle lower-body stretches on the mat. The girls groaned and complained and sometimes giggled when one of them let out an expletive, and she let them do all those things freely, not correcting their words or behavior. Just letting them feel what they felt and be where they were. During some of her own teenage struggles, that had been her mother's approach, and it seemed to have worked.

"I think that's enough for tonight," she said after Tallie swore her hamstring muscle had torn in half. "We still have some time, though. I don't have any other plans this evening. So we can just chat and get to know each other a little better."

Four pairs of heavily made-up eyes blinked at her.

Yeah, they probably didn't get too excited about chatting with a thirty-year-old adult. "Or we could watch a movie?" she suggested. "If you don't have to rush off, I can hook up the projector in here. Oh! And we can order takeout from the café." If all other efforts to make them like her failed, she could resort to bribery.

"That might be fun," Cheyenne said.

"Yeah. Especially if there's free food," Skye added.

Lyric held back a cheer. They actually wanted to spend extra time hanging out with her? That was a win.

"I can't stay." Elina pushed to her feet, wincing the whole way. "My boyfriend is picking me up in a minute." She hurried to the shelves and steadied one hand against the wall while she put on her shoes.

"Are you sure?" Lyric approached her. "Can't he pick you up later? A movie would probably be over by nine." This could be her chance to bond with all of them.

"I said I can't stay." The girl lowered her eyes away from Lyric's. Her movements were suddenly shielded, guarded. "I already told him I'd be ready. He'll be here any minute and won't want to come back and pick me up later. I can't let him down."

"Oh." Concern prickled under her skin. She'd felt that same way once. Afraid to let a man down. "Okay," she said gently. "Well, maybe next time then."

"Maybe. See ya." Elina shot out the door without looking back.

A heaviness draped over her shoulders as Lyric set up the projector screen and called Minnie to put in their take-out order. Twenty minutes later, they had their food and they were all settled on their mats getting ready to start a true classic from her generation—*How to Lose a Guy in Ten Days*.

But Lyric couldn't shake the feeling she'd gotten when

Elina had left. "So who's Elina's boyfriend?" she casually asked before pushing play.

"He's a senior." Cheyenne popped a fry into her mouth. "His name is Franco."

"He's kind of a jerk if you ask me." Tallie sipped on her milkshake. "They argue a ton and she never hangs out with us anymore."

"We hardly ever get to see her since they started dating," Skye added.

The trickle of concern she'd felt earlier gained momentum. "Have you talked to her about that?"

"Sure. But she's in *love*." Tallie drew out the word and fluttered her eyelashes while the rest of them laughed.

"People aren't rational when they're in love," Skye said wisely.

That had been Lyric's experience. Love had blinded her to so many things. It had made her weak and vulnerable, and her ex had taken advantage of that. Before long she'd lost herself somewhere in the middle of all those emotions. "What do Elina's parents think about Franco?"

The girls all wore varying degrees of sardonic expressions.

"Her dad took off a while ago, and her mom's a mess," Cheyenne said. "I don't think her mom cares what she does."

"I'm sure that's not true." Rather than allowing the gossip to continue, Lyric started the movie. But the romantic comedy didn't make her laugh the way it usually did. The girls laughed and ate and seemed like they really enjoyed the story. She tried too, but worry weighted her heart. Elina's story was a little too similar to her own. Lyric's own father had left her mom when she'd only been a baby and she'd never had the chance to know the man. Her mom hadn't been a mess, though. She'd always given Lyric a sense of love and security. After her mom had remarried, Lyric had a wonderful relationship with her stepfather until he passed away a few years ago.

But like Elina, she'd been all too obsessed with making a man happy—tiptoeing around so she didn't upset him. She'd learned how unhealthy that kind of relationship dynamic could be.

"What else do you know about Franco?" Lyric asked the girls when the movie had finished. Worry had gotten the best of her.

"Not much." Skye hopped up from her mat and threw away her cup. "He plays basketball. Lives on a ranch about ten miles outside of town."

"He's gotten into a few fights at school," Tallie offered.

Her heart took a sharp drop. So he was violent?

"Anyway, thanks for the movie and the food." Cheyenne rolled up her mat and stashed it on the shelf with the others following.

"I'm glad you all stayed." She walked them out of the studio and through the clinic's hallway and reception area. "We could do it again sometime, if you'd like." Maybe she could even get Elina to join them next time. If the girl was in an unhealthy relationship, Lyric could help. She'd been through that too.

"Maybe." Tallie was the first out the door.

"See ya." Cheyenne left next, and right away another car pulled up to collect Skye.

"Thanks again," the girl called as she ran down the sidewalk.

"Anytime." Lyric shut the door, her worries still focused

on Elina. What if this Franco guy was really bad news? All the signs of a seriously unhealthy relationship were there. She knew them better than anyone. But she didn't know much about Franco and she had no way to find out about him.

Unless...

Thatch. He'd offered her a favor in exchange for yoga sessions. Now she knew exactly how he could help her.

Lyric hurried back to the studio and quickly swept the floor before grabbing her purse and turning off the lights on the way out.

Thatch's house sat on a few acres just on the outskirts of town. For years, the place had been a dilapidated boxy structure, but the man had flipped it completely and now even the outside had a lovely stone facade with log beams as accents. Thankfully, the lights were on, so she didn't have to get him out of bed.

Lyric followed the stone path to his front door, a strange sensation humming through her. Nerves? She tried to shake them off. This was Thatch. She couldn't be nervous to see him. She saw him all the time. Or at least she used to see him all the time. She wasn't sure if she'd been avoiding him or he'd been avoiding her up until they'd seen each other at happy hour.

Clearing her throat, she tossed her hair over her shoulder and knocked. It took a few minutes for him to open the door.

"Lyric?" He started to smooth his hair down and moved aside. "Come in."

"Thanks. I, uh, won't stay long." She stepped onto the slate-tiled foyer of his home. She'd been here before for game nights along with their other friends, but now it was just her. And him. Did he have to look so hot? Slightly disheveled in joggers and a ripped long-sleeved T-shirt. Even though he'd run his fingers through it, his dusty-blond hair was still slightly mussed. Maybe she'd interrupted a workout or something. It didn't matter. She would be leaving soon. "I, um, just came to tell you that I'll help you. With the yoga. We can meet for a few sessions every week." Why were the words rushing out? She *sounded* nervous. "But I need your help with something too."

"Sure. Yeah. Like I said, I'm happy to trade." He walked away and waved her into his living room, which smelled nice. Similar to her eucalyptus essential oil. Not surprisingly, everything in this space was orderly, from the uniform black leather furniture to the naval magazines positioned on the coffee table.

"You want something to drink?" he asked. "A beer?"

"No." She stood at the very edge of the room, maintaining a clear path to the front door. Her heart was thrumming and her body was heating—not good signs for keeping a neutral distance from him. "I need you to help me keep an eye on a kid in town. Franco Vaughn. He's a senior at the high school."

"Uh..." Thatch's head tilted while he studied her. "You want me to spy on some kid for you?"

When he said it that way, the request sounded completely irrational. "He's dating one of my sixteen-year-old students," she rushed to explain. "I have some concerns." Every time she looked into Thatch's eyes, her brain stalled. "So I just want to keep an eye on him. I figure maybe you could even, like, reach out to him or something? Mentor him? Offer him a job?" Thatch, Silas, and Aiden were always looking for labor help with their various projects in town.

"Maybe." Confusion still pinched at his mouth. "I guess that's a possibility. What're your concerns about him?"

"He seems a little controlling." She knew from personal experience that was how abuse started. But she couldn't tell Thatch that. She couldn't tell anyone. Her friends all knew she'd been divorced a long time ago, but she'd always been too humiliated to give them the details. Except for Kyra. But they were stepsisters. "He's gotten into some trouble at school. I just don't want her to end up in a bad situation." Like she had. "Please, Thatch? This is really important to me."

"Okay. Yeah. Of course I'm willing to help." His tone gentled. "I'll figure something out. Maybe I can call the school and see if he'd be interested in becoming an intern for Cowboy Construction or something."

"Great." She could've hugged the man, but she held back. She'd already made up her mind about dating him...even if he was a pretty wonderful guy. She quickly headed for the door. "Why don't you come to the studio on Friday night? My last class is over at seven. We can do your first session after that."

Thatch opened the door and stepped out onto the porch with her. "Sounds good. I'll be there."

She told him goodbye and hurried to her car before he could tell that her heart was racing. That he'd *made* her heart race. Would her heart do this every time she was with him?

She'd have to figure out how to deal with that problem later.

CHAPTER THREE

"That's the last of it." Thatch slid the box of vinyl plank flooring out of his pickup and set it onto the leaning stack inside the rec center's main door. "Hard to believe we're ready to start the interior work."

"About time." Silas cut open the box and inspected one of the planks. "Leave it to us to do most of the exterior work in the winter."

"At least we had a crew helping on the outside." Aiden assessed the open room that would eventually serve as the main lobby. "Finishing off this much square footage is going to take us forever."

"Nothing we can't handle." Thatch was up for the challenge. When the town council had approved the new rec center project, Cowboy Construction had gone from mainly doing odd jobs around town to looking like a real professional outfit. "The detail work has always been our specialty." They'd developed a reputation in the region for being the best with interior renovations. Besides, there was also another potential employee he hadn't told them about yet. He still didn't know what he was getting himself into with this Franco kid, but he couldn't tell Lyric no. Not when she'd looked at him with those imploring dark eyes. So he'd better get Aiden and Silas on board with the new hire.

"I may know someone who could help with the grunt work." When he'd called the school, the guidance counselor had been ecstatic to hear that they were interested in an intern. He believed the woman's exact words were "Franco could use some special guidance." Which gave Thatch the feeling that bringing the kid on might be more work than he'd bargained for. Whatever trouble the arrangement brought into his life might be worth the effort, though. Especially if this act of goodwill could help convince Lyric that Thatch was worth a yes. Not that he'd ever admit he had ulterior motives.

"Who's gonna help with the grunt work?" Aiden took a swig from his water bottle.

From the other side of the boxes, Silas was giving him a skeptical glare.

"There's this kid. Franco." He had to be careful about what he said. He couldn't tell them about his deal with Lyric, or they'd find out he was going to yoga on a regular basis, and he didn't feel like explaining that. "I was thinking we could give him an internship, teach him the ropes. He could help with the measuring, cutting, and painting." Those were good skills for anyone to have going into adulthood, right?

Aiden shot him a suspicious frown. "How do you know this kid?"

"I don't know him. Yet." Shit. He really should've

come up with a solid cover story before springing this on them.

"Then why would we give him an internship?" Silas demanded. "We've already got enough on our plates with this project. We don't need to be babysitting some kid you don't even know."

When he put it that way, this arrangement sounded like the last thing Thatch wanted to do. He'd never babysat anyone. But the deal was done. "I'll supervise him." That was all Lyric had asked him to do anyway. To keep an eye on the kid. How hard could that be?

"This makes no sense." Aiden marched up to him with a familiar glare. "Why would you want to take on a kid you don't even know?" His friend knew something else was up, so there was no point in denying it.

"Lyric knows him. Or knows *of* him." His tone wrote the definition for *casual*. "She said he could use an internship. That he has potential." Not exactly her words, but telling them the kid might be trouble would not help his cause.

"Ah." Silas's head tipped back slightly, as if it all made sense now. "Lyric asked you."

"You could've just said that in the first place," Aiden added with a laugh. "Why don't you ask her out already instead of taking on an intern for her?"

Thatch ignored the question and ripped open a box to start unloading the planks. He'd asked Lyric out. He'd put himself out there and approached her at Aiden and Kyra's Christmas party. He'd had a whole spiel and everything. Told her he was attracted to her. That he loved how she was so good with people, kind, and thoughtful. Hell, he'd spent ten minutes going over her attributes before getting to the point. Then when he had, she'd said thanks but no thanks. Yet here he was still trying to impress her.

"You should ask her out." Silas echoed Aiden, opening the next box.

Those two didn't know how to let something go. "I'm not into Lyric." He didn't look up from the planks he was stacking. More accurately, Lyric wasn't into him. Yet.

"Bullshit." Aiden stepped into his line of vision. "You can't lie to us, Hearst. We've got too much history together."

They were also worse busybodies than the elderly ladies who gossiped at the salon. "Seriously." Thatch tossed the empty box into a corner. "Maybe I was into Lyric at one time, but I've moved on. She wasn't interested, and I've got other things to focus on. Don't really have time for being so tied down like you two are." He kept going before they could get a word in. "Speaking of, do you think you can actually grab a beer tonight without the wives?"

His two friends shared a sheepish look.

"It's country-western night at the café," Aiden said.

Thatch served up a smirk in their directions. "So that's a no then."

Silas shrugged. "Tess has been looking forward to country-western night all week. You know how much she loves to dance."

"And Kyra's been so busy at the clinic lately that I've hardly seen her," Aiden added.

"Another time then," he said drily. He didn't really mind that they'd rather be with their wives than him. That was how it was supposed to be, but he couldn't resist giving them shit and distracting them from all the Lyric talk. Hell, he'd like to distract himself from thinking about her.

"We can still have a beer at country-western night." Silas tossed another empty box out the door.

"I'm not going to country-western night." Thatch had made that mistake once and had been passed around as a dancing partner to every woman over age fifty in Star Valley—from Doris to Minnie to Nelly and every other member of the Ladies Aid Society.

"Why can't you make it?" Aiden had finally started to help them unload the vinyl planks from the boxes.

"I'm not big on dancing." That wasn't exactly true. He didn't mind dancing when he had someone to dance with. Someone who wanted to dance with him. At this point in time, exactly zero other single women—around his age— intrigued him in Star Valley. "I've got other stuff to do tonight."

Silas snorted. "Now you're just lying."

"You asked us to have a beer but now you're suddenly busy?" Aiden shot him an interrogating gaze. "What're you so busy with lately anyway?"

Thatch shared a look with Silas and gave his friend a slight shake of the head. He'd tell Aiden about his bronc riding soon. He already knew the revelation wouldn't earn his friend's approval. Aiden didn't exactly like taking risks anymore. Since he'd married Kyra, he'd become a grounded family man.

Silas, however, understood Thatch's quest. Last year, Silas had considered going back to work in the Middle East, but that was before he and Tess had acknowledged their feelings for each other.

"I've been working on the house," he decided to say. "You know that."

"Yeah, and you've already replaced pretty much

everything," Aiden countered. "What work is there left to do?"

He didn't have an answer to that question. Last week, he'd put the finishing touches on his remodeled bathroom—the last project in his house. "Fine. I'll stop by the café for a while." But he wouldn't stay long.

And he wouldn't dance.

An hour later, Thatch was questioning his decision. Country-western night always drew a huge crowd at the café. Most of the tables had been stacked and pushed to the corners of the dining room so Louie and Minnie could set up a dance floor right in the center of the space. Some people sat at the bar along the back wall, but the majority were out getting their boot-scootin' boogie on.

So far, Thatch hadn't had a beer with his friends because they'd been too busy dancing with their wives. Shocker.

"Hey, Louie." Thatch signaled the bartender. "I'll take a beer." Looked like he'd be enjoying an ale on his own tonight.

"You got it." The older man set a frosty mug in front of him.

"Hi." Lyric slid onto the stool next to him.

He startled but tried not to show it. Usually, he was aware when she walked into a room. "Hey." Something happened to him whenever the woman got this close. He couldn't even really describe it. His senses heightened. She brought more vibrance to his vision, to sounds. And he always caught her intoxicating scent—something that reminded him of his mom's prized lilacs blooming in the spring. Thatch cleared his throat. "How's it going?"

"Pretty good. How come you're not out there?" She tipped her head toward the dance floor.

"I've never mastered the art of line dancing." He'd grown up in farm country. Some of this cowboy stuff was new to him. Though he'd already embraced the boots and the hats and the riding. "I'd rather watch everyone else and point out Silas and Aiden's screwups."

Lyric's laugh had the best melody.

"Come on, man," Silas called, moving his feet as he and Tess shuffled past. "Ask Lyric to dance."

No one excelled in the art of beating a dead horse more than Silas Beck. "I probably shouldn't." Thatch should've told his friends that the woman had flat-out rejected him so they'd lay off. Being turned down privately had been bad enough. He'd rather not put himself out there again in public.

"Hey, Lyric, why don't you dance with Thatch here?" Tess stopped two-stepping and marched over to them. "He's bored."

"Oh. Uh." *Spooked* was the only way to describe Lyric's wide-eyed expression. "Well—"

"That's okay," he interrupted. "I'm not a great dancer."

"Lyric can teach you! She's an *amazing* dancer." Tess nudged her closer to him. "Come on. You two are literally the only people in here who aren't dancing."

"Okay. Yeah. We should dance." Lyric's smile faltered, but he was probably the only one who noticed. He doubted anyone studied her face the way he did.

"Sure." Thatch stood and abandoned his beer. Everyone else would get suspicious if it became too obvious they were avoiding each other. They couldn't avoid each other much longer anyway. He'd better get used to being around her one-on-one seeing as how he'd be doing yoga with her on a regular basis. The key would be to act like everything was normal between them. Like he'd never asked her out in the first place. He'd never been good at pretending, but he could learn.

Thankfully, Minnie put on a fast song, and they fell into an easy two-step with a little extra distance between their bodies.

He couldn't help but notice how soft her hand felt in his, though.

"I called the school and told the guidance counselor I'd heard great things about Franco's work ethic and wondered if he would have any interest in being an intern," Thatch said before things could get awkward.

"That's brilliant." Lyric followed his lead, her feet keeping time with his. "Good thinking."

"They already got back to me." He did his best to block out the scent of her perfume or whatever it was that made her smell so delicious. "Franco is interested, so we'll do an interview on Wednesday."

"Perfect." Lyric's tense shoulders seemed to relax. "I can't tell you how much I appreciate this." Her gaze held his long enough to stir a craving in him. He spun her real quick to get his head back together. He couldn't look into her eyes for too long or he'd stumble.

"Happy to help," he said when they'd resumed their two-step. "So...how're things at the clinic?" Small talk was always a safe bet.

"Good. Very busy." The words ended in an abrupt, awkward silence. "And the rec center project," Lyric murmured after a few beats. "How's that all coming?"

"It's moving along." He wouldn't bore her with the details. "We're a little behind schedule, but I think now that we've moved to the interior, we'll get back on track."

They had to get it back on track, since the grand opening was slated for the Rodeo Days weekend.

The song ended—finally—and they drifted back to their seats at the bar. "Can I order you a drink?" Thatch asked, but she didn't seem to hear him. Her eyes were trained on something across the room.

"That's Elina," Lyric half whispered. "Right over there. With Franco."

He turned his head, scanning the tables to their left until he saw the teenagers sitting across from each other. The girl with dark hair seemed to be scowling.

"Don't stare." Lyric nudged him. "They can't know we're watching them."

She sure seemed to be staring a lot, but he didn't argue. "You don't think Elina will find it suspicious that one of your friends asked Franco if he wanted an internship out of the blue?" Everyone in town knew the six of them hung out all the time. In his opinion, the whole arrangement with Franco had *surveillance op* written all over it, but Thatch had also been trained in the art of skepticism.

"Hopefully, she'll think it's a coincidence," Lyric muttered, still looking away from him. "All I want to do is see them together a few times. I'll know if something's off."

Thatch noted the twitch in her jaw. "How will you know?" He hadn't meant for his voice to soften so much, but her surety had to come from somewhere. In his view, the deepest convictions were born out of experience.

"Do you see how he's looking at her?" Lyric asked, disregarding his question. "He looks angry."

Thatch snuck a peek at the couple again and then focused on her before she could accuse him of staring. "They both look a little angry to me." Maybe *angry* wasn't the right word. "I'd call them angsty." He'd had his angsty moments as a teenager, that was for sure.

"I wish we could get closer so we could hear what they're talking about." Lyric swiveled her barstool to face him. "Maybe we could have a party and invite them to come."

"Not sure teenagers would want to hang with a bunch of thirty-year-olds." At least he wouldn't have wanted to at that age. "But, hey, we could always pretend to be a couple and then follow them on dates."

He'd meant the words as a joke but Lyric's spine straightened. "That's a bad idea." A flush crept up her neck. "I mean, no. I don't think that would work. Nope. We can't pretend to be a couple."

"I know." Talk about playing with fire. Thatch smirked at her. "Relax. It was a joke. We'll figure out something else." Because he already knew that pretending to date Lyric when he had real feelings for her would be worse than all the torture he'd been trained to withstand.

CHAPTER FOUR

All right, ladies. Let's bring it into a warrior one pose." Lyric lunged into her right leg, bending the knee while straightening her left leg and lifting both arms up toward the ceiling.

Groans chorused through the room, competing with the percussive music coming through the speaker.

"My leg is about to give out," Skye complained.

"This has been so hard." Cheyenne stood upright. "My muscles are tired."

"Okay." Lyric had thought she could get one more challenge in tonight, but from the sound of things, they would revolt if she made them finish the whole flow. "Let's sit in our butterfly pose instead." Tonight she had pushed them a lot more than she had during the first session—balancing the flow between some stretching and strength training. But she remembered being new to the practice, too, and if you weren't used to holding poses, the muscles could fatigue easily.

Uttering a collective sigh of relief, the girls sat on their mats, bringing the soles of their feet together.

"This might be my favorite pose." Elina finally spoke up. Lyric had been observing the girl. She didn't talk much compared with the others. But she didn't seem shy as much as she seemed...cautious. That would likely make it difficult to get to know her.

"I'd rather stretch than do lunges," Tallie mumbled.

Warrior one wasn't exactly a *lunge*, but Lyric let the comment go. "You all did great tonight." She'd led them through a full beginner's flow, and while they'd moaned and groaned some, they'd also chatted and giggled and tried. That was what mattered. Physical exercise should be fun—that was the only way they'd make it a lifelong practice.

"Well, I need to get going." Elina hopped up. "Franco will be here any minute." She rolled up her mat and paused on her way past Lyric. "Hey, did you ask your boyfriend to give Franco a job?"

"My boyfriend?" Did she mean Thatch? Lyric hopped up too. Elina thought she and Thatch were together? "Um—"

"Because that's really cool of him," Elina went on. "Franco said Thatch told him you thought he'd be good at construction."

"Oh. Yeah." Lyric took her mat and stashed it on the shelf. "But Thatch and I aren't really toge—"

"Go, Lyric!" Tallie interrupted. "Those SEAL guys are *so* hot."

"Hey, maybe the four of you could go on a double date," Cheyenne suggested. "Since Franco and Thatch are working together."

Huh. Maybe Thatch's joke the other night wasn't so off base. Sure, when he'd mentioned being a pretend couple, Lyric had experienced a sudden adrenaline rush followed by an onslaught of panic, but the ruse apparently could work. A double date would be a great way to see Elina and Franco interact. In fact, that might be her only opportunity to get a glimpse of their relationship given the girl had never said more than five words to her before this moment.

"Well, thanks again." Elina actually smiled at her. "He needs the money. So a job'll really help."

"You're welcome." She hesitated. She didn't want to scare the girl away, but this could be her best chance to find an opening. "Maybe the four of us *could* hang out sometime." She and Thatch could pretend for a short time, right? What harm would that cause? Surely Thatch would agree. This was his idea in the first place. Pretending to be together for a while was a small price to pay for making sure Elina was safe with Franco.

"Maybe." The girl shrugged. "He'd probably want to. He's pretty excited about the job."

"Okay." Lyric, however, did her best to appear not overly excited. "We can talk about it—"

The door opened, and Thatch stepped inside the studio before coming to an abrupt halt. "Hey. Didn't realize you had a class now."

"Oh. Yeah!" The panic flooded her, sending a warm rush through her chest. She hurried to meet him before he blew their cover in front of the girls. "But we were just finishing up. Come here, you." She pulled him into a hug while her students serenaded them with catcalls.

"Uh." Thatch's body tensed, but hopefully no one else

noticed. "Hey?" He gave her back a weak pat and she let him go so no one else could pick up on the awkwardness between them.

"We were just telling Ms. Valenza how hot her boyfriend is," Skye said demurely.

Uh-oh—

Thatch visibly flinched. "Boyfr—?"

"Yep. I was telling them how happy we are together, shnookems," Lyric said quickly.

He jerked his head to stare at her, eyes blinking faster.

"Elina and I were thinking maybe we could go on a double date with her and Franco sometime." She murderously squeezed his hand so he would take the hint. "Wouldn't that be a ton of fun?"

More blinking, and then after another squeeze on his hand, he stood straighter. "Sure. That sounds...good?"

"I'll ask Franco." Elina was already halfway out the door.

"And we should get going so you two can make out or whatever it is you're doing tonight." Tallie snickered.

"Yoga," Thatch mumbled while the girls stashed their mats. "We're doing yoga."

"Sure. That's what all the kids say these days." Skye led the way out of the room, all of them laughing hysterically.

Thatch faced her the second the door closed, hands posted to his hips. "We're *together* now?"

Whew. Lyric turned away from him so she could buy a moment of clarity. "Well, yeah," she murmured as though this were no big deal. Just another normal day in Star Valley. "Fake-dating was your brilliant idea. Remember?"

"I said that as a *joke*," Thatch said behind her. "And I

distinctly remember you saying that pretending would be a bad idea."

"That was before I thought it through." She dragged two mats to the center of the floor, her hands fumbling to distance them a few feet apart. "This could help both of us, actually."

"Yeah?" He marched to her, jaw set in a hard line, his sneakers squeaking on the bamboo floor. "How do you figure?"

"Well, you don't want anyone to know you're doing yoga or bronc riding." She rushed to a shelf and selected two yoga blocks. "So a pretend relationship would explain why you're coming to see me all the time. And it'll help me to really see what's going on with Elina and Franco. So I can make sure she's safe." She pointed to the bench with shoe storage. "Can you please take off your sneakers?" So he didn't mark up her beautiful floors.

"Franco seems like a decent enough kid to me." Thatch sauntered to the bench. It was hard to imagine he could look even better in a pair of sweats and a fitted tattered T-shirt than he looked in his typical cowboy jeans, but here they were.

Lyric tore her gaze away from the man while he removed his shoes.

"I mean, I didn't get any red flags during the interview." Thatch came back to the mats.

She couldn't remember ever seeing him barefoot. It was almost too intimate.

"Nice guys know how to pretend," she told him, fighting to keep her focus on the conversation. Thatch had some serious sex appeal, but she had to treat him like any other client. At least when they were alone together. Now, when they were in front of other people, she'd have to treat him like her boyfriend.

She shook away the thought. "Trust me. I know how men can pretend. If you and I are supposedly dating, then maybe we'll have an excuse to hang out with Franco and Elina sometimes."

"Why is this so important to you?" Thatch asked quietly.

He looked at her differently than most people. Maybe that was why her heart started to pound harder. An open curiosity defined his gaze. But there was something else in his eyes too. Tenderness.

A breathless yearning to share her burden with someone else gripped her, but she couldn't. She'd never been able to tell anyone about the worst moments. The moments that still haunted her.

The abrupt change in energy between them threw her off. It was like he truly saw her, but she couldn't let him in. No one knew except for Kyra, and her friend wouldn't have betrayed her confidence. "I just have this feeling something's not right." Her throat tightened, but she managed to grin at him. "I know you don't work from feelings, but I do." Thatch was all plans and logic.

He still stood on his mat, facing off with her, studying her closely. "So how's this going to go?" he finally asked. "What about Kyra and Tess and Silas and Aiden? They know we're not together."

"We'll tell them we've been secretly dating for a while. Everyone in town will have to believe we're together, or this won't work." Lyric traipsed to the Bluetooth speaker and started the music again. Mostly to drown out her inner panic. "And then we'll break up in a few months after we spend some time with Franco and Elina." When she got back to the mat, Thatch met her with a skeptical expression.

"You really want to go through with this?"

She couldn't tell if a warning or amusement hid in his tone.

"You'll be taking quite the risk. Because we'll have to spend a lot of time together. And I'm pretty hard to resist, Valenza."

Okay, definitely amusement. "I think I can manage." Maybe. Hopefully. Normally, she didn't like to play with fire, but this time she refused to get burned. "A fake relationship between us doesn't have to be a big deal," she lied. "And it's for a good cause."

"So you're completely fine with acting like a couple in front of our friends?" This time, the amusement made it all the way to his eyes.

"Thankfully, you haven't been hanging out with us much lately anyway," she said curtly. Ever since she'd told him she didn't want to date him, Thatch had made himself scarce. "I'm busy at the clinic. You're busy at work and with your riding thing. It's totally believable that neither one of us can go out much."

"Okay." He delivered the word with a singsongy cadence and might as well have added, *We'll see.*

Yes, they would see. She would show him she could resist him, cowboy charm and all. "All right, Hearst. Let's get down to why you're really here." She lowered herself to her mat and sat cross-legged. "We'll start with some breath and focus work."

"I don't need to work on breathing—"

"Breath and focus are the foundation for flexibility and strength," she informed him. "So that's where we start every session." She smiled up at him sweetly until he sat his butt down.

"Now hands on your knees," she instructed, closing her eyes. "Pull your heart forward, chin up, and inhale deeply." Lyric demonstrated, lifting her head, drawing her chest forward. "And then round the back when you exhale." When she opened her eyes, Thatch was staring at her. "What?"

"Nothing." He quickly looked away. "Okay, so heart forward." He jutted out his chest.

"Careful. Try to make smooth, flowing movements." Or he'd pull a muscle.

"And inhale," he murmured, his muscled chest expanding even more while he lifted his chin. "Exhale and round the back." Thatch hunched forward with a sigh. "How was that?" He sat upright, gazing at her expectantly.

"Um. Well. We'll keep working on it. The biggest thing is you want to feel the connection between your body and your breath. You want to feel how your breath moves your body." She demonstrated again, feeling a calm settle over her. This time, she kept her eyes open to make sure he was watching. Yes, he was watching all right. Especially as she pushed her chest forward.

Okay, maybe this wasn't the best exercise to start with, especially when she was wearing a skintight sports bra. "Now you try."

Thatch seemed to refocus himself and went through the breath pattern—somewhat clumsily—but they would keep working on that too.

Next, Lyric walked him through some side bends.

"My body doesn't move that way." He stretched his arm over his head but could hardly bend.

"That's because you haven't developed any flexibility yet." Lyric got on her knees and crawled onto his mat to press her hand against his arm. "I'll assist you with this one. Just tell me if it hurts."

"Oh, it hurts." He winced. "But I guess it's also a good stretch?"

"It's a great stretch." She pressed a little harder. "Especially for riding. Lateral flexion will be really good for you."

Thatch merely whimpered in response.

She urged him a bit deeper into the stretch, and his shirt came up, revealing a set of toned abdominals. *Don't check out the client*, she reminded herself. But it was hard to stop.

"If you're wondering why I'm so tan, it's because I was working with my shirt off last week at the request of the Ladies Aid Society."

Busted. He'd totally caught her. "I wasn't looking. Or wondering." Lyric quickly scrambled back to her mat. "Let's move on."

"I could do yoga shirtless too, if you'd like." The innocence in his voice was such an act.

The man knew he had a nice body.

"No thanks. You should save your abs for the old ladies. They appreciate them more than I do. How about we try crow pose?" She'd make him hold it for five minutes.

Maybe that would wipe the cocky smirk off his face and encourage him to stop teasing her. Because they both knew she wasn't as immune to his magnetism as she pretended to be.

CHAPTER FIVE

Dear God. Perspiration dripped down Thatch's temple. How was it possible to sweat this much while *stretching*? A grunt threatened in his throat, but he couldn't let it out. He couldn't give Lyric the satisfaction of hearing him voice his discomfort and frustration. After progressing through the poses, he'd been holding warrior III for less than a minute—or thirteen years—and his standing leg had already started to cramp.

Who the hell knew yoga was so hard? He'd take riding a bronc over this shit any day.

"How're we doing?"

Ha. That sugary tone didn't fool him. Lyric was a sadist. He never should've teased her at the beginning of the session. He'd underestimated her penchant for torture.

"I'm great." So great he could feel the vein in his forehead bulging. He gritted his teeth and swallowed a groan. "I could do this all day."

"Oh, good," she sang. "Because I think to get the full benefit, we should hold it for another three minutes."

Three minutes? She might as well have said five hours. He wasn't gonna make it.

Meanwhile, the woman standing next to him effortlessly held the pose, perched on one leg with her other leg outstretched behind her and her arms reaching out in front of her, somehow not trembling at all.

His body convulsed. Every muscle. Muscles he didn't even know he had. *Ahhh...* he was losing it. Screw this. Thatch lowered to his knees on the mat. "You're trying to kill me, aren't you?"

"I don't know what you're talking about." Lyric continued to hold her perfect warrior III pose.

Thatch shouldn't have looked at her. Because now it was hard to look away. Those skintight yoga clothes kept snagging his focus. Lyric always dressed in leggings and formfitting tops, but he'd never seen her body work this way. She had such strength and control. Graceful but powerful. He wasn't sure he'd ever seen such an intoxicating combination.

"You won." He rolled over onto his back and stared at the ceiling. "I'm done. I can't move anymore."

Laughing, the woman finally broke her pose to sit on her mat next to him. "It's a common misconception to think that yoga is just a bunch of light stretching."

"Trust me. I have a whole newfound respect for what you do." He hadn't counted on this session being such a workout. But he had to admit, his body felt good. Tired and worked over, but good. "I can see how this practice would help with staying on the back of a bronc." Every sport he'd ever played before, football and lacrosse mainly, had been about powering through. But Lyric had told him yoga was about control—muscle control and mind control. Which was why he sucked at it.

"This practice will help your mind and body be more in sync when you're riding." Lyric lay down on her mat too. "It helps you stay in control in the midst of the chaos around you." She raised a leg in the air and pulled on her calf with both hands. "In fact, I always like to end a session with the good stretch." She turned her head and raised her eyebrows at him until he raised his leg too. "Yoga is very calming."

"Mm-hmm." He could barely grab the back of his leg. Seriously. His hamstring might rip. He might have found yoga calming if it didn't hurt this much. If the woman lying next to him didn't have such a direct impact on his pulse. But he planned to keep all the chaos inside his own head. "How'd you get into yoga anyway?"

Lyric pulled her knee nearly to her nose. "I went through some things that left me drifting and lost. I needed to feel centered in my life again, so I joined an online yoga community." She released the stretch. "From there I traveled to do the trainings in Costa Rica and was eventually certified."

She didn't offer anything more about what she'd gone through that had left her feeling lost, and he didn't push. It was none of his business anyway. Even with this brand-new arrangement pretending to be her boyfriend, there were boundaries he wouldn't cross.

"You're not stretching." Lyric scrambled to get up and stood over him, her hand pressed against his calf.

"Ow." Yes, that was a stretch. Suddenly the back of his leg was on fire.

"Breathe deep," Lyric reminded him.

He tried, but breathing didn't take the edge off the agony. And he was all too aware of her hands on him.

"Why is this upcoming competition so important to you?"

He stopped wincing to peer up at her. "I told you. I have a lot to prove." And just like her, he would withhold the details of his own experience with being lost. "My brother will be here. We've always had a sibling-rivalry thing." That had peaked when Liam had married Sienna. Since then, the two of them had hardly talked. They'd been in the same room plenty, they just opted not to have any meaningful conversations.

"So you're going through all this pain because of a little sibling rivalry?" Lyric let go of his right leg and motioned for him to raise the left.

Did he have to? "It's not just a little rivalry." He grunted when she pushed him into the stretch. "We haven't spoken much in eight years."

The pressure on his leg subsided as the woman angled her body so she could see his face. "You haven't spoken to your brother in eight years? What happened?"

"It doesn't matter." Thatch brought his leg down and pushed off the floor. He shouldn't have even brought up Liam. "I need to run. I promised my mom I'd call tonight. It's her birthday." He'd sent her a pair of earrings from a fancy jewelry shop in Jackson, but a phone call always meant more. Plus that gave him the perfect excuse to take off. Before he bared any more of his soul to Lyric.

"Right. Okay. Sure." Lyric knelt down to roll up their mats before he could read her face. "That was a good first session," she said formally while Thatch pulled on his shoes.

"I wasn't good." He grinned at her. As long as they could keep things light, he would do his best not to get any ideas in his head about this fake-relationship thing becoming real. "But the session was good. I'll try to do better next time." He got up off the bench and followed her out the door.

Lyric shot him an evil grin over her shoulder. "I didn't exactly go easy on you. I'd say you held your own—"

"What're you two doing here?"

Thatch jerked his head to see Kyra standing behind the reception counter in the main lobby of the clinic. "Uh, um…"

An awkward pause pounded his ears before Lyric threaded her arm around his waist. "It's okay, hon. We should tell her."

"Tell me what?" their friend asked in a high-pitched screech.

Yes. Tell her what? Alarm itched on the back of his neck. They couldn't seriously convince their friends they were together, could they?

"We're dating," Lyric announced.

He had no idea how she could say those words so casually. They seemed to roll right off her tongue. He sucked at pretending. He wouldn't be able to say anything to anyone about this supposed relationship without stumbling over every word.

"I knew it was only a matter of time!" Kyra flew to them and hugged Lyric, squealing. "I'm so happy!" She pulled back and hugged him next.

Thatch returned the embrace, grateful she couldn't see his face.

"Does Aiden know yet?" she asked when all the hugging ended.

"No." That question he could answer. "We're trying to keep this on the down low." Staying quiet would be best for him. Silas and Aiden knew him. They were basically his brothers. They'd spent months together on covert missions. They'd dodged bullets in some pretty sketchy situations. If he tried to lie to them face-to-face, they'd see right through him.

"But you're going to tell him, right?" Kyra desperately tugged on his arm. "Because I can't keep this from him. I can't! I mean, he'll be thrilled! He's talked about you two getting together forever now. Actually, we all have."

Yeah. He'd heard the talk. Which was why he'd asked Lyric out at the Christmas party. *Surely she'll say yes*, they always told him. Everyone else thought they should give it a try. Just not the person who'd mattered the most. She'd said no. She didn't want him. Not for real. He couldn't lose sight of that fact in this facade.

"Why don't you share the news with Aiden for us?" Lyric suggested. "But tell him not to make a big deal about it or anything."

"Yes. You tell Aiden." And then he'd avoid his friend as much as possible for the next month.

"Of course I'll tell him." Kyra rushed back behind the desk and slipped on her coat. "I was just getting ready to go home anyway. Had some paperwork to finish up. But I'll tell him right when I see him." She hardly took a breath between the words.

"But you don't have to make a big deal out of it," Lyric reminded her.

"I get it." Kyra dug her keys out of her purse.

Did she? The woman looked a little too excited to him.

"You two don't want any pressure. That makes total sense. Aiden will be on board with that." She gasped. "We'll have to go on a triple date soon! Maybe we should go to Jackson to celebrate! We could all stay in a hotel and have a fancy dinner and—"

"We're pretty busy." Lyric finally stepped away from his side, panic registering on her face for the first time.

Well, good. Now she was on the same page as him.

"We're all busy, but we can find time for this." Kyra hugged her again. "When are you telling Silas and Tess?"

Lyric glanced at him. How the hell was he supposed to know? None of this had been his harebrained idea. "I guess soon." Because it wasn't like Aiden would keep the news to himself once he heard. Did Lyric even realize what she'd started? She'd lit a match now, and there'd be no stopping the impending inferno. News like this spread through town like a forest fire. Damn. Too late to go back now. At least he could escape tonight. "I should get going."

"That's right. You have to call your mom." Lyric was nervously knotting her hands together in front of her waist. "Yes, you'd better go. Tell her I said happy birthday."

"Will do." Or not. His mom would be a little too ecstatic to hear he and Lyric had discussed her birthday. She'd get all kinds of ideas in her head. "See ya." He turned to leave but hadn't even taken a step before Kyra cleared her throat.

"You two can kiss in front of me, you know."

No, they couldn't. They really couldn't.

"Oh, that's okay." Lyric's laugh was about as authentic as the plastic ficus in the corner. "Thatch is super shy about PDA."

Oh, sure. Blame him. If he was with someone like Lyric, he wouldn't be shy at all about showing her some love in front of anyone and everyone. "I'm not shy." He whirled back to her.

Her eyes widened, and her lips formed the most perfect *O*.

She wanted everyone to think they were dating? Fine. He scooped his arms around her waist and drew her to him, those exotic eyes growing larger with each inch. "Bye, honeybunch." Before she could respond, he laid one on her—pressing his lips against hers. He wasn't anticipating how soft they would be. Or how the subtle strawberry taste of her lip gloss would hit him. Against his will, he lingered there, holding her, inhaling her, letting his lips lull hers into a rhythm. She didn't push him away. In fact, her hands gripped his arms tight, as if trying to hold him there.

"My, my, my." Kyra hummed from someplace nearby. "I really should leave you two alone."

Lyric pulled back, her eyes wide and unblinking.

He couldn't look away either. Hell, he couldn't even see straight after that kiss.

"I can give you two the room." Giggling to herself, Kyra gathered up a pile of files.

"Not necessary," Lyric finally said. "Thatch has to go." She waved him away. "See you soon."

"Yes, you will." A growl was all he could manage with the heat climbing up his throat.

He trotted out the door and down the steps, welcoming

the cold air that slapped him in the face. Not the smartest move to kiss the woman who'd rejected him, but he couldn't say he regretted the impulsive decision either.

Mouth still scorching, he climbed into the driver's seat and started the engine. His phone chimed in his back pocket. He dug it out and glanced at the text from Lyric.

Honeybunch?????

Thatch laughed out loud as he drove away.

CHAPTER SIX

Was the coast clear? Lyric rolled through the café's parking lot, identifying each vehicle she drove past, but Thatch's truck was nowhere to be seen. Good. She could go in and meet her friends for an afternoon coffee break without having an awkward run-in with her pretend boyfriend. This conversation with Tess and Kyra was going to be hard enough without bringing Thatch into the mix.

Heat zinged across her cheeks. Who knew? Maybe he'd kiss her again, and then she'd get all weak-kneed and breathless like she did the last time, and who knew how long it would take her to stop having flashbacks.

Check that. She was still having flashbacks. She would likely never stop reliving that kiss.

Lyric swung her SUV into a spot and hopped out. Hopefully, the man wouldn't show up while she was here. Though if the radio silence of the last few days was any indication, it didn't seem like Thatch was all that keen on seeing her either. Which was just as well.

With one last look around the surrounding streets, she ducked inside the door. About half the tables were full, but there was no sign of Kyra or Tess yet, so she wandered to the long bar counter where Minnie was chatting with Doris and Nelly.

"Well, if it isn't the fine Ladies Aid Society of Star Valley." These three women had formed a committee tasked with organizing an effort to take care of anyone and everyone who found themselves in a time of need. They cooked and cleaned and mobilized and donated. And they usually gossiped while they did so.

Minnie, who'd been in the middle of saying something, suddenly clammed up.

Lyric assessed each of their expressions, which were all guilty. "What were you discussing?" She already had a pretty good idea.

"Oh, nothing. Nothing at all." Doris patted her hand and smiled with her teeth. That woman never smiled with her teeth.

"Nice weather out there today." Nelly stared out the window. "So warm for this time of year, don't you think?"

"Yeah. It's the perfect day for a little gossip." She aimed a knowing look at Minnie. "Don't *you* think?"

"We weren't gossiping." The woman wrinkled her nose. "Thatch was just here. That's all."

"Quite a looker, that man. Wouldn't you say?" Doris peered at Lyric over her mug before she took a sip.

"You're looking mighty lovely yourself today," Nelly added. "I mean, it would appear you're positively glowing with happiness."

Did these three have to be so obvious? They had a habit of implying something they didn't want to outright say.

They'd obviously heard something about her and Thatch. "I don't think I'm glowing."

"But you are." Minnie stole the mug from the place setting next to Doris and filled it for Lyric. "You're positively glowing."

"What've you been up to lately, hon?" Nelly peaked her eyebrows into overly innocent arches. "I haven't seen you around much."

Oh, sure. Now they wanted her to spill all her secrets to them. "I've had a pretty busy schedule at the clinic."

"Mm-hmm," Nelly murmured. "And what else have you been so busy with, hmm?"

"I don't know." She pretended to think. She could play this game every bit as well as they could. "The usual, I guess."

"Oh, come on," Minnie whispered. "We know about you and Thatch, so you might as well fess up."

"Of course you know." These three single-handedly powered the gossip mill in Star Valley. "A few days ago, only Kyra knew."

Minnie picked up the carafe and refilled Nelly's mug. "Well, Doris was talking to Janie at the market who'd just run into Bessy at the library—which you know is right next to the rec center project Cowboy Construction is working on—and Bessy happened to go in and take a peek at the progress on the rec center."

Most likely to see if Thatch was working shirtless, but Lyric let her continue.

"And that's when Bessy *overheard* Kyra and Aiden talking about going on a triple date with you two."

"So Bessy was basically spying." Kyra and Aiden probably hadn't even realized she was there.

"Is it true?" Doris hopped off her stool. "Are you and Thatch finally an item?"

"I don't know if you could call us an item, per se." They were more like an...arrangement.

"But you're dating?" Nelly dumped a sugar packet into her coffee. "Finally? After all this time?"

"That's the rumor." The rumor she'd started herself. Faking a relationship had seemed like the best option at the time, but the complications were starting to stack up.

A customer down the bar signaled Minnie for a coffee refill, but she waved him off. "I'm busy right now." She leaned in closer. "How long has this been going on?"

"It's still pretty new." Lyric lowered her voice. "And we're keeping things pretty low-key. I'm sure you can understand." She smirked. "You gals know how people talk in this town."

"Oh, yes. Well, your secret is safe with us." Doris twisted her fingers in front of her mouth. "Lips are sealed. Don't you worry. We won't tell a soul."

Lyric almost laughed. "Glad to hear—"

"There she is!" Tess rushed at her with Kyra not far behind. "I hear you have news to share."

Yes, and the Ladies had practically shared it with the whole café already. Lyric turned to Minnie. "Can we get our coffee to go today?"

"You bet." The woman scurried away humming the tune to "Chapel of Love."

"I'll need the decaf," Tess called. Then she frowned at Lyric. "Apparently, I missed all the juicy details about you and Thatch. I can't believe I didn't pick up on something sooner. I'm usually very observant. I want to know everything right now."

"We have all afternoon." And she'd rather not talk about Thatch here. "I thought we could wander through that new consignment shop and maybe check out the boot selection at Ranchers Outfitters."

"I'm game." Tess peered over her belly at her tennis shoes. "I feel like my feet have grown three sizes with this pregnancy."

"Perfectly normal," Kyra assured her.

"Oh, yes." Doris had settled herself back on her stool. "With my third baby, I had to buy all new shoes."

Thank God. Talking about babies and shoes would keep them distracted.

Tess smiled. "I guess there are worse things."

"Three coffees to go." Minnie handed Lyric a drink container with three cups. "Decaf's on the right."

"Got it." Tess stole the cup and, after a quick goodbye to the Ladies, the three of them paraded outside.

Spring was Lyric's favorite time of the year in Star Valley. Most of the snow had melted off the mountainsides, making room for the emerald-green grasses to carpet the landscape. Pops of color dotted the slope with wildflowers that had already begun to bloom. And today, the slight breeze carried the scent of lilacs. The sunshine seemed to have drawn most people outside, luring them to the quaint benches that sat underneath the blossoming ornamental cherry trees lining Main Street. Lyric walked along with her friends smiling at the familiar faces passing by and drew in a lungful of the mountain air before slowly exhaling. "So it would seem the entire town knows about Thatch and me."

"You had to figure that was going to happen." Tess slung an arm around her as they meandered down the street past the last arched windows of the Meadowlark Café and Hotel. "There's no hiding anything around here."

"Thatch sure didn't seem to mind people seeing you two kiss." Kyra turned to Tess. "You should've seen him smooch her. It was adorable. Very tender."

If Lyric hadn't known better, she would've agreed. The kiss had shocked her. But instead of wanting to push him away due to the sheer surprise of it, she'd sunk into him, held on to him.

"It's not fair that I wasn't there," Tess whined. "You're going to have to re-create that for me. Silas and I have had a bet going on how long it would take you two to get together. He said with how stubborn Thatch is, it could be another year, but I said no way." She pumped a fist in the air. "And I was right."

"You had a bet?" That revelation was reason 532 this fake relationship had been a bad idea. It seemed everyone in town had been discussing Lyric and Thatch's future behind their backs. This ruse would only feed those big expectations.

"The bet was just for funsies." Tess squeezed her hand. "All I really care about is your happiness, of course."

"That's good because Thatch and I are just having fun. There's probably no future there." Lyric held open the door to the ranching supply store, which also had a nice women's apparel selection. She might as well start setting the stage for their impending breakup now. Before things got out of hand. "You know me. I like my independence."

Both of her friends merely laughed.

"That's what I said too," Kyra muttered.

Lyric ignored her friend's teasing. "So how're you feeling, Tess?" Nothing like an abrupt subject change to steer the conversation away from things she'd rather not talk about.

"Huge." Tess's hand rested on her rounded belly. "But also elated. I mean, I never thought I would get to do this again." Her eyes got all misty. She might've blamed the pregnancy hormones, but Lyric's eyes were misty too. When her friend's husband died on a mission in Afghanistan, the light had gone out in Tess's eyes. Lyric had walked through much of that time with her, helping where she could—taking the girls for an evening, cleaning their house, bringing them meals. In fact, the whole town had come together to get Tess through. And now her friend had her joy back. That kind of restoration was beautiful to see.

Tess paused at the rack of new cowgirl hats. "And pregnancy is way better this time around because I don't have to drive all the way to Jackson for my appointments, thanks to the clinic."

Kyra plunked a flowery hat onto her head. "I've loved being a part of the journey."

"I have too." Lyric removed the hat for her, lest she get any ideas about purchasing the monstrosity. As a transplant from Florida, their friend was still getting the hang of authentic mountain style. "Speaking of, when are you coming for another prenatal yoga session?"

"Soon." Tess shifted her hips with a wince. "I really need to stretch out. My hips are so tight."

"Well, you're welcome anytime." Lyric spotted a rack of new sunglasses. "Oh, I need some new shades." She moved in that direction and then stopped suddenly. Elina and Franco stood a few feet away from the display. It appeared they were in the middle of an intense discussion, with hand gestures and everything, but she couldn't hear what they were saying.

"What's up?" Kyra glanced at Lyric over her shoulder.

"That's one of the girls in my class." She moved behind the hat display so they wouldn't see her. "Elina. And that's her boyfriend." He had that textbook bad-boy look, from the black spiked hair to the many tattoos coloring his arms to the scowl on his face.

Tess and Kyra hid with her, both of them craning their necks trying to get a better look.

"Yikes. I'm not sure he's being very nice to her." Tess frowned.

Lyric peeked through the space between two black cowboy hats. "That's what I've been worried about."

"They might be yelling at each other," Kyra observed. "I can't tell."

"We have to get closer." Lyric moved along the rows of hats and then hurried to take cover behind the first rack of sunglasses.

"Stop it. Just stop it," Elina was saying. "Don't talk to me like that."

Lyric shared an intense gaze with Tess.

"Shut up," Franco growled.

Oh, no, he didn't. Before she could think it through, Lyric stepped out from behind the sunglasses. "Hey, Elina." It was impossible to muster a smile with her blood boiling this way. "Everything okay over here?"

The girl's eyes registered a panicked shock.

"Who the hell are you?" Franco demanded, squinting at her.

"I'm her friend." *So take that.* Elina had backup—

"She's my yoga teacher," the girl corrected in a

horrified tone. Lyric might as well have been her embarrassing mother.

"I'm a customer at this establishment who is concerned
that we might have a problem here." She stared the kid
down. She no longer caved to bullies.

"Oh, my God." Elina hid her face in her hands.

"What the hell is your problem, lady?" Franco hissed,
looking around as though embarrassed.

Lady? She didn't even have one gray hair yet! "I
don't have a problem," she said calmly. "Do you?" She
addressed the question to Elina. "Because I'm here to
help—"

"I don't need your help." She was definitely staring at
Lyric the way an irate teen girl might stare at her mother.

"Come on. Let's get out of here." Franco tugged on
Elina's arm, and Lyric found herself in motion again,
stepping between them while some other force took over
inside of her. "You don't have to go with him. I can take
you home." Her skin prickled from the icy hot adrenaline the same way it had when her ex Luke used to grab
her arm.

"Leave me alone." Elina lurched away and practically
ran for the door with Franco trailing behind her. The fight
instinct that had risen inside of Lyric nearly sent her chas-
ing them out the door, but that wouldn't do any good. So
instead, she tried to even out her breathing and returned
to her friends, her heart thudding.

"You okay?" Kyra put an arm around her. She was the
only one who knew the whole story behind Lyric's past.

"I'm fine." The wheeze in her voice exposed the lie.
Her stomach was sick.

"I don't understand," Tess said. "Why would she want

to leave with him if he was talking to her like that? So rude."

Lyric couldn't explain. She'd done the same thing once. She'd ignored all her friends' careful questions. She'd let other relationships go in favor of the one that was hurting her the most. "She's probably never going to talk to me again now."

"She has to keep going to your class to get the school credit, right?" Kyra asked.

"I guess so." But, after making such a scene, Lyric had no idea how she would ever earn the girl's trust.

CHAPTER SEVEN

This radio silence between her and Thatch had gone on long enough. Lyric parked in front of the rec center and tried to see through the slightly tinted windows. Running into Elina and Franco at the store a few days before had really shaken her, and she needed to know if Thatch had spent any time with the kid.

Between a busy week at the clinic and the lingering awkwardness after the kiss they'd shared, she'd been avoiding seeing her "boyfriend" as much as he'd seemed to avoid her, but it was time to get back to her mission. Before Elina got hurt the way Lyric had.

Thatch had to be in the rec center because his truck was parked in the alleyway, along with Aiden's and Silas's. That meant the man wasn't sick or maimed or in a hospital somewhere because of a bronc riding accident. He simply hadn't called or texted or run into her all week.

Ever since that damn kiss.

His lack of attention shouldn't bother her. They were

faking it, after all. But how could he kiss her like that and then ignore her? The contact hadn't simply been a little peck on the lips. Maybe that was the problem. Maybe he hadn't *liked* kissing her. She shouldn't have liked kissing him either. But everyone was going to start to get suspicious if they weren't seen around town together once in a while. Starting with their friends.

Lyric lifted her head so she could see herself in the rearview mirror. She brushed on some lip gloss and then pushed out her car, a rogue anticipation swirling.

The glass door had been propped open, so she followed the whirring sounds of a saw until she found Thatch, Aiden, and Silas in a big half-drywalled room.

Thatch finished cutting a piece of drywall before shutting off the power tool to greet her. "What're you doing here?" was all he said.

She wrangled a smile for the benefit of the two other men watching them. "Can't a girlfriend visit her boyfriend at work?"

"No one around here's gonna stop you." Silas checked his watch. "I've gotta head out anyway. Tess has a checkup at the clinic."

Aiden removed work goggles from his eyes and threw them onto a nearby table. "Then I might as well take off early and make Kyra a surprise dinner tonight. Don't tell her," he said to Silas.

"It's not even four o'clock." Thatch stacked the cut of drywall against some two-by-fours.

"Good thing your new intern is coming in." Silas clapped him on the back. "He can help you hang some drywall."

Aiden removed the tool belt from around his waist

and set it next to his goggles. "Since you're all here, Kyra and I want to have you four over for dinner. Saturday night work?"

"I don't know," Thatch said at the same time Lyric said, "Sure. Sounds great."

Ugh. No one was ever going to buy that they were really a couple. They simply had to flirt more. "We can make it work." She sidled up next to him. "Right, *honeybunch*?"

A smile flickered across his lips. "Yeah. Sure."

"Great. It's all set." Aiden pulled out his phone and started tapping away. "Four o'clock. We'll grill out if the weather's nice."

"Sounds good." Silas disappeared down the hallway. "See ya tomorrow."

"I'm out too. You kids have fun." Aiden turned and hurried in the same direction Silas had gone.

Now that they were alone, Thatch crossed his arms. "What're you really doing here?"

A few different explanations crossed her mind. *I'm trying to convince people we're really together. I needed to know if kissing me disgusted you.* She finally gave voice to the most rational one. "I need to know if Franco has said anything to you. About me."

"No." Thatch hauled another piece of drywall to the cutting table and lined it up. "Why? What did you do?"

Uncanny how the man seemed to be able to read her. "I saw him being mean to Elina in a store a few days ago, and I kind of made a scene and confronted them."

"Subtle." He turned the saw on and ran a perfect cut through the piece of drywall before giving her the chance to explain.

"Well, I had to do something." She marched to him, her face firing up like it had in the store that day. "He was *yelling* at her."

Thatch carried the drywall across the room and leaned it against the other sheet. It seemed he had no desire to stand close to her. "Did you hear what they were talking about?"

"No. But I know what I saw." Their body language had been all too familiar. She was sure Elina had been cowering slightly. Maybe no one else would've noticed, but she knew.

"Listen." Thatch seemed to give up on his work. "I've already spent two afternoons with Franco, and he was actually pretty respectful and polite. We talked some. I got to know him a little—"

"He told her to shut up." Thatch thought he'd gotten to know Franco, but with guys like him, no one ever really saw the truth until it was too late. They knew how to charm and manipulate people into thinking they were good. "Would you ever talk to a woman that way?"

Thatch didn't answer until he came back to face her directly, his eyes all fiery and intense. "You really have to ask me that?"

"No." Her voice weakened. The man likely never played poker. Those eyes would always give him away. She could read him as easily as he seemed to read her. She could see the emotion there. The mix of hurt and intrigue when he stared at her this way. "I know you wouldn't talk to a woman that way. But I'm worried that Franco will avoid me now. And I want the four of us to hang out so we can keep an eye on them."

"Well, you can talk to him about it if you'd like."

Thatch lined up another piece of drywall. "He'll be here any minute."

"Right. I'll apologize to him." If she wanted to earn Elina's trust and learn what was really going on between her and Franco, then she'd have to earn his trust too. Or at least clear the air between them so he wouldn't run in the opposite direction whenever he saw her.

"You're sure you still want to go through with this whole thing?" Thatch made another cut with the saw and then continued. "The pretending?"

"Sure." Second thoughts might have been her constant companion the last few days, but she didn't have to tell him that. Because the man seemed all confident and unaffected. She could play that part too. "Why wouldn't I want to go through with it?"

Thatch pulled the pencil out from behind his ear and made some marks on the drywall, his lips hinting at a smirk again. "You seemed a little taken aback when I kissed you."

"What?" She wished he would turn his head so she could read his eyes again. Was he teasing her? Or trying to figure out how she felt about him kissing her? "I wasn't taken aback." Maybe she'd been *taken in*, but he didn't need to know that. "I mean, kissing you was *so* not a big deal. We're going to have to kiss occasionally so everyone thinks we're together." They would get used to it, and eventually, her pulse wouldn't even kick up.

"I guess we will." Thatch continued his work, marking off sections of the drywall without paying her much attention.

But this conversation wasn't over. They had to hash out all these details now so they didn't come across as awkward and unsure. "Why didn't you want to go to dinner at Kyra and Aiden's on Saturday night?"

"Our friends know us better than anyone else." He stashed the pencil behind his ear and faced her again. "Don't you think they're going to see through this?"

"We won't let them." They simply had to power through and get past any awkwardness. "We can be convincing." He'd certainly been convincing when he'd kissed her.

Thatch's deep sigh sagged his shoulders. "They won't tell anyone. If we tell them the truth. That we're only dating so we can hang out with your student and her boyfriend. Maybe it would be better to be honest with our friends. I don't like lying."

"We're not doing this so we can *hang out* with them." Her voice rose despite her best effort to restrain the anger. "We're getting to know Franco so we can protect Elina." That was the bottom line. "We're watching out for her." She couldn't let someone else go through the pain she'd experienced when she had the power to step in and do something. She fired up her right eyebrow into her most skeptical glare. "Besides, do you really want to tell Silas and Aiden you're doing yoga with me so you can become a better bronc rider?"

His silence answered for him.

"I didn't think so." They were only pretending. That wasn't quite the same as lying.

Uttering another sigh, he glanced past her shoulder at the windows. "Franco pulled up. You might want to meet him on his way in if you're going to apologize and all."

"Right." She eased out her own sigh as she left the room and hurried down the hallway. "Hi, Franco."

The kid froze inside the doorway and raised his hands. "I'm only here for work, lady."

"I know." She turned up the wattage on her smile. "I wanted to apologize. I probably jumped to some conclusions that I shouldn't have at the store the other day." Or not. "I'm sorry we got off on the wrong foot."

"Okay." Without smiling back, he sidestepped her and continued down the hall.

She followed behind him. "I really feel bad about making such a scene." She kept her tone chipper so she wouldn't come across as desperate.

They walked into the big open space where Thatch had just finished cutting another sheet of drywall. "Thatch and I were thinking maybe we could take you and Elina out to dinner at the café to make up for it."

"No thanks." The kids sauntered to a shelf that held a tool belt and slung it around his waist. "Hey, Thatch. Are we hanging more drywall today?"

Lyric shot the man a desperate look behind Franco's back. She needed his help here.

"Uh. Yeah. We'll keep working on drywall." Thatch lifted the piece he'd cut and hauled it to the opposite corner of the room while Lyric gestured at him the whole way.

Thatch sure seemed to be sighing a lot today. "Hey, Franco. I don't suppose you and Elina would want to come out to the arena to watch me take a practice ride sometime, would you?"

The kid slipped on a pair of work goggles. "That might be cool."

"I've got a time set up for Saturday morning. Ten o'clock. Show up at Kirby Leatherman's place if you can make it." Thatch slid her a sideways glance as if to say, *See how it's done?*

"We'll be there." Franco said the words almost with awe. "Definitely."

"Great." Thatch sidled up alongside Lyric. "I'm going to walk her out to her car. I'll be right back." He nudged her along down the hallway.

"How did you know he'd agree to come and watch you ride?" she asked when they'd stepped outside.

"We've talked about it some." He opened the car door for her. "He's interested in bronc riding. I told him I've been dabbling."

Really? It had been that simple for him to connect with the kid? "But you haven't told hardly anyone about riding." She climbed into the driver's seat.

"He's not going to say anything." Thatch glanced at the windows. "I think he's scared of me. He does seem to respect authority."

That made sense. There was no authority figure quite like an ex–Navy SEAL.

Thatch leaned into her car. "I know you said you want nothing to do with my riding, but that was the only thing I could think of to get him motivated enough to show up."

"It's fine." If their double date had to be at the arena, she would make it work. She needed to see Elina and Franco interact to figure out if her instincts were right. "I've been to plenty of arenas. I've seen plenty of cowboys ride." She used to watch her ex ride every weekend. "I can handle it."

As long as she stayed focused on helping Elina.

CHAPTER EIGHT

Thatch had never been nervous before a practice ride. It wasn't like he lived to impress Kirby. But with Lyric walking into the arena alongside him, a tic worked in his jaw. It didn't help that she'd been nearly silent since they'd met at the café and then during the whole drive to Kirby's. Lyric was never silent. Desperation flooded through him. What was she thinking? Why was her face so expressionless?

He glanced at her again while they paused at the fence around the corral. "You okay?"

"Mm-hmm." Her eyes were trained in front of her, focused on something he apparently couldn't see.

There was no sign of Kirby yet. Nothing else to distract them. Nothing to interrupt the awkwardness between them.

This was ridiculous. He and Lyric talked all the time. So he'd kissed her. He'd have to get past that and move on. There had to be something they could talk about.

Thatch cleared his throat. "You said you've been around the rodeo a lot?"

"Uh, yeah." She paused, seemingly lost for a second. "It was years ago, though."

As much time as he'd spent with Lyric in the last couple of years, she'd never really talked about her history. He knew the basics—that she'd lived in Fort Myers until her mom had married her stepdad, who happened to be Kyra's dad. Apparently, their affair had been quite the scandal. Lyric and Kyra had been best friends, and then Kyra's dad had cheated on her mom with Lyric's mom. The three of them had moved to Wyoming when Lyric was in elementary school. But past that, she'd never revealed anything. "Did you grow up watching bronc riders?"

"No." She ran her dainty fingers along the top run of the fence. "I didn't get into the rodeo world until I moved here with my mom and stepdad." Her gaze toured the corral in front of them. "Believe it or not, I was a rodeo queen."

It wasn't much, but for some reason, that revelation felt like a gift. "Yeah?" Though she was beautiful—with her soft long black hair, her silky skin, her curious dark eyes hiding beneath long lashes—he couldn't quite picture Lyric as a beauty queen. She didn't do herself up like so many of those women did. From what he could tell, she wore little to no makeup. Her clothes were understated; when not teaching or working out, she mostly wore flowy tops with jeans or shorts. These were some of the things he liked best about her. They told him that appearances didn't seem to matter.

He quickly looked away. He'd been studying her too long. "How'd you like being a rodeo queen?"

"I wasn't that into it." She collected her hair in her hand and pulled it on top of her head with an elastic band. "Star Valley didn't have any candidates willing to compete. Kenny taught me how to handle a horse, and I was pretty good. So he talked me into entering the pageant. And I won."

He spied a hint of pride in her smile. But it wasn't a full smile, not her real one. It was hiding something. "Anyone else know about this beauty queen business?" Because he was having a hard time believing no one in their group of friends had ever discussed this tidbit.

"Only Tess, and she's been sworn to secrecy." Lyric walked along the fence a few paces. "I don't exactly remember a lot of my time around the rodeos fondly." She said the words so quietly, he almost didn't hear them.

"What happened?" Had she wanted him to ask? He didn't know. He didn't know what the rules were when they were supposed to be faking it. But he couldn't pretend he didn't want to know about her. She made him wonder.

"I met my ex-husband at a rodeo. And then we went to college together." Now she fully turned away from him, rubbing her hands up and down her bare arms. "He's a bronc rider."

Lyric had been married to a bronc rider? She'd never said anything. Even when he'd told her what he was training for. She'd never brought up her ex-husband. "What's his name?"

She hesitated. "Luke Copeland."

Copeland? The guy wasn't just a bronc rider; he was a pretty big deal in that world. "I know the name. He's good." From the articles Thatch had read, her ex had won plenty of competitions. "So what happened—?"

"I wonder where Franco and Elina are."

He could take a hint. This conversation was done. "I'm sure they'll be here. The kid asked me about a million questions after you left the other day. I think he wants to get into riding too."

"He'd probably fit in with the rest of those cowboys," she muttered with clear disdain.

Thatch nudged her. Usually Lyric was so buoyant, so light and carefree. But ever since he'd picked her up today, she'd been off. "You say that like cowboys are a bad thing." He couldn't help but tease her, bring that real smile out of the shadows.

"Sorry." A half smile flashed, giving him a glimpse of the woman hiding behind the curtain today. "I guess I think of you a little differently. You weren't born and bred a cowboy."

"Nah. I've always been more of a farm boy." And then when Jace had died, Thatch's life had taken a turn. He'd found himself building a life in the mountains. "But I've met some pretty stellar cowboys through all my training. So they're not all bad."

"No." Her eyes went downcast. "I guess they're not."

She didn't seem convinced, but he would gladly show her. He would show her how a man should treat a woman—with respect and reverence. Hell, he'd put her on a pedestal. If she'd ever let him.

"Hey, Hearst, you ready to ride?"

Thatch hadn't even seen Kirby sneak up on them from the other side of the stacked barrels.

"Just about." He walked to meet one of the best cowboys he knew. "First, I want you to meet Lyric. She's my yoga instructor. She's going to watch the ride and then tell me everything I did wrong." That statement earned another smile out of her.

"You're going to have your work cut out for you," Kirby informed her.

Lyric laughed. "Don't I know it?" She sidled up closer to Thatch. "I'm also his girlfriend, by the way. In case he hasn't told you."

Sometime soon, he would have to stop flinching when she introduced herself that way. It shouldn't be so jarring. He knew their arrangement. Yet this stirring sensation inside him took him by surprise every time.

The old man's gaze gave him a good chastising. "You ain't never said nothing about a girlfriend."

"I don't advertise my love life." Because things had been pretty quiet in that department since his engagement had fallen apart. There'd never been much to talk about. Not commitment-wise anyway. And he and Kirby didn't exactly have heart-to-hearts when he was training.

"Well, it's nice to meet ya." The man shook her hand. "Lyric, you said? Hoping you can work a miracle with this fella. Otherwise, we're about out of options." He gave Thatch a surprisingly strong clap on the shoulder. "Lemme know when you're ready to ride. I'll have Rich put Notorious in the chute today."

"You can go ahead and get everything ready." Thatch checked his watch. "I invited a kid who's working with me to come and watch too. So we'll wait a few more minutes to see if he shows."

"Great," Kirby mumbled. "It's a party. You'd better step it up today so you don't disappoint your fans." He walked away, his left leg dragging a little.

"Why'd you tell him you're my girlfriend?" Thatch

asked Lyric when they were out of earshot. Now Kirby was one more person he'd have to keep this lie straight with.

"I didn't want him to say something in front of Elina and Franco." Lyric spoke in a hushed whisper. "It'll be less confusing if *everyone* believes we're dating."

Less confusing for who? He didn't have a chance to ask before Franco wandered in through the open doorway. A young girl—presumably Elina—followed behind him but stopped abruptly when she saw Lyric.

"What is *she* doing here?" The girl nodded in Lyric's direction with a clear frown.

Franco shrugged. "Watching Thatch ride, I guess. Same as us."

"Great." Elina folded her arms. She rolled her eyes and cocked one hip at the exact same time. Thatch had seen the same stance from his younger cousins when they'd been in their teens. It appeared Elina wasn't one of Lyric's biggest fans.

"Hey." He stuck out a hand in her direction. "I'm Thatch. You must be Elina. I've heard a lot about you." Franco had two favorite subjects while they were working: rodeo and his girlfriend.

"Yeah, I've heard a lot about you too," Elina muttered, still glaring at Lyric.

Yikes. The girl had quite the cutting stare.

"Hey, man. Can I see the bronc?" Franco asked, already heading toward the chute.

"Sure." Thatch followed him. It would likely be a good idea for Lyric and Elina to have a minute alone anyway. He was getting chilly from the ice in the girl's stare, and it wasn't even directed at him.

"So this is Notorious." He gestured to the animal standing behind the fence.

"Damn." Franco walked the length of the chute. "He looks mean."

"They're not mean." Thatch had thought the same thing until he'd spent time around the animals. "They're strong and competitive. They love the thrill of the arena. They're athletes just like the riders."

Franco had stars in his eyes. "Think I could ever give it a try?"

"Maybe in a few years." As gruff as he was, Kirby was also a great teacher. He might take on a student like Franco if he showed promise. But the kid would have to prove he was a hard worker first. Thatch had renovated half the man's house before he'd agreed to take him on as a client.

"A lot of riders start out younger than me even." Franco's tone made it sound like he was offended Thatch thought he couldn't do it. At least the kid had some drive, a competitive spirit. That was a good start.

"It's best to get through high school first." He wouldn't miss a chance to steer Franco in the right direction. "And then get good training. That's the key. When I moved here, I could hardly even ride a horse."

Franco laughed. "Then I've already got a head start. I've been riding since I was four."

"That is a good start, but bronc riding is completely different." Thatch caught a glimpse of Lyric and Elina. It appeared, based on the girl's body language, that they were having a one-sided discussion with Lyric doing most of the talking.

Since he had Franco as a captive audience, he might

as well do a little recon work and find out more about their relationship. "So how long have you and Elina been dating?"

"I don't know." The kid was still eyeing Notorious. "Eight months maybe."

"You didn't tell her Lyric was going to be at the arena today, did you?" He was surprised the girl hadn't taken off yet.

"That lady's intense. No offense, man. I know she's your girlfriend and everything, but…" Franco looked over his shoulder at Lyric. "She freaked out on us in front of everyone at the store. Like she thought I was gonna hurt Elina or something."

So Franco knew exactly what Lyric thought of him. Interesting. "I hope you'd never hurt a woman." Thatch watched the kid's face intently for any sign of guilt.

"Man, I'm not that stupid. I know I shouldn't have told her to shut up, but she said much worse to me right before that. We were arguing because she wanted me to steal a pair of sunglasses, and I told her hell no."

Say what? "She wanted you to shoplift for her?" That was a red flag if he'd ever seen one. "Does she ask you to do that a lot?"

"Never. But things have been really tight for her family money-wise." Franco walked closer to the fence, staring at the bronc again. "Don't worry, dude. I wouldn't shop-lift, and I wouldn't lay a hand on her. Elina would hurt me back if I ever crossed a line. She's much stronger than she looks. Trust me."

"I do trust you." Granted, he didn't know the kid well. But from what he'd seen so far, Franco had a good head on his shoulders. As good as a teenage boy could have anyway. He wasn't perfect, but nothing about him indicated violence. So why would Lyric assume the worst before she'd gotten to know him?

Thatch wasn't sure he wanted to know the answer. But he was also starting to put the pieces together. Lyric didn't want to be here at the arena. Her ex-husband had been a rider. It wasn't too hard to figure out that the man had hurt her somehow. Maybe it was none of his business, but he'd be lying if he said he didn't care about her, fake relationship or not.

"Hey, I'm gonna go find Kirby so we can get this party started." And so he could ask the man a few questions.

"Sounds good to me." The kid climbed up on the fence like he wanted a front-row seat.

Thatch wandered behind the barrels until he found Kirby and his assistant Rich talking near the feed storage.

"You finally ready?" the old man grouched. "'Cuz I don't got all day here."

"In a minute." Thatch nodded for Kirby to walk with him. "What do you know about Luke Copeland?"

The man didn't even hesitate. "Lives in northern Colorado. Still competes some. He's an asshole from what I've heard. Been in trouble with the law a few times earlier in his career for getting violent. Why?"

"I heard his name and got curious." He glanced to where Lyric and Elina had joined Franco by the fence. So Luke had been the violent type. Now he had a more complete picture.

"Sounds like Copeland will be right here in Star Valley for the Rodeo Days. So you can see him for yourself." Kirby motioned for Rich to move to the chute gate. "You'll get to compete against him." He snorted. "Good luck."

"He's competing?" Thatch's stomach clenched. Lyric's ex-husband was coming to Star Valley?

"He's on the list," Kirby said impatiently. "Doubt he's gonna be here for the scenery. Now let's get moving. I've got another client coming in half an hour."

"Right." Thatch had to battle for focus. Whatever had happened between Lyric and her ex-husband had been a long time ago. Before he'd known her. And she'd made it clear that her past was none of his business. She hadn't wanted to talk about it, so he would have to let go. But he would be watching over her while Luke was in town.

"Just about ready," he called to his cheerleaders at the fence. He walked to the bench and pulled on his chest protector.

"You got this." Franco gave him a thumbs-up.

"Any day now, hotshot." Kirby stood with Rich at the gate.

Was anyone ever ready to climb onto the back of an irate bronc? He didn't know what being ready would feel like. Same as when he found himself walking into a fight as a SEAL. There was no way to prepare. Instinct had to take over. Maybe that was why he was here, why he'd been drawn to this sport. He'd always excelled at following his instincts.

Before he could think too much, Thatch climbed the fence, wrapped his gloved hand in the rope, and swung his leg over, sliding into the saddle. Notorious lurched and swayed, already gunning for him.

Kirby did a countdown from three, and then they threw open the gate.

Notorious bucked immediately, but Thatch stayed

loose, not fighting the horse's momentum. They went air-borne and then thudded back to the dirt, sending a spray of mud behind them.

"That's it!" Franco yelled. "What a badass!"

"Straighten up," Kirby instructed.

Even with a few good jackknives, Thatch was able to hold his posture. Work the spurs, arm raised above his head. The constant bucks jolted him, but he let his body whip forward and back instead of snapping. This was it. The best ride he'd ever taken.

Notorious went into a series of spins, and he fought to hold on, engaging his core for balance and stability the way Lyric had taught him in their yoga session.

"Eight seconds!" Kirby sounded thrilled for once.

Notorious went into a jackknifing spin in the opposite direction and then put on the brakes. Momentum pitched Thatch off the bronc sideways and a hoof caught him in his chest on the way to the dirt, knocking the wind clean out of him.

"Thatch!" Panic raised Lyric's voice.

He opened his eyes to stare at the metal ceiling over the arena but didn't even try to breathe yet. He knew better. Whenever he got the wind knocked out of him, he waited a few seconds before taking a small, shallow breath. The harder he struggled, the worse his lungs would hurt.

Rich already had Notorious corralled on the other side of the fence, thank God. Because one more blow from that hoof might end him.

"Are you okay?" Lyric lowered to her knees beside him. "That looked awful. He kicked you! Are you breathing?"

"That was my best ride ever," he wheezed. Maybe he

wouldn't try to sit up just yet. The pain in his ribs sent stars circling in his vision.

"Dude, you totally rocked that!" Franco stood over him. "He threw you off like a rag doll."

"That's usually how it ends." Thatch slung an arm around his chest. Well, he usually didn't get kicked on the way down. That was new.

"I would've scored that ride in the top ten percent." Was that pride in Kirby's voice? "Maybe there is something to that yoga shit after all."

"Can you sit up?" Concern still pinched at Lyric's mouth.

"Sure. I can sit up. No problem." It likely would've sounded more convincing if he hadn't gasped between the words.

"You can't even breathe." Lyric gently pressed her fingers into his chest. "Does this hurt?"

Of course it hurt. "I'm good." He shooed her hands away.

"Do I need to call nine-one-one or something?" Elina had crept over to stand next to Franco.

"Nah." Kirby nudged Thatch's shoulder with his boot. "He'll be fine. Give him a minute."

"I'll bet that bronc threw you thirty feet," Franco marveled.

More like ten, but he let the kid exaggerate. "Top ten percent ride, though." Thatch looked up at Kirby to make sure he'd heard that right.

"For sure." His mentor reached out a hand to help him up. "Best ride of your career so far, kid. I think you've finally got the feel for it."

Instead of reaching for Kirby's hand, Thatch turned

over on his side and then pushed onto his knees, bracing his rib cage against the spiraling pain.

"You need to go to the hospital." Lyric's hands were on him again, supporting his back while he stood. "I don't understand why you're doing this to yourself."

"Because it's awesome." Franco gave him a high five. "You watch. That'll be me someday."

"Whatever." Elina started to walk away. "This has been real fun and all, but I have to get home."

Thatch tried to stretch out his upper body, but his ribs locked him down. He was gonna be sore for a while.

"Let me know when you're riding again," Franco called, following his girlfriend to the doors. "Next time, I'll take a video."

"Great." Thatch made sure to stand up straight and not wince. He grinned at Lyric. "See? I'm good." His voice went a little too high.

She shook her head at him.

"You did it, kid." Kirby gave his shoulder a good whack.

Owwww.

"See ya next week." The older man hurried away to meet up with Rich by the chute.

"I don't think you'll be riding next week," Lyric told him while he painstakingly removed his gear and stashed it in his bag. "I think you should see a doctor for your ribs."

"I'll give it a day or two." He couldn't take a break now and risk moving backward. "Besides, after a few yoga sessions, I'll probably be as good as new."

"Not sure about that." Her hand pressed against his chest again.

Thatch did his best not to wince, but he couldn't hide from her probing gaze.

"It hurts right here, doesn't it?" she asked.

"I mean, I guess. A little." But he sure didn't mind her touching him. Feeling her hands on his body was totally worth a kick to the ribs.

CHAPTER NINE

Thatch was not fine. She didn't care what the man said. Every time they hit the slightest bump in the road, a subdued groan rumbled in his throat, and his jaw tightened like he was gritting his teeth. Only he evidently didn't want her to notice because ever since they'd gotten into his truck, he kept trying to make small talk.

"Did you get things all straightened out with Elina?" he asked in a raspy *my ribs are killing me* kind of voice.

"Not exactly." *All straightened out* would've been Elina actually talking back to her. Instead, the girl had mostly ignored her and acted like she hated her the entire time they were at the arena. "I apologized for what happened at the store in quite a passionate monologue. But she didn't say much."

Thatch shifted in the driver's seat with a suppressed grunt. "I'm sure she'll come around. Give her some time."

If she gave *him* some time, would the man admit he was hurting right now? "I overreacted." She could own up to her mistake. "I never should've confronted them in public like that." She could've asked Elina to talk privately for a minute instead of embarrassing her in front of whoever happened to be in the store at the time. "I just . . . I know how it feels to want to be loved by someone so much that you overlook things you shouldn't." She wanted to stop the girl from making the same mistakes she'd made in the past.

Thatch brought the truck to a stop at the intersection and turned his head to her. "I know how that feels too." There wasn't as much rasping in the words this time. His low tone hinted at empathy.

Most of the time, Thatch stayed in the realm of joking around, teasing, lighthearted conversation, so this show of compassion was new for him. "Really?" Lyric didn't mean to be skeptical, but he'd never exactly divulged such a personal emotion.

"Yeah." He turned his gaze back to the road and accelerated again. This stretch happened to be one of her favorite drives in all of Star Valley—the way the pavement curved and bent and dipped with the rugged landscape as they crawled down the mountainside back into the valley. But right now, she couldn't seem to look away from the man sitting beside her. Could he truly relate?

"It's like you almost think you can make everything okay if you just stay the course," he finally said. "Like all the problems in the relationship will disappear if you can work hard enough. Like the other person will love you if you love them enough."

"Exactly." Now she was the one rasping. She couldn't help it. She never could put her relationship with Luke into those terms, but Thatch's description was exactly what she'd experienced. Every time he mistreated her, she told herself she simply had to do better. To be better. And she could fix him. She could fix their marriage. "Elina's so young. I don't want her to get into a bad situation because she's overlooking things she shouldn't." If she could save one other woman from going through the hell she'd gone through, making a fool out of herself in a store would be worth it.

"It's easy to overlook things." Thatch slowed the truck, his expert hands turning the wheel to wind down a set of Star Valley's infamous switchbacks. "She's lucky to have someone who wants to watch out for her."

"Elina doesn't necessarily see it that way." The girl had treated her like an overbearing mother. "She pretty much told me to butt out of her life." And Lyric had told her mother the same thing a time or two at that age.

"Why not take a different approach?" He eased on the brakes and paused at the stop sign before turning onto the main highway. "I mean, I've gotten to know Franco a little bit already. Why don't you see if Elina wants a job at the clinic or something? Do her a favor so you can hang out with her in a different context. Then she could see a different side of you. The fun, caring, thoughtful side."

Had the heat suddenly come on in the truck, or had the man made her blush? She didn't realize he saw her as all those things. But it felt good to have someone recognize that her motivation was in the right place. "You're right. I need to try something different." Begging the girl to hang out like they were besties wasn't going to work.

Thatch turned onto the highway, and they hit a pothole, jostling them both. A whimper escaped his lips.

"That's it," Lyric declared. "We're going back to my place."

His head swiveled, and he stared at her with wide eyes. "Say what?"

She laughed. "So I can wrap some ice around your sore ribs, silly." As if she'd really hit on him when he was injured. "And don't tell me your ribs don't hurt. I can see right through you."

"Fine." His shoulders slumped. "They're killing me."

"I thought so." The man wasn't as good at pretending as he thought he was. "I have ice wraps in the freezer for when I overdo it at yoga. They work wonders on soreness and bruising." Hopefully, he hadn't cracked any of the bones.

"A little ice might be good," Thatch said begrudgingly. "I have a hard time seeing you get hurt doing yoga. You're pretty good at it."

"It happens less frequently now, but yeah." During the rest of the drive to her house, she entertained him with the story about the time she was doing a headstand and toppled over, landing on her coffee table.

When they walked through her front door, Amos, her faithful husky, was there to greet them. The dog growled at Thatch, as usual, letting the man know it was his job to protect Lyric. But all it took was one scratch behind the ear, and Amos was leaning into Thatch's leg, practically purring.

"All right, boy. Go easy on him. He's injured, after all." She nudged the dog away and led Thatch into the kitchen.

"Not necessarily *injured*," he clarified. "It's only a bruise."

She wasn't so sure about that. Lyric pointed to a kitchen chair. "Take a seat. And you need to lose the shirt."

His jaw dropped. "Usually, a woman offers me a drink before she asks me to start stripping."

"Stop being cute, Hearst." Lyric reached into the freezer and found the elastic bandages. Nice and frozen.

"I'm not trying to be cute," the man muttered, peeling off his shirt with a grimace. "Trust me. No man ever wants to be called *cute*."

Yes, *cute* didn't really fit Thatch. Typically, she liked to downplay his overall sex appeal, but that proved to be more of a challenge when he was shirtless. Her gaze spent a little too much time appreciating the washboard abs, broad chest, and sinewy biceps before he cleared his throat. "Would you like me to get *you* a drink?" Amusement glinted off his grin.

"No." She added an eye roll for good measure. "I was trying to figure out the best way to wrap you." Little white lies never hurt anyone. "I've never actually had to wrap my ribs."

Amos wandered between them, whining and nudging Thatch's hand with his nose. "I know, boy. It's gonna hurt."

"You might have to stand up." She backed up to keep a healthy distance between them. "And then I'll wind the bandage around your rib cage."

"Sure. No problem." He pushed out of the chair with a pained murmur.

"Okay. Hmm. I'll just reach this way…" Holding the wrap in one hand, she snaked her arms around him, giving herself as wide a berth as she could, and managed to grab the end of the bandage with her other hand. "There we go." Her hands were brushing his skin, but so far there hadn't been any contact with their bodies, which was a good thing. "Now I'll fasten the Velcro, and you should be good."

"Whoa. That's cold." Thatch's upper body stiffened, all his muscles flexing.

"You can sit back down." So she wasn't eye-level with his impressive pecs anymore. "I'll get you a drink. How about some kombucha tea?"

Wariness worked itself into lines in his forehead. "Kom what?"

Ah, yes. She'd forgotten that his beverage menu consisted only of water, beer, and the occasional soda. "It's a healthy drink. Full of probiotics." She made a show of pouring herself a glass from the pitcher in her refrigerator. "Vitamins keep the inside of your body healthy." He already had a good grasp on the outside of his body.

"I think I'll stick with water, thanks." Thatch shifted to the right and then to the left. "I hate to say it, but I think the ice is helping."

"Because ice takes away inflammation." She set a water bottle in front of him and took her kombucha to the other side of the table. "You'd better get used to inflammation if you're going to be a bronc rider. Maybe you should pick up a different passion."

"Like?" His gaze homed in on her with that intent laser focus that made her all flustered.

Not her! She wasn't suggesting *she* should be his passion. "Fishing," she sputtered. Her stepdad had loved fly fishing on the river. "Fishing is a good hobby."

"I'll have plenty of time for fishing when I'm sixty," he deadpanned.

Right. The man was an adrenaline junkie. "Okay. What about mountain climbing? Bungee jumping? Paragliding?

Because those activities would probably be just as safe as riding a bronc anyway." She didn't know why she was lecturing him. If he wanted to break his body, what business was it of hers? They weren't really together.

"I'll take my chances with the broncs." Thatch picked up the water bottle but hesitated before taking a drink. "By the way, I should probably tell you that I talked to Franco about him and Elina while we were at the arena."

"Oh." He'd managed to have a conversation about their relationship with that kid that easily? She hadn't even gotten past *how long have you been dating?* with Elina. "And?"

"He told me he'd never hurt a woman." Thatch delivered the words almost apologetically, like he was afraid they would disappoint her. "Franco explained that they were only arguing at the store when you ran into them."

"He told her to shut up and grabbed her arm." The same fiery urgency she had at the store started to take over again. "I saw him. You don't believe me?"

"I believe you." Thatch set down the bottle and leaned into the table, his mouth soft. She seemed to notice his mouth a lot more these days. "He said she was mad at him. Because he wouldn't steal a pair of sunglasses for her, Lyric. He didn't want to get in trouble."

"That's not true." That couldn't be true. "He's lying." There was no way a teenage boy would confess to mistreating his girlfriend. Especially to an intimidating ex–Navy SEAL like Thatch who wouldn't put up with that kind of thing. "I know what I saw." She replayed the scene again. "He was intense with her…" She couldn't have misread the situation, right?

"Did you happen to hear what they were fighting

about?" he asked, focusing on swirling his finger around the rim of the water bottle like he didn't want to look at her.

"No. But she was upset. I could tell." Her heart thumped harder. Except she couldn't be sure, could she? "It looked to me like the kid has an anger issue. That type of thing is easy to hide." She would know.

"Right." His small smile wasn't convincing. "Well, maybe we can hang out with them again. I'll invite them next time I ride. We can keep an eye on things."

He didn't believe her. She could tell. He thought she was wrong about Franco. "We might have to come up with another plan too. I don't think you're going to be riding for a while." Without the ice pack, he couldn't even rotate his upper body without groaning and grimacing. "You'll probably need a few weeks off at the very least. Especially if you want to go into this competition healthy."

"They're only bruises." Thatch pressed his hands against the ice pack. "And they feel better already."

Likely because his rib cage was numb. "The bones could be cracked." Back when Luke had been riding, he'd cracked a rib or two at least once a year.

"I have to be good to get past the competition." He hesitated, gaze darting before looking at her again. "Speaking of, did you know your ex-husband is competing in the Star Valley Rodeo Days?"

Lyric startled, accidentally knocking over her glass. "What?" She jumped up to grab a towel. "Where did you hear that?" Her fist squeezed the cloth too tightly. Luke was coming here?

"Kirby told me." Thatch watched her while he spoke. "I asked him about Luke Copeland. I got curious after you told me his name. And he said Luke is slated to compete that weekend."

"Oh. Huh." Shock jammed her throat. She hadn't seen Luke since the day her stepfather and mother picked her up from the hospital after the man had broken her arm. After three months of ignoring his apologies and hiding out in Star Valley, she'd managed to work up the courage to file for divorce. Only with Kenny and her mother's help. And they'd made sure she never had to face him. Kenny had wanted her to press charges at first, but she couldn't. She'd only wanted the whole ordeal to be over.

Thatch still stared at her from across the table, his head slightly tilted as though he was trying to read her.

She shouldn't be readable. She shouldn't feel the fear that had started to pump through her again. "That's… interesting news." Her perky tone cracked. She tossed the damp towel into the sink to wash later and then busied herself with emptying the dishwasher so she wouldn't have to look at him.

"I didn't know if you knew," Thatch said softly. "Or if you'd care."

"I don't care." She slid the stack of clean plates into the cupboard. She didn't want to care. She didn't even want to be thinking about Luke right now. Why would Thatch even bring him up? "We got divorced a long time ago. It's not like he's coming here to see me." Surely he wouldn't try to find her. Not after all these years. She wouldn't have to see him. She didn't plan on going to the rodeo events anyway.

"Have you seen him?" Thatch brought her glass to the sink, and she couldn't avoid his gaze anymore. "Since your divorce? Have you talked to him?"

Blood whooshed through her ears. She couldn't discuss this right now. This was none of his damn business. Instead of answering, she pretended to be distracted by the clock. "Oh, wow. We should get going. I told Kyra we would be at the barbecue early to help get the food ready." Lyric closed up the dishwasher and breezed past Thatch to retrieve the salad she'd made earlier from the refrigerator. "You can leave the wrap on underneath your shirt." She tossed him the garment on her way.

"Yeah," he grunted. "Sounds good."

While he pulled on his shirt, Lyric fed Amos and then bustled out the front door as if everything were normal, as if her stomach weren't all twisted and painful. "We should drive separately." She needed some space to pull herself together before she had to spend the whole evening acting like a woman in love.

"You don't think they'll wonder why we drove separately?"

She paused in her driveway. God, he was right. They were supposed to be dating. It didn't matter that her hands were shaky or that her legs moved like wooden planks. She had to pretend. How had everything gotten so out of control? "Fine. I'll ride with you."

Maybe she could turn up the radio so they wouldn't have to talk.

*   *   *

Lyric clicked in her seat belt and pretended to be fully occupied with her phone. Just as Thatch started to back down the driveway, his Bluetooth rang. "Sorry. It's my mom. I better answer."

"No problem." She shoved her phone in her back

pocket. At least she wouldn't have to make small talk right now. She could focus on some cleansing breaths instead.

"Hey, Mom." Thatch put the truck into gear and drove slowly down her street.

"Thatch! Finally, you answer your phone." Lyric had only met Thatch's mom once when his parents had visited last summer, but she recognized her friendly, boisterous tone.

"Sorry. I've been a little busy this week." He turned onto the highway. "By the way, you're on speaker. Lyric is in the car with me."

She sat up a little straighter. Uh-oh—

"Lyric!" Nancy Hearst squealed a little. "How are you, darlin'? Where are you off to? It's only the two of you in the car?"

The questions came at her rapid-fire. "Uh, yes." She shot Thatch a silent desperate plea for help. Even if the rest of town thought they were dating, they didn't need to get his parents involved too.

"We're headed to Aiden and Kyra's house for a barbecue," Thatch said casually.

"So you're *carpooling*?"

Lyric detected a big grin in the woman's voice.

"Did you need something, Mom?" Thatch didn't answer the question. "I sent you the confirmation for your house rental while you're in town."

"Oh, yes. I got that. I was only calling to say thanks."

Thatch hoovered his finger over the end button. "Okay, then I'll talk to you—"

"But how fun that I have Lyric on the phone too," Nancy interrupted. "How are you, honey? Still teaching yoga? Maybe I could do a session with you while I'm in town for the Rodeo Days. And then I'll take you out to lunch!"

"Oh, boy," Thatch muttered under his breath.

"That would be nice." At the man's questioning glare, she raised her hands. What was she supposed to say? His mom seemed great.

"And maybe we could all go to dinner together too!" Apparently, once Nancy got going with the planning, it was hard to stop her. "It would be like a triple date with you and Lyric, Dad and me, and Liam and Sienna!"

Thatch's expression darkened. "We have to go, Mom. I'll call you later."

"Oh, all right," she relented.

"Love ya." He clicked the off button and stopped the truck before turning into Aiden and Kyra's driveway. "This is getting out of control. I don't want my parents thinking we're dating."

"I don't want them to think we're dating either." Though she did like his mom. Nancy Hearst was a sweetheart. "I didn't tell her we were dating," Lyric reminded him. "She came to that conclusion all by herself."

"She's going to come to all kinds of conclusions if she knows we're spending time together, and that'll make my life a lot more complicated." He sighed heavily. "This fake relationship needs to be over before my family gets into town. I'm not going to bring them into the middle of it."

"I'm more than fine with that," she said with a huff. "All I want is for us to hang out with Franco and Elina a few times so we can make sure she's safe. Then we can be done." And it wouldn't be a moment too soon for her. In one day, Thatch had dredged up more emotions in her than she'd experienced since her divorce had been finalized. He was complicating her life too. The faster they ended this, the better off she'd be.

"Good." Thatch steered the truck the rest of the way into the driveway and cut the engine.

"Good." Lyric hopped out and got the salad from the back. She beat Thatch up to the front door by a good ten paces.

Kyra greeted them with hugs, all smiles and positive energy.

"Hi!" Lyric returned her hug. "We brought a salad." She handed over the ceramic bowl.

"Oh, great." Her friend held the door open for them and guided them into the kitchen. It felt strange walking through the house Lyric had once known so well. She'd grown up here with Kenny and her mom after they'd moved from Florida. She couldn't have been more thrilled when Kenny had left Kyra the house after his death and they reconnected. It was nice having something so close to a sister in town.

"How about a glass of wine?" Her friend waved a bottle of Sauvignon Blanc in front of her.

"Perfect." Thankfully, she hadn't had to look at Thatch once. Maybe this whole *pretending in front of her friends* thing would be easier than she'd thought. They'd both be so distracted and busy chatting, they would hardly have to interact at all.

"So, what've you two been up to today?" Aiden walked in from the patio wearing an apron, a grilling spatula in his hand.

"Oh, you know…" She looked to Thatch to fill them in, since he likely wouldn't want to admit that he'd been bronc riding.

"Uh—" Her pretend boyfriend looked a little spooked. "We did some hiking," he finally said.

"Right. Hiking." Lyric patted his shoulder. "And

Thatch took a fall. Off some rocks. So we have him all wrapped up with ice packs."

"What?" Kyra quickly handed Lyric a full wineglass and turned to Thatch. "Are you okay?"

"It's no big deal." He backed away from the off-duty nurse practitioner. "My ribs are sore, that's all."

"They're pretty bruised from what I could tell," Lyric said sweetly. Her friend would never let him off the hook without a full checkup.

"You don't want to mess around with bruised ribs." Kyra approached him again. "Let me take a look. You'll run into all sorts of problems if you're not breathing right."

"I'm breathing fine." Thatch sidestepped her and accepted a beer from Aiden. "It's your night off. I'm not going to make you work."

"But maybe it wouldn't hurt to get a checkup at the clinic tomorrow morning. I'm sure Kyra won't mind stopping by on a Sunday morning for a friend." Lyric beamed her smile directly into Thatch's annoyed glare. She was only playing the part of the concerned girlfriend. And a checkup was in his best interest.

"That's not nec—"

"I can be there at nine if that works for you." Kyra reached for her phone, which was sitting on the counter. "Actually, I won't take no for an answer. I'm putting you on the schedule right now. You really need to take care of yourself. Especially having such a physical job."

Ha. If her friend thought construction was a physical job, wait until she found out about Thatch's new hobby. Though he likely wouldn't disclose the real source of his injury, even to a medical professional.

Down the hall, the door clattered open.

"Hey, everyone!" Tess called. "Sorry we're late." She appeared in the doorway with Silas behind her. "We were chatting with Minnie. She came to watch the girls."

"And before that Tess fell asleep on the couch," her husband added. "I didn't have the heart to wake her up." Silas brushed a kiss across his wife's cheek.

Weren't they adorable?

"She needs all the rest she can get." Kyra handed Tess an Italian soda.

"I'm getting enough rest," their friend assured them. "What with Silas, Morgan, and Willow doing pretty much everything for me right now, I have plenty of time to nap. This man is a saint and lets me sleep in every morning." She peered adoringly at her husband.

Aww. Lyric couldn't be more thrilled for her friends. That was what a marriage should look like. Not the nightmare she'd endured. But she wasn't thinking about Luke. That chapter in her life was over.

So why couldn't she seem to close the book?

"But enough about me." Tess sashayed over to where Lyric stood. "I need to know all the deets about you two. When did you guys cross over that friend line?"

"Why don't you tell them?" Thatch nudged her to the center of their circle—the last place she wanted to be standing right now.

"Oh. Well." A laugh bubbled out. "It wasn't too big a deal." She sipped from her wine, her mind racing. "We, um, well, I guess it was at the Christmas party."

"That's right!" Kyra gasped. "I seem to remember you two were dancing quite a bit that night."

Yes, they had been. And then they'd taken a break to get a drink by the bar before meandering near the fireplace, where Thatch had asked her out. And for a split second she'd wanted to say yes. Her cheeks had been warm and rosy, her heart buoyant from dancing and laughing. But peering up at him that night, she knew she'd never be able to give him her heart. Not her whole heart anyway. And he deserved more. So she'd said no.

"You were at the Christmas party..." Kyra prompted.

"And then we, uh, kissed under the mistletoe." It was the only thing she could think to say. Instead of telling them what had really happened. That she'd quickly left the party after Thatch had asked her out.

"How'd we all miss that?" Aiden asked, handing Silas a beer.

"Everyone else was a little busy." Lyric snuck a glance at her pretend beau. He was awfully quiet.

"So then you started going out on secret dates?" Silas rubbed his wife's shoulders.

"Mm-hmm." Before Lyric could change the subject, Tess jumped back in.

"How did you hide that from all of us? I mean, it's impossible to hide anything in this town. The Ladies knew I was pregnant before we even told my parents."

"Wait a minute." Aiden pointed at Thatch. "That's why you've been disappearing so much. On the weekends."

"And you've been teaching in Jackson a lot more frequently," Kyra said to Lyric.

She tried to laugh. "Busted, I guess." She looked to Thatch for backup, but he seemed content to stay silent and let her handle the interrogation.

"Now that you two are an item, we should plan a trip together." Kyra held up her glass of iced tea for a cheers.

"Yes!" Tess clinked her bottle with their glasses. "But

if we can't fit it in this month, it can't happen until next fall. After the baby's old enough to stay a few nights with Grandma and Grandpa."

"Sure." Lyric tried not to think about how disappointed everyone would be when she and Thatch broke off this fake relationship. "How're plans with the nursery going?" It was time to get them all talking about something else.

Her stratagem worked. While Tess filled her and Kyra in on the nursery and birthing plans, the men went outside and gathered around the grill. All through dinner, everyone was too busy talking about the upcoming Rodeo Days to focus on her and Thatch. But after they'd finished eating, they all ended up on the outdoor couches around the firepit. And, naturally, the only open seat had been next to Thatch.

"Here's a blanket, you two." Kyra dropped the throw into her lap. "It's cool tonight. Feel free to snuggle."

Lyric was chilly, but she'd been sitting as far away from Thatch as she could without raising suspicions.

"You need to share the blanket with him," Tess told her, already cuddled up with Silas.

Now all four of them were staring.

Thatch draped his arm around Lyric's shoulders and nestled her into his warmth. From the outside, they looked like the rest of these couples. Sitting in front of the crackling firepit with the diamond-studded sky overhead. Close and happy and in love. But sitting here with him only made the emptiness expand inside her until she felt hollow.

Sometimes she wanted what Silas and Tess had. Or Kyra and Aiden. Both couples had developed this trust, this bond that could withstand any test. They'd found the magic somehow. The right person or the right time in their lives. All the stars had aligned for them.

Maybe she was so desperately trying to keep some physical distance between her and Thatch because it would be too easy to pretend with him. Spending more time with him lately had revealed the qualities she'd never noticed before. His thoughtfulness. His wisdom in how he interacted with Franco. And even her, in truth. He somehow sensed when she needed space or needed to change the subject and never pushed her.

"You okay?" Thatch murmured near her ear.

She nodded and turned her face to his because that's what a girlfriend would do. A girlfriend might also brush a sweet kiss across his lips whenever she found herself this close to the man she loved. And she wanted to. A distinct urge to be close to him—to be close to someone that way again—pressed into her breastbone, filling her whole chest with a yawning ache.

But anytime she'd had that urge before, with any other man, fear overtook it eventually. She couldn't go there. For years, she'd found her safety in distance and independence and control.

She didn't know how to drop any of those shields now.

CHAPTER TEN

For the second time in twenty-four hours, Thatch had to take his shirt off for a woman.

"Yikes." Kyra inspected the bruising on the right side of his rib cage. "This seems like a strange injury for a fall on a trail. The discoloration is really concentrated in this area." She brushed a finger over the damage.

That was because he'd taken a direct shot from a bronc's hoof to the bones right there. But he wouldn't tell her that. "I landed right on a rock." He tried not to sound impatient, but he didn't need to be here. Bruises were a part of this gig. He could handle them. Kyra and Lyric didn't understand that, in his previous line of work, he'd endured far more than a kick to the chest. If he could survive a gunshot wound, he could handle bruised ribs.

"How does this feel?" Kyra gently probed the area with her fingers.

"Fine," he lied before holding his breath. The pain had a razor-edge sharpness, but, again, he didn't need to be sitting here on the exam table in Kyra's clinic like a little kid.

"Take a deep inhale for me." She stood back to watch his face.

Did he have to? Thatch braced himself for the pain and drew in a slow, long breath, trying like hell not to wince when his rib cage expanded. Okay. Yep. That hurt.

"You *are* in pain." The nurse practitioner shot him the same frown she probably used on her five-year-old patients. "Don't bother pretending otherwise."

He shrugged, but even that small movement made his sternum throb. "Nothing some over-the-counter painkillers can't help with." Though he hadn't taken anything yet.

"Well, I'd like to finish the exam, at least." Kyra slung a stethoscope around her neck. "Take your blood pressure, listen to your breathing to make sure there's no pneumonia setting in. You know, all the important stuff."

Thatch knew better than to argue. Kyra wasn't about to let him out of here without torturing him. "Whatever you have to do, Doc."

"I'm not a doctor, remember?" She pulled a blood pressure cuff off a nearby hook on the wall and clamped it around his biceps. "So was everything okay with Lyric last night?"

Uh-oh. He should've been ready for this line of questioning. Of course she'd want to discuss his relationship with Lyric. They were best friends. "Sure. She was okay last night." But he wouldn't call his interactions with Lyric at dinner exactly convincing for a new romance. "Why do you ask?"

"Something seemed off." She paused and put the stethoscope's earpieces in her ears and pumped the blood pressure cuff, cutting off his circulation. "Blood pressure looks great." She jotted something on his chart. "Lyric wasn't herself last night. Especially after dinner. She was too quiet. It seemed like she had a lot on her mind."

Thatch had noticed that too. He'd even asked her if everything was okay, but she brushed away his concern. Lyric didn't want to share anything personal with him. "I think she was tired. From the hike." He tried to think of a way to distract Kyra from discussing their relationship. "And she's worried about one of her students too. Elina."

"Oh, that's right." She paused again and pressed the cold metal of the stethoscope against his chest, instructing him to take deep breaths. "No pneumonia." Again, she recorded the declaration on her clipboard. "We ran into Elina and Franco at the store when we went shopping."

"Did it seem like Franco was treating her aggressively?" Maybe he shouldn't ask, but he had to know if the kid was simply telling him what he wanted to hear when they'd talked about Elina.

Kyra gave the question some time. "Actually, I didn't notice anything too off between them," she finally said. "I mean, they both looked mad to me. But I also don't know either one of them well. I can see why it triggered Lyric to see Franco grab Elina's arm, though."

Triggered. That was a good word to describe Lyric's physical demeanor whenever she talked about Franco and Elina. "You can?"

"Well, yeah." His friend placed the stethoscope on a hook by the blood pressure cuff. "I mean, after what she went through with Luke—" Kyra stopped abruptly, concern suddenly radiating in her wide eyes. "She *has* told you what happened with her ex, right? I mean, you're together. That's something you tell your significant other."

If they had something real, Lyric might've trusted him with her past. But here he was trying to help her sort out Franco and Elina's relationship problems when he had no context for Lyric's reactions. He didn't want to pry behind her back, but he did need to understand. "I know some of what happened between them." Now his biggest concern was whether this jerk would come to Star Valley and create problems.

"You don't happen to know if she's seen him or had any contact with him since the divorce, do you?" He tried to ask casually, but if the woman were to take his blood pressure now, she likely wouldn't give him a clean bill of health.

"I don't think so." Kyra reached into a cabinet and found an Ace wrap. "This will put some compression on your ribs." She gestured for him to hold his arms out and then started to wrap the bandage tightly around his chest. "I'm pretty sure Lyric hasn't seen Luke since before the divorce when her mom and Kenny picked her up from the hospital."

Hospital? Thatch nearly jolted off the table. Jesus. So the asshole had hurt Lyric bad enough to put her in the hospital and now he was coming to Star Valley. "Luke is competing at Rodeo Days this year."

Kyra bolted upright and dropped the wrap. "Oh, God. Does Lyric know?"

"I told her." He would've told her more carefully if he'd had any idea of the hell that man had put her through. "Kirby said he was on the bronc riding schedule. Lyric acted as if his coming to Star Valley wasn't a big deal."

Because she didn't trust Thatch enough to tell him the truth. But he'd read past her words. The tremors in her voice, the sudden desire to stop talking about Luke and escape the conversation. He should've realized how deeply fearful she was of this guy.

"She doesn't like to talk about her past." Kyra started winding the bandage around his ribs again. "She's only told me snippets. I don't know many details. But I don't think she's ever gotten over what he did to her."

What *had* he done to her? Thatch couldn't ask because Kyra assumed he already knew. And what good would details do anyway? Hearing the play-by-play would only make Thatch want to hunt Luke down the same way he'd hunted down international terrorists.

"That's why I'm so happy for you two." Kyra secured the wrap with Velcro and then stepped back. "It seems like maybe she's finally putting all that heartache and fear behind her."

He wished that were true. He wished he could be a part of Lyric's healing. He would do anything to help her. But she was keeping him on the outside, even when they were supposed to be together. When she'd told him she didn't want to be with him, he'd let go. He wouldn't push her now.

But he would still damn well protect her.

"Do you think Luke will try to see her?" Kyra sank to her rolling stool, worry locking her jaw.

"That won't happen." He would make sure. Thatch pushed off the exam table and pulled on his shirt. "I'll be around that weekend, and I won't let him get near her."

"What if he's coming for revenge or something?" She pushed her hair out of her eyes. "As far as I know, she never pressed charges when he broke her arm. Right? But maybe he's still angry she left him."

His stomach clenched. From the little Lyric told him, he'd assumed her marriage to Luke had been ugly, but he hadn't realized she'd lived through a genuine nightmare.

"Thank God you'll be around." Kyra was on her feet again, pacing. "We'll have to make sure she's never alone that weekend. You'll have to stay with her. Or she could even stay at your place."

"I'll take care of it." He would take care of Lyric. "Luke won't have the chance to—"

"Knock, knock." Lyric poked her head into the exam room. "How's the patient?"

"Oh. Um." Kyra suddenly went back into medical professional mode, her eyes scanning his chart. "He has a pretty serious contusion, but I don't think there are any broken bones." She raised her eyebrows at him. "However, the only way to be sure is to drive to Jackson and get an X-ray."

"No thanks." Right now, Thatch couldn't look away from Lyric. He'd always admired the strength in her, her genuine compassion and concern for people, the way she made everyone feel valued. But now he knew where those traits had come from. They were born from her own trials and pains.

"You sure?" Lyric nudged his shoulder. "I could drive you to the city for an X-ray right now."

"That would be a waste of time," he assured her. "I'm feeling better already."

The two women shared an exasperated look.

"I can give you a prescription for a pain med, if you'd like," Kyra offered.

"Nah. I'll tough it out." He didn't like any of those meds messing with his mind, and he never remembered to take pills anyway. He needed to be fully alert and aware right now.

"You Navy SEALs." Kyra shook her head. "It's like they don't feel pain. But I guess when you've been shot in the leg, suffering from a few bruises is kind of a walk in the park."

Lyric whirled to gape at him. "You got shot in the leg?"

"They've all been shot." Kyra gave her a funny look. "Aiden in the hand, Silas in the shoulder, and Thatch in the leg. I'm surprised he hasn't told you all his war stories."

"He has told me," Lyric said quickly. "I mean, some of them. Maybe not all of them." Her eyes were silently questioning his.

"If I gave up all my secrets, I'd lose my sense of mystery." That sounded better than saying he didn't exactly like talking about his past either. Being a soldier meant he'd lived in a different world. A world no one else could understand unless they'd been there. Maybe that was why relationships had eluded him. "Thanks again, Doc." He headed for the door before they could try to unpack any more of his baggage.

"I'm not a doctor," Kyra reminded him. "And you're welcome. I'd advise you to rest for a few weeks. No hiking. And be careful at work."

"Sure thing." He grinned. She hadn't said anything about staying off the back of a bronc.

He'd made it into the reception area of the clinic before Lyric caught up to him. "Do you have time for a few gentle stretches?" Her hands were fidgeting with the zipper on her fleece vest. "That might help you loosen up a little."

Thatch checked his watch. Aiden and Silas likely wouldn't miss him at work for a while. They'd all agreed to get in a little overtime today, but those two were always taking off for secret rendezvous with their significant others, so why couldn't he? "Sure. I've got some time."

"Go easy." Kyra breezed out the door with some folders and started to file them in the reception desk. "No overdoing anything because you're trying to impress your girlfriend."

"I think I'm past that." He couldn't impress Lyric if he tried. And he had. Plenty of times.

Thatch followed his fictitious girlfriend down the hall to her studio.

"I need to know all your war stories." Lyric closed the door behind him.

Ah. And there was the reason she'd randomly wanted him to do some stretching. "That would be a lot of ground to cover." He sat on the bench and took off his boots so he wouldn't scuff up her fancy bamboo floor. "It would take me more than a quick yoga session to tell you everything." Yes, he was stalling, but he didn't have war stories. He had tattered memories. Painful memories. Horrific things he'd witnessed and experienced.

Thanks to the movies and television, people tended to forget that those scenes in his head weren't images of glorified violence where the good guys always won. His flashbacks were ugly and real. He didn't only remember the victories they'd had. He remembered every impossible life-or-death choice he'd made, every selfless soldier he'd watched die, every person he couldn't save on both sides of the war. And while he'd dealt with most of those things over the last few years, they were still a lot to carry.

"You can start by telling me about when you got shot." Lyric took two mats off the shelf and unrolled them on the floor side by side.

He dragged himself to the mat and stood the way she showed him—feet hip distance apart, spine straight.

"Now raise your right arm out to the side, and I'll carefully pull you into a stretch." She pressed on his arm. "Keep your chest open, and tell me if it's too much."

All of this was too much. Spending time alone with Lyric, feeling her hands on him, sharing all his secrets with her.

"So?" she prompted. "Did you get shot on a mission?"

"Yeah." At least he could face the windows and not her. "It was on our third mission as SEALs. We were going in to take out a target." In trying to separate himself from the memory, he probably sounded like a robot. "We thought it would be a surprise ambush in the compound during the middle of the night, but somehow they were tipped off and ready for us."

"That's frightening." Lyric pressed his arm another centimeter back while he fought a groan.

"Anyway, there were three terrorists waiting for us outside the gate. One of them got me before we could get them."

She seemed to wait for him to continue, but he didn't have a whole lot more to say on the subject.

"You must've been so scared," she half whispered.

"I was scared for my brothers. For Aiden and Silas and Jace." But not for himself. That was right after he'd found out about Sienna and Liam. At that time, he'd believed he had nothing to go home to. "I was afraid one of them would go down next." But Jace had managed to get behind a wall and neutralize the threat.

Lyric gestured for him to raise his left arm out. "Did you think you were going to die?"

"Yes." Every time he'd dressed in his uniform, he knew death was a possibility.

"I can't even...I mean, that's terrifying." She gently eased him into the stretch, which didn't hurt nearly as much as the right side. "The things you went through. I don't know how you made it. How you're such a positive and happy person."

"That's who I choose to be." Everyone had a choice. It had taken work for him to reconcile his past—for all of them, including Aiden and Silas. But reconciling didn't mean forgetting. "I guess that's part of the reason I want to ride broncs. I know how fragile life is, and I want to live it to the fullest." So he'd found a new passion that gave him an outlet.

"I can understand that." She let go of him, moving in front of him to see his face. "You must've had a lot to work through after you retired."

His eyes locked on hers—he couldn't stop the pull, the gravitational force bringing them together. He couldn't suppress the hope that she would see more of him, enough to really know him. "For me, part of moving on and processing came when I relocated to Star Valley so I could help Tess." He hadn't anticipated how much healing would come by being a part of this Star Valley family. Jace had given him that gift. In honoring a promise to his friend, he'd unexpectedly found his restoration. "And by trying new things. Taking on new challenges. Because there's still so much life for me to live, and I don't want anything to hold me back."

"I know exactly how it feels to have things from the

past hold you back." Lyric didn't look away from him. If anything, she looked at him more intently, her dark eyes a maze he could easily get lost in.

"It's hard to let those things go," he murmured. He understood how difficult past traumas were to work through.

"But I want to." Her voice had gained strength. "I have to."

He wanted to kiss her every bit as much as he'd wanted a glass of water that time he'd been trapped in a desert hovel for five days, pinned down by enemy fire—so much that he physically ached. But he didn't dare move his face to hers. He only grabbed her hand and held on. "I'm here for you, Lyric." That was all she needed from him right now.

And he would always give her what she needed.

CHAPTER ELEVEN

"Yoo-hoo? Lyric? Hello?" Tess waved a hand in front of her face.

"Sorry." Lyric shook herself out of the daze she'd been stuck in for who knew how long. One minute she'd been guiding her friend through a breathing exercise, and the next her thoughts had drifted to a certain cowboy. She hadn't been able to focus all day.

Earlier, she'd kept calling a client by the wrong name, and she'd forgotten to take the mail to the post office like Kyra had asked her to do before lunch.

"Okay. That's it. Something's on your mind." Tess sat up on her mat, stretching her legs out in front of her and reaching for her toes over her belly with a wince. "Spill it, sister."

What was she supposed to say? That she was developing complicated feelings for her fake boyfriend? Ever since she'd talked with Thatch earlier, she'd been distracted. Normally her clients were her sole focus during sessions, but today her thoughts had kept meandering back to Thatch. To what he'd said. To what she'd seen in him when he'd told her about his past.

Lyric groaned in frustration. "This is supposed to be a relaxing prenatal stretch session for you. We don't need to talk about me." She needed to clear her mind.

"I'm a good multitasker," Tess insisted. "I can stretch and breathe and talk all at the same time. But you do know I really only come here to hang out with you, right?"

That made her smile. "And here I thought you had goals to get stronger and more flexible." At least that was what her chart said.

"I'm plenty flexible." Tess brought the soles of her feet together and hinged into a butterfly stretch with a whimper. "When I'm not pregnant. Just ask Silas. I've impressed him with my flexibility on more than one occasion."

"I probably shouldn't ask him." She didn't need details about her friends' sex lives, especially when she had nothing to share on that front.

"Right now, we have to be careful in the bedroom, or I'll throw out a hip," Tess complained.

"Why don't we focus on relieving some hip tension then?" Lyric grabbed the foam roller she'd set aside earlier. "Bridge your hips, and I'll slide this under your pelvis for a good hip flexor stretch."

"Yes, ma'am." Tess lay on her back and planted her feet on the floor, elevating her hips.

"There." Lyric got the roller positioned. "Now stretch your legs all the way out."

"Oh." Tess sighed happily. "I'm never moving. This is amazing."

"One of my favorite ways to lengthen the hips." Lyric

lay down next to her, staring up at the ceiling. At least her friend's session wouldn't be a total waste of time.

"Is everything okay with you and Thatch?" Tess turned her head to look at her. "I mean, I'm sure the dynamics are a little different now that everyone knows about your relationship. Has that been hard?"

"Not really." Most of the difficulty came in figuring out how to act around him now, how to keep the lines from blurring any more than they already had. Despite her best efforts, the time they spent together was slowly erasing certain boundaries that had been her lifelines for years. "I feel like there's still so much I don't know about him." Sometimes she forgot Thatch had had this whole life before becoming a cowboy in Star Valley. He'd lost a best friend on the battlefield. He'd been shot. He had trauma, pain, and regrets too.

"So that's what's up, then?" Tess shimmied her hips side-to-side slightly, as if looking for a deeper stretch. "You keep zoning out on me today because you feel like you don't know your boyfriend well enough?"

"Not exactly." A heaviness pinned her to the mat. "What changed for you when you started dating Silas? I mean, how did you let go of the pain of losing Jace?" How did everyone else make it look so easy to move on and grow and really embrace life while she stayed still?

Tess took her time answering, the meditative music playing softly in the background. "I've never fully let go of it," she finally said. "Losing Jace is part of me. That time in my life has shaped who I am."

"But you've found love again. You've managed to risk your heart, even with everything you lost before." And that was the one thing Lyric couldn't seem to do. She couldn't take risks when it came to love. Not after having someone crush her when she'd been at her most vulnerable.

"I think Silas and I connected at the right time." Her friend brought her feet back to the floor and pushed the foam roller away before turning on her side to face Lyric. "At that point, I was ready to step into the strength that my past pain had produced. If that makes any sense."

"But aren't you afraid of losing Silas?" Because she was afraid. Not of losing a man but of losing herself to a man, of becoming the unrecognizable helpless woman she'd been when she married Luke.

"There are moments I'm afraid." Tess's smile shone in her eyes. "But the other moments—the good moments, the laughing moments, the hugging moments, the joyful moments—are more powerful."

"I'm not sure I can open myself up to those moments. With anyone." Lyric sat upright and then reached out her hand to help Tess move into a more comfortable seated position on her mat.

"When you've been through something painful, like losing a spouse or getting a divorce, I think it's normal to want to retreat from ever feeling those emotions again so you can protect your heart." From anyone else, the words might have come across as a lecture, but Lyric knew how hard-earned Tess's wisdom was. "Give yourself some time. You and Thatch haven't been dating too long."

"We're not dating," she blurted. Because she had to tell someone. She had to process her confusion with a rational person.

"What?" Tess studied her. "But I thought—"

"It's all a lie." Lyric shielded her face with her hands, her eyes tearing up. "I wanted to pretend we were dating so the two of us could hang out with Elina and Franco. I'm concerned about her, and I thought if we spent time with them as a couple, I'd be able to tell if something was off. Or if he wasn't treating her right."

"Lyric." Tess pulled her hands away from her face. "You know you don't have to lie to *us*."

"I didn't mean to." Everything had snowballed out of control. "It started with letting the girls I'm teaching just assume we were together, and then I didn't want to tell some people we were and others we weren't. I thought it would be easier this way." But she'd complicated everything.

Confusion set into her friend's features. "And Thatch agreed to this?"

"He has his reasons." But she couldn't share them. She'd promised his secret riding career would be safe with her and the least she could do was honor that vow.

"Is his reason because he's totally head-over-heels in love with you?" Tess's voice rose, and Lyric quickly shushed her.

"Please don't tell anyone else about this." She'd needed someone to know, so she had an ally. But she wasn't ready to tell Kyra yet. "Thatch isn't in love with me. He's pretending."

"Like hell he is." Tess's mouth briefly scrunched with indecision. "Listen to me. That man has had feelings for you for a long time."

Lyric opened her mouth to argue, but Tess raised a hand between them. "It's *so* obvious. Even to his best friends. Hell, I don't even know him very well and I can see it."

Lyric didn't want to see his feelings. That was the

bottom line. Because if she truly acknowledged they were there, she'd have to explore her own feelings for him.

"It can't be easy for him pretending to be with someone he actually has feelings for," Tess said gently. "Just be careful. Don't hurt him—"

The studio door swung open, and Skye, Cheyenne, and Tallie all paraded in.

"Oh!" Lyric shot up to her feet. "Hey, girls." She'd totally forgotten they'd rescheduled their session during their gym class hour. "Wow, you're right on time." And she was so unprepared to teach a class.

"Shoot. I'm going to be late for my date with Silas." Tess got on her knees, and Lyric rushed to help her stand.

"If you two need more time, we could always just say we did our yoga class and go play video games instead," Skye said hopefully.

"No, you can't." Lyric walked Tess to the door. "I'll be right back, girls." She would rally and get herself together and actually accomplish something worthwhile today. "I'm sorry," she whispered to Tess in the hallway. Hopefully her friend considered it a blanket apology for everything—the crappy session, the little white lie…

"I love you." Tess hugged her tight. "And I understand more than you think I do."

"I know." That was why she'd told her the truth. "You won't tell Silas, Kyra, or Aiden yet, right?"

"That's not my place." She glanced around them. "But you do know they're going to be able to tell eventually. Those three have the tightest bond and the most heightened sense of awareness I've ever witnessed."

"I know." She shook her head. "I'll talk to Thatch."

She never should've pushed for this arrangement in the first place.

After making sure Tess got to her car okay, Lyric found the girls in the studio rocking out to a playlist on one of their phones.

"We thought it would be more fun to have a dance party today." Tallie turned down the music.

"Actually, that's not a bad idea." Lyric started to set out their mats. "I did a whole course in dance yoga. I can teach you all a routine and then we can practice it for the next few weeks." Maybe that would help to ramp up their enthusiasm.

"That's cool." Cheyenne kicked off her shoes and claimed a purple mat.

"Is dance yoga harder than regular yoga?" Tallie asked warily.

"Not really." Lyric dragged her mat front and center. "Where's Elina?"

"She said she doesn't want to come to the class anymore." Skye moved her mat closer to the Bluetooth speaker.

Lyric's heart sank. "But she needs this class to graduate."

"She's going to ask if she can do a summer school class instead." Cheyenne rolled her eyes. "Personally, I have no idea why she'd want to take a class in the summer. This is at least *kind of* fun."

"It's better than playing basketball and dodgeball, that's for sure," Tallie added.

"I'm glad you feel that way." But Elina's absence dampened her energy. She never should've confronted her at the store. She should've kept her suspicions to herself and built a relationship with the girl first. Elina couldn't quit yoga. Lyric would find a way to convince her to stay. Later. Right now, she had to make sure she didn't lose the rest of these beauties.

"All right, get ready to dance, ladies." She took over control of her speaker again and put on pop music. "Let's start with some arm movements."

She walked them through the warm-up slowly and then added tempo as they got the hang of the rhythm.

The faster movements helped steer her thoughts, keeping her in the moment with these girls. Their laughter and chatting lightened her heart again.

"That was pretty sweet," Tallie said after the cooldown.

"Can we dance every week?" Cheyenne paused from rolling up her mat. "That's way more fun than holding poses."

"Sure. I can plan a new dance each class." She wanted them to learn that working out could be fun. The best part was, they were getting in some good cardio when they danced and they didn't even realize it. "All right, girls. I'm going to head out with you." She helped them stash the mats on the shelf and then they all walked outside. "Who can tell me where Elina lives?" She locked up the door. "I'd like to stop by and try to convince her to stay in the class."

Everyone else got into idling cars, but Skye waited for her on the sidewalk. "Good luck. No offense, but she doesn't like you."

That comment hurt probably more than it should've. But ultimately, she didn't need Elina to like her. She needed her to be safe and to make good decisions for her future. That was all that mattered. "Not liking me shouldn't force her into summer school." What if she didn't finish that class? Then she might not graduate on time.

"That's what I told her." Skye started to back toward the idling car waiting for her at the curb.

"So where does she live?" Lyric asked again. She needed to settle this tonight.

"You know that mobile home down the block from the gas station?"

"I think so." The only mobile home in that area she knew of was run-down and decrepit. "Is it the one with the broken window?" That hadn't been fixed in at least a year?

"That's the one. But don't tell her I sent you." The girl got into the car and drove away.

Lyric waved and then climbed into her SUV and started the engine. The mobile home sat on a large lot outside the main downtown area, only seven minutes from the clinic. She parked at the edge of a dirt driveway and walked around a patch of weeds and then up a set of peeling and battered wooden steps.

Beyond the door, loud music played, and it sounded like a baby was crying.

Lyric knocked as loud as she could. Mass chaos broke loose inside—kids' voices and yelling.

The door opened a few inches, and Elina peeked out. "Who is it?"

"Hey." Lyric craned her head so she could see through the crack. "I thought I'd stop by since you missed class today."

"Oh, great." The girl walked out onto the first step and closed the door behind her. "I'm quitting yoga." She stuck a hand to her hip, a sassy pose Lyric had used herself back in the day. "I'll take a summer class to make up the credit."

"You shouldn't quit because you don't like me." She only had one chance to get this speech right, and she didn't want to send the girl running again. "Coming to a few more sessions is going to be a lot easier than taking a whole class over the summer."

Hesitation flickered in Elina's deep scowl.

Lyric took the opening. At least the girl hadn't shut her down completely. "Look, I know I overstepped at the store. I get that. But I'll back off. I promise. The yoga class is an easy way to make up the credit you're missing. If you stop coming, you'll only be hurting yourself."

"Fine." Her gusty sigh fluffed her bangs. "I'll come back to the class, but only if you chill about me and Franco. What I do outside of class is none of your business." She moved to step back inside.

"Wait." Thatch was right. She needed more time with Elina. A chance to show the girl she really did care about her and want to help. Kyra had been talking about hiring someone for months anyway. "I also came by because Kyra and I could use part-time help at the clinic. Just cleaning, light paperwork, scheduling, and stuff. I thought maybe you'd be interested in earning a little money for yourself. The hours would be super flexible." She stopped there so she didn't come across too desperate.

"Really?" Elina closed the door on the noise behind them again. "You want to hire me?" Genuine interest replaced the annoyed scrunch around her eyes.

"Elina!" a woman shrieked behind her. "Who's out there?"

"No one," she yelled. "Just my yoga teacher, Lyric."

The door opened wider, and Elina's mom stepped out to join them. Cathy, she believed her name was. She was young—probably a few years older than Lyric—and her dark eyes and black hair were identical to her daughter's.

"Hey there, yoga girl." The smell of alcohol enveloped Lyric's senses. "Why don't you come in? Elina needs to make dinner before the kids completely lose it."

Elina needed to make dinner? Lyric glanced at the girl's downturned eyes and saw past the irritable teenage shield. She was genuinely embarrassed right now. "I'm coming in a minute, Mom."

"Thank you for the invitation," Lyric said brightly. "But I really can't stay tonight." She held out her hand in the woman's direction. "It was nice to meet you, Mrs. Mills. I'll see you soon, Elina." She turned to leave to save the girl from any more embarrassment, but Elina followed her halfway down the drive. "Wait. I could only work a few hours after school every day. Maybe a little on the weekends when I'm not babysitting my brothers and sisters."

"That would be fine." An ache worked through her heart. This girl seemed to shoulder far more responsibility than Lyric had realized. "We're flexible."

Elina nodded, her scowl back in place. "How much would you pay me?"

"Twelve dollars an hour to start." At least that was what Kyra had mentioned a few weeks ago. "With the opportunity for a raise later if everything goes well."

"Okay." She peered over her shoulder and then said quietly, "I'll take the job."

"Great!" Lyric toned it down. "Good. Why don't you come by tomorrow, and I can show you around? We'll get you a key so you can work whenever it's best for you, even if we're not there."

"I'll stop by after school." Elina turned to walk back to the house but then stopped. "Thank you, Lyric," she said quietly.

She blinked back the tears before they gave her away. "You're welcome."

By the time she made it to the car, she'd started to sniffle. No wonder Elina maintained such a tough exterior. The poor girl was trying to take care of everyone—her mother and her siblings. Lyric slid into the driver's seat and automatically pulled out her phone to call Thatch.

"Hey, what's up?" he answered cheerfully.

"I'm just leaving Elina's." The tears were flowing now, making her voice wobble.

"What's wrong? What happened? Are you okay?" He spoke with tender concern.

"I'm okay." She exhaled slowly. "It's sad, that's all. I think Elina is trying to take care of her entire family. Including her mom." She used her shirtsleeve to mop up her cheeks. "But I offered her a job and I think she's going to take it."

"That's good." Thatch's tone was still gentle and soft. "Maybe that'll open the door for you to really be there for her."

"I hope so." A sudden fear gripped her heart. He wouldn't back out of their arrangement now that she had an in with Elina, would he? "So you'll get closer to Franco, and I'll have more time with Elina, and maybe we can still hang out with them together to watch them interact."

"Oh. Yeah. Sure." An awkward silence followed the response.

"I think seeing them together as a couple is still important." Yes, that was why her heart had dropped at the thought of him bailing. Never mind that talking to him always seemed to make her feel better. Never mind that she had immediately called him for comfort in her sadness. Never mind that she was getting used to him being a bigger part of her life. "We have to stay together—er, I mean in this fake relationship—for Elina," Lyric said with conviction.

And maybe a little bit for her too.

CHAPTER TWELVE

Thatch finished nailing the last sheet of drywall into place and briefly considered collapsing to the ground out of sheer relief. It turned out hanging drywall with bruised ribs was its own special torture.

Silas stuck out a hand to help him off his knees. "Seeing as how you're injured, you could've taken a few days off, you know. We would've handled it."

"I'm good." He couldn't take a few days off and leave all the work to these two. He didn't do that. Pain or no pain, he'd stick it out and help his comrades get the job done.

"At least it's quittin' time." Aiden pulled off his work gloves and tossed them onto the table.

"Really?" Thatch checked his watch. How was it already after six? "Time flies when you're having fun." But at least most of the heavy lifting was done. They'd hired out the mudding and texturizing work to a contractor, then they'd be able to get moving on the floors.

"I wouldn't call hanging drywall fun," Aiden muttered. "Hey, Kyra's hanging out with Tess and the girls tonight, so let's head over to my place and play some pool. It's been a while."

Weeks had passed since the three of them had hung out solo. They used to head to Jackson and hit the bars every weekend, but times had changed. "Sure, I could stop in for a quick game."

"Stop in?" Silas unplugged the reciprocating saw and wound the cord. "You got big plans later or what?"

"Lyric and I have a date." They were really meeting up for a yoga session at the clinic, but his friends didn't need to know that.

Aiden started to sweep up the debris around the cutting table. "Man, you're a goner. Look at that grin on your face."

Was he grinning? He hadn't meant to. "You two would know all about being goners."

"You've got us there." Silas dragged over the trash can, and Aiden dumped the dustpan, shooting him a grin. "Welcome to the club."

Thatch grabbed his coat off the rack and headed for the door. No matter what they thought about him and Lyric, he wasn't an official member of their club. Not that he wouldn't like to be. "See you two over there," he called on his way down the hall.

When Thatch climbed into his truck, a text buzzed his phone. The sight of Lyric's name brought a simmer of anticipation, which wasn't a good sign. When this fake relationship had started, he'd sworn to himself that he wouldn't get confused about the boundaries. But now Lyric was opening up to him, confiding in him, trusting him. And damn it if he didn't feel hope creeping in to stamp out any doubts he'd had. When she'd called him the other night, he'd almost suggested they end their ruse, since she'd be seeing a lot more of Elina, but Lyric had insisted they stay together. *Together*, she'd said, before correcting herself. So maybe the lines were blurring for her too.

See you at 8!

Looking forward to it. He fired off the response and then started the engine, driving off before Aiden and Silas had even gotten into their trucks.

Aiden and Kyra's house sat on a picturesque ranch nestled in the hills outside of town. The place had once belonged to Kenny, Kyra's dad, but after he passed away he'd left the land and half the town to her. That woman was another one who hadn't anticipated staying in Star Valley when she'd first come. But then she and Aiden had fallen for each other, and everything changed.

Could everything change for him and Lyric? That wasn't something he could figure out tonight.

Thatch parked in front of the outbuilding the three of them had renovated last year. Aiden had sectioned off enough space for a small bar and a few pool tables, enclosing one side of the barn for a den. It'd be a good spot to hang out regularly if either Aiden or Silas had any time to hang out.

While he waited for his friends, another text arrived. This time a smiling emoji from Lyric.

He'd never been an emoji kind of guy, but he sent Lyric back a wink. Why the hell not? They'd had a moment the other day when she'd been stretching him out in her studio. And then she'd called him when she was crying. She could've called Tess or Kyra but she'd called him. Maybe they could build something off that.

When Aiden and Silas arrived, they all walked in together.

Aiden went behind the bar. "You want a beer?"

"Nah." Yoga was hard enough without alcohol. Besides, he needed to accelerate the healing in his ribs as much as possible. According to Lyric, he needed more nutrients and to really pay attention to what he was putting into his body for the next several weeks.

"I'll take one." Silas slid onto the stool. "Man, how long's it been since we've hung out here?"

"About two months." Not that Thatch was counting. He went directly to the pool table. "I know you're just afraid I'll kick your ass again." He and Silas always had a rivalry going with something. Battleship, mostly. But pool had been another point of contention between them back in the day.

"You've never kicked my ass." Silas grabbed a cue off the wall rack.

That was one of the things Thatch loved most about his friend. He was so easy to bait.

"I'll sit this one out because I've kicked both of your asses." Aiden dragged a stool to the table.

"Or you'll sit because you're out of practice." Thatch couldn't miss a chance to harass him. "You even remember how to play?"

"I've got more important things on my schedule these days." Aiden tipped his beer in their direction. "In fact, there's something I wanted to tell you." The tone suddenly turned serious.

Thatch paused from racking up the balls and gave his friend his full attention.

Silas had frozen too.

"We're having a baby." Aiden said the words like he almost couldn't believe them.

"Hells yeah!" Silas rushed him and nearly took him down.

"Hey, congrats, man." Thatch shook his hand and then pulled him in for one of their half hugs—the only kind either of them ever offered.

"It's still early." Aiden wore the stress in his eyes. "And it wasn't easy to get to this point, so we're not making any huge announcements. But I figured it was only a matter of time until you two figured it out."

Because they didn't lie to one another. They didn't hide things. Thatch snatched up his pool cue again. "You guys are gonna make awesome dads. Both of you." That was a club he wasn't going to be a part of for a long time. He wanted in. Don't get him wrong. Family had been everything to him once. He'd grown up around his grandparents, aunts and uncles, and a whole lot of cousins in Iowa. They'd gotten together for birthdays and holidays and sometimes even random Sunday suppers. In his estimation, family was the best kind of chaos. But he was nowhere near building one of his own.

"Since we're on the subject of family..." Silas rested his pool cue against the table. "Now that I'm gonna be a dad, I want to make that same pact with you two that we all made before we went on our missions. That if anything happens to me, you'll take care of Tess, Morgan, Willow, and Baby Beck."

"It goes without saying," Aiden added. "I'd ask the same for my family."

Thatch lined up the cue ball and prepared to take his first shot. "Nothing's gonna happen to either one of you."

Both Aiden and Silas had found their places. At one time, Silas had been the most restless of them all. He didn't have much family growing up and had never put down roots in his life before he'd moved to Star Valley. Aiden had been plenty wild too. They all had. But they'd sacrificed and worked hard, and now look what they both had to show for it.

"We'll all pitch in and help each other out." That was what these last few years had been about. Thatch hit the ball, sending the others scattering while he pocketed the striped eleven.

"Exactly." Silas took a good long look at the table before aiming his cue. The solid seven ball missed the side pocket by a mile. "You know I'll return the favor for both of you. I'll be watching out for Kyra and the baby. And for Lyric too. That's my sworn duty now."

After serving in an elite branch of the navy, none of them knew how to let go of duty. But Aiden and Silas didn't owe anything to Lyric. She wasn't part of his life like that. "You don't have to make any blood oaths to me yet," Thatch told them. He took another shot, this time sending the striped fourteen ball too wide. "I'm not sure what the future will hold for Lyric and me."

"Oh, come on." Aiden walked to his side of the table. "It's so obvious you're head-over-heels."

He wished they would stop saying that. The truth hurt. "It's complicated." He had seen a possible future with Lyric. Before the Christmas party. Before she'd looked him in the eyes and told him she wasn't interested. Though now he understood why. After the kind of abuse she'd endured during her marriage, he didn't blame her for not wanting to be with anyone.

"Bro, I married our late best friend's wife." Silas pocketed the five. "*That* was complicated."

Yeah, but both Tess and Silas had been willing to work through the mess to find something worth building on. "I think Lyric is still dealing with a lot from her divorce." Enough said. It wasn't his place to divulge the details.

Aiden went back to his stool. "I thought her divorce happened a long time ago."

"And it doesn't sound like they were even married that long," Silas added.

A protective instinct pulled his jaw taut, but he couldn't lash out at them. They didn't know what she'd been through. "It doesn't matter how long they were together. Sometimes betrayal sticks with you." Even he understood that. "I don't know if we can get past everything she's been through." That was the bottom line.

"Bullshit." Silas marched to him and stared him down. "I know you. Because you're like me. Like us. Loyal to a fault. You would do whatever it takes to get her through whatever it is she has to deal with."

"Yeah. I would." But what if his loyalty didn't matter? Lyric had started to open up to him in the studio the other day, but could he go all-in and get rejected again?

"Then there's your answer." Silas gestured for him to take his turn. "You'll do whatever it takes."

Thatch lined up his shot but found it difficult to focus. He hit the cue ball too far on the edge and sank the eight ball, scratching the game. Yeah, he couldn't play right now. He hung up his pool cue. "I might do whatever it takes, but I don't know if she would say the same thing." And he hadn't been enough for Sienna. He'd tried. He'd been loyal. He'd been understanding. He even might've forgiven her for cheating on him.

"So ask Lyric if she's in for the long haul." Silas hung up his pool cue too, for once letting go of his competitive nature.

"No, no, no. You can't ask her and put all that pressure on her," Aiden countered. "Be patient. See how the next few months play out. It's not like you two have to head straight to the altar or anything."

"But communication is key," Silas insisted.

Thatch shook his head at them. "You two are a lot of help." Though he already knew there was no simple answer. No magical piece of advice for navigating relationships.

"Either way, it's obvious she has strong feelings for you." Silas retrieved his beer from the bar.

Thatch went to sit down between them. "You think?"

"Oh, yeah." Aiden got up and found Thatch a Coke. "The other night she couldn't keep her eyes off you."

"And she laughs at all your lame jokes," Silas added.

"My jokes aren't lame." Everyone laughed at his jokes because they were funny.

Silas rolled his eyes. "Dude, Morgan can tell a better joke than you."

"Whatever. Uncle Thatch taught her everything she knows about good comedy."

For the next half hour, they settled into their usual banter and insults. He'd missed this. Hanging out with these two. Not only harassing one another but talking about life too. Still, he had to get going so he wouldn't be late for his yoga session. "Sorry to cut out early."

"You don't have to apologize to us," Aiden said. "We've both been there."

"We'll all be there for a long time." Silas clapped him on the back. "And Aiden's probably right," he said begrudgingly. "Just let things happen."

"I actually think I can do that." *Let things happen.* The simplicity of that mantra was freeing.

By the time he made it to the clinic, he'd managed to let go of the what-ifs, the plans, the complications he hadn't even realized he'd been holding on to.

"Hey." Lyric greeted him at the front door, her dark eyes looking up at him shyly from underneath her lashes.

Before responding, he took a few seconds to appreciate her. She'd pulled her hair up loosely on top of her head, and her face was makeup-free and lovely. "Hey." He stepped inside the reception area with her. "You might need to go easy on me tonight. I've been hanging drywall all day."

"I thought *you* were going to take it easy." Lyric waved him down the hall to the studio.

"We're on a schedule." And truthfully, he didn't know how to take it easy. "The town council wants to open the rec center right after the Rodeo Days." They'd make it, but they'd be cutting it close. He lurched ahead to open the door for her. "But I figured we can do some strength work. And stretching, of course." If they had to. Stretching wasn't his favorite.

"Sure. We can do that." Lyric seemed a little distracted. "But before we get started, we need to talk."

Uh-oh. He'd heard those words delivered in that same serious tone before.

"Sure. Hang on." He took off his boots before he slipped into the changing room to put on his sweats.

When he came back out, Lyric was waiting for him on the bench.

"What's on your mind?" He sat down next to her, their shoulders brushing.

"I wanted to discuss our *arrangement*." She kept her gaze straight ahead. "On the phone the other night, it kind of sounded like you didn't want to continue pretending." She clasped and unclasped her hands in her lap. "The thing is, I don't want to force you to be in a fake relationship. Especially if you don't want to be. I mean, I know this is not ideal. So we can break up if you want."

Huh. He hadn't seen this coming. The truth was, he'd thought she would let him off the hook when she connected with Elina. Only he didn't necessarily want to go their separate ways now. That would mean they'd go back to avoiding each other, hardly talking. He liked hanging out with her. "*You* want to break up?"

"I want what's best for you." Lyric stood and walked to the shelf of mats. "I mean, I'm fine either way. As long as you are. I wanted to give you an out. In case you don't want to keep on pretending." She pulled two mats down and unrolled them on the floor, but if you asked him, her movements seemed a little frantic. She was nervous. He didn't want her to be nervous with him. Ever. But he also had to be honest with her.

"I'm not pretending all that much." In case she hadn't noticed. He waited for her to turn and look at him. "But if you want out, I'm fine with that. Whatever you need." He'd already told her he'd be there for her either way. As a friend. Or as more if she wanted.

"I don't—I mean—" She tugged at her sweatshirt a few times, exposing the strap of her sports bra. "Um, I'm not sure what I want, Thatch." This time, her eyes braved a good long look into his. "I don't know."

"That's fine." He gave a little shrug. "There's no pressure here either way."

True concern appeared in the faint lines of her forehead. "I don't want to hurt you. If things don't work out. Or if we keep pretending and then the whole thing falls apart."

"My happiness and well-being aren't your responsibility, Lyric." He almost touched her, brushed a tendril of hair away from her temple, but instead he fisted his hand at his side. "I wouldn't put that on another person. If I've learned anything over the last few years, it's that you have to be good on your own before you can ever be good with someone else."

Maybe that was what he'd been missing with Sienna. Back then, he hadn't been good on his own. And neither had she. She'd missed him too much when he'd joined up, she'd said. She needed someone who could be with her all the time. But he wouldn't be the man he was today if he hadn't become a SEAL. He was better for all of it, even though he'd lost out on who he'd thought was his dream.

"I want to be good on my own," Lyric half whispered. "And with someone else. I want to let myself feel something again." With her eyes locked on his, she took his hand, weaving their fingers together.

The gentle but firm contact radiated all through him. He held her hand tighter, letting her know her confusion didn't scare him off. "Let's not try to define anything right now. We'll keep our cover. But there're no strings, no obligations, no expectations on my side." He only wanted to keep spending time with her.

The start of a smile chased away the traces of worry on her face. "Okay." She shuffled her toes closer to his. "But if we're keeping our cover intact, we should probably work on our kissing. I'm not sure we convinced Kyra the first time."

Thatch accepted the invitation and set his hands on her waist. "I'm all about practicing." He lowered his mouth to hers, following her eyes until they closed, and then started with a slow brush against her lips.

Lyric sighed against his mouth, enticing him with the scent of cinnamon.

"How was that for convincing?" he murmured, breaking away for only a second.

She made a noncommittal noise. "I mean, it was a start..."

He cupped her jaw with his hand and guided her face back to his. This time, he let his lips linger over hers, teasing her by kissing her and then pulling back slightly.

She uttered a groan of frustration and moved her hands to the back of his head, holding him there. Maybe he'd been trying to tease her, but that had backfired because he was the one sinking into her, suddenly intoxicated by the softness of her lips, the feel of her curves against him. He was the one pulling her closer, unable to stop himself. He was the one opening his mouth to taste more of her. He was the one finding it hard to breathe, but maybe she did, too, because she was holding on to him tighter, her chest rising against his so she could probably feel how hard she had his heart pounding—

A crash sounded somewhere down the hall.

Lyric jolted back. "What was that?"

"Dunno." Right now, he didn't care. He pulled her

closer, studying the mystery in her eyes. God, she was pure magic, those dark eyes, and the soft contour of her lips—

More clatters came from the reception area. This time, Thatch woke up.

"No one's supposed to be here right now except for us." Lyric darted away from him and rushed out of the studio.

Thatch caught up to her in only a few steps. They made it to the reception area and found the front door standing wide open.

"What the hell?" He scanned the room.

"Oh, my God. The safe." Lyric pointed to the small box on the floor behind the reception desk. She knelt down and typed in a password combination to open it, and then rifled through the contents.

"Is anything missing?" Thatch lifted the safe onto the desk.

"I don't know." She pulled out checks and cash. "I'll have to call Kyra. She was doing the books this week. We alternate."

Well, damn. This night just took a turn. "We should call the police too. Get Natalie over here." Though could it technically be considered a break-in if the front door had been unlocked? It didn't matter. He typed in the number for the station and talked with the chief herself. "Natalie will be right over," he told Lyric after hanging up.

"I texted Kyra too. She's on her way." Lyric sank into the chair behind the desk. "Who would break in here at nine o'clock at night?" She shoved the cash and checks back into the safe and closed it up.

Exactly. This didn't make any sense. Especially in a place like Star Valley. "Maybe it was a client or a patient who forgot something earlier today?"

She seemed to consider the possibility. "But then why would they take off running out the front door when they heard us coming?" Lyric started opening drawers. "And none of our clients would touch the safe. It doesn't look like they messed with anything else."

So the person was only after money? "We should walk through Kyra's exam rooms. Just to be sure." He led the way down the hall opposite from the studio, but they didn't find anything that looked out of place. Even the locked medicine cabinet hadn't been tampered with. When they went back into the reception area, Kyra was walking through the door.

"Are you sure someone broke in here?" She looked around the space. "Everything seems fine to me."

"We're sure." He might've been dazed from kissing the woman, but they'd heard the safe fall. "The door was standing wide open, and I know I closed it when I came in."

"You need to check the safe." Lyric hurried to punch in the code again. "I looked, but I didn't know what all was supposed to be in there."

"You found it on the floor?" Kyra went to the desk and collected the contents, looking through every paper, check, and dollar bill.

"Yes. It was on the floor right here under the desk." Lyric pointed out the spot. "But it was still closed."

The front door opened again, and Natalie entered, looking as confused as Kyra. "You need to report a break-in?"

"Someone came in here while Thatch and I were in the studio," Lyric said impatiently. "We heard a crash and came running, but by the time we got out here, the person had taken off, leaving the safe on the ground and the front door wide open."

"Nothing's missing from the safe," Kyra announced. "I counted earlier. All the money is still here."

"I'm sure they didn't have enough time to take anything." Lyric sat on the small love seat. "We ran out here as quick as we could."

"You were in the studio?" Natalie focused on Thatch. "Doing what? Yoga?" She laughed.

He didn't take offense. If someone had told him even a year ago he'd be doing yoga, he would've laughed too.

"Yes," Lyric said with a huff. "We were doing yoga."

"But you didn't hear the front door open when the person came in?" The police chief had her interrogation face on. Thatch had seen the same expression once before when she'd busted him for speeding.

"We had music on," he explained in a neutral tone. Well, he tried for neutral anyway.

Color seeped into Lyric's cheeks.

"What kind of music?" Kyra asked with a snicker.

"Oh, my God." Natalie gaped at them. "Are you two *dating*?"

Busted. Thatch hung back and let Lyric take the lead on answering. He still wasn't quite sure what they were doing.

"We are, as a matter of fact." Lyric stubbornly lifted her chin, but she was still blushing.

"That's fun!" Natalie leaned over the reception counter and glanced at Kyra. "How did I miss this news?"

Thatch had no idea how she'd missed the news when most of the town knew.

"Um, maybe we should focus on finding the person who broke in?" Lyric interrupted before Kyra answered.

"Sure." The chief didn't lose the smile, though. "Well, nothing's missing. And the door wasn't locked, so maybe someone came in looking for one of you and accidentally knocked the safe off the shelf."

Lyric gritted her teeth. "If they had been looking for us, they would've come into the studio."

"I guess so," Natalie said noncommittally. "I'll take a drive around and look for anything suspicious. Then I'll head back to the station and put in a report. Do you guys have a security system?"

Thatch snorted. No one in Star Valley had a security system. A lot of people left their front doors unlocked when they weren't home.

"We've never needed a security system." Kyra stood and put on her coat.

"You might want to think about getting one. Just in case." Natalie opened the front door. "Keep me posted if you notice anything else."

"We will," Kyra promised.

Lyric still looked a little steamed or embarrassed. It was hard to tell.

"You two should probably get back to your yoga now," their friend teased. "I'll take the safe home with me tonight. That way, there's really nothing of value sitting around."

"I should get home too." Lyric looked at him apologetically. "It's late, and I'm tired."

"Sure. We can call it a night." Like he'd told her earlier, he'd never expect anything more from her than she was willing to give.

CHAPTER THIRTEEN

Lyric sat in front of Nelly, Doris, and Minnie the way one might face a firing squad. These three never scheduled a chair yoga session unless they wanted to gossip, and she had a feeling she and Thatch would be the topic of choice today.

"This stretch is doing wonders for my arthritis," Minnie said innocently.

"Seated cat cow stretch is great for spinal mobility." No matter what they threw at her, Lyric was prepared to keep them focused and on task. "Now let's go back into that cat stretch one more time." She stood so she could correct their forms. "Bring this shoulder down a touch, Doris. There you go." She moved on to Nelly. "That's it. Get some good flexion into that spine."

"Oh, this is wonderful." The woman sighed happily. "We simply don't make it here for yoga enough. But that'll have to change."

"Starting today," agreed Minnie.

"I always love having you three." Even if they did tend to veer off track from time to time. Lyric sat back down in her seat, facing them. "Let's move into our chair pigeon now." She brought her left ankle up and crossed it over her right thigh. "Go slowly here. Be nice to the knees."

All three of them grumbled and groaned, but they managed to find the position.

"So how's Thatch?" Minnie asked, her face still scrunched in a grimace. "It helps get my mind off the stretch if we talk about other things."

Uh-huh. "He's good." Lyric hinged forward. "Let's deepen the stretch by placing your elbows on your shins."

"No thanks," Nelly muttered.

"Come on, Lyric," Minnie whined. "Don't we get more than *He's good*? We're counting on you to keep us distracted."

"We like to live vicariously through you." Doris exhaled loudly. "My God, stretching is harder than walking."

Lyric gave them all a good, long chiding stare. "Are you here to do yoga or are you here to learn about my love life?"

"Both," Minnie assured her.

"I'm more interested in the love life." Nelly was always overly honest. "What's it like to be able to see Thatch's abs whenever you want?"

"Switch legs." Lyric glanced at the clock. They still had ten minutes left? She was running out of ways to distract them.

"Is he a good kisser?" Nelly had abandoned the stretching altogether and stared at her with stars and hearts in her eyes.

"Of course he's a good kisser." She wouldn't deny that. Thatch was such a good kisser that one brush of his lips made her forget all about her carefully guarded personal space and independence. One brush of his lips had her begging him to give her more last night before they'd been interrupted. And it was a good thing too. Not that she wanted to be a burglary victim, but the kissing and the spending time together wasn't nearly as simple as Thatch liked to pretend it was.

Because she could develop real feelings real fast. And she didn't want to.

On that note... "Let's finish up with chair savasana." She straightened her posture and reconnected with her breathing. "Spine tall and stacked, shoulders weighted down, chest opening with a big inhale."

"So how serious are you two?" Minnie had no respect for meditative postures.

"We're not serious at all." She might as well start spreading the word. "We're only having fun." Wasn't that what the man had said himself? No expectations. "Not everyone is headed down the church aisle right after they start dating." Just because Aiden and Kyra and Silas and Tess had didn't mean she would follow. "There is such a thing as casual dating still." Yet there was nothing casual about the responses the man seemed to drum up in her.

"Whoa, darlin'." Nelly's shoulders went rigid and completely took her out of the pose. "You don't have to tell us as much. Trust me, if I were younger—and single—I'd be playing the field myself."

"Amen," Doris echoed.

"Sorry. I'm a little uptight today." Forget savasana.

Forget calm and meditative. Memories of that explosive kiss had her panicking again.

"I'm sure it's a lot to balance." Minnie bounced up from her chair with her usual energy. "Working and having this new relationship. Just don't forget to enjoy it, honey."

Lyric was more worried about enjoying Thatch too much. "Thanks, ladies." She moved her chair back to the corner of the room. "I know I can always count on you for a good chat."

"Let's do it again next week," Doris suggested, dragging her chair next to Lyric's.

"I'm in." Nelly stashed her chair, too, and then they all put on their shoes.

"Sure. We can do next week." Why not? Maybe their wisdom would help her sort out the complications she'd introduced into her life.

Lyric followed them into the reception area. Elina sat behind the desk, typing away at the computer. "Hey," she greeted her new favorite employee before hugging the Ladies goodbye. After they'd walked out the front door, she went to hover near the desk. This would be Elina's second shift, and already the girl had a sense of control about her. She'd also dressed up, which was fun to see. "Do you have any questions or need help with anything?"

"I don't think so." Even her tone was business-like. "I scheduled two appointments for you next week. The client wanted Tuesday and Thursday." She pointed to the calendar on the screen.

"Perfect." She couldn't believe how smoothly this was all working out.

"I also finished filing the paperwork for Kyra and swept the floor out here as well as in the kitchen."

Wow. She didn't bother to hold back her surprise. "I have to tell you, I'm really impressed with your work so far."

"Thanks." Elina didn't smile much, but she wore one now, proud and bright. "I like having a job. It'll be nice to have some of my own money. I want to save up for a car."

That was the first time Elina had ever shared a personal desire with her. But Lyric didn't want to make too big of deal about it. They were simply co-workers chatting. Yet she couldn't help but feel like she was making progress with this girl. "Do you have any fun plans this weekend?"

Elina glued her gaze back to the computer screen. "Not really."

"No dates with Franco or anything?" Lyric regretted the words right after speaking them. She couldn't come on too strong again.

But the question didn't seem to faze Elina. "I don't know. We'll probably hang out or something. But I thought I'd work late tonight. If you're cool with that."

Nope. After the break-in, she wasn't cool with Elina working here alone anymore. "I know I said you could work whenever you wanted, but I'd rather you're not here at night by yourself right now." Lyric hesitated. She didn't want to scare the girl off, but Natalie hadn't seen anyone after patrolling the neighborhood, so whoever had tampered with the safe was still out there and they had to assume the person could come back. "Someone messed with the safe the other night."

"Really?" Elina's hands jerked away from the keyboard. "Do you know who it was?"

"No." She'd lain awake all night wondering. "They took off when Thatch and I came running out of the studio, but we have the police looking into it." Surely the crime wouldn't be that hard to solve in this small town.

"The police?" Elina spun her chair to face Lyric, her eyes wide.

Great. Now she probably wouldn't want to work here anymore. "Natalie filed a report and is investigating. I'm sure it'll all be fine." Whoever had broken in didn't seem to be violent or confrontational.

Elina didn't look too convinced. "They probably won't find anything, though, right? I mean, there are no cameras or anything, are there?"

"No, but Natalie's good at her job. I'm sure she'll do her best." At least they hadn't lost any money in the incident.

"I need to go." Elina stood up suddenly. "I forgot I promised my mom I'd be home after school. I have to babysit."

"Oh. That's fine." Lyric stepped aside so the girl could get around her. "Do you babysit a lot?" In addition to making her family dinner while her mom drank? Lyric didn't mean to be judgmental, but Elina seemed to be under a lot of pressure for a fifteen-year-old girl.

"Sometimes." The girl hoisted her backpack off the floor and hurried to the door. "I might not be able to come in tomorrow."

"Okay—"

She was gone before Lyric could finish her response. Elina's shock wasn't a surprise. Break-ins typically didn't happen in Star Valley. It probably made her nervous to think it might happen again.

"Hey." Kyra appeared in the hallway that led to her office. "I'm so glad you're here." She gave her a long probing look, frowning. "What's wrong?"

"Elina just ran out the door." She took a seat at the computer so she could add the Ladies' chair session next week to the schedule. "I told her about the break-in, and then she got all freaked out. I told her I didn't want her here alone at night until we know who was snooping around in here. But I think she's scared."

"I'm not sure we need to be scared, but it's probably smart to make sure we always have two people here." Kyra dragged over another chair and sat beside her. "So, I have the *best* news."

"Perfect." She could use some good news right about now.

"You know that patient I have who owns the bed-and-breakfast between here and Jackson?"

"Oh, yeah. Marie Billings." She did yoga occasionally too, though Lyric hadn't seen her in a few months.

"That's her," Kyra sang. "She had three cabins open this weekend, and I successfully treated her gout, so she offered them to me. We can all go stay Friday and Saturday night for free! We're going on a triple date!" She made a *ta-da* gesture with her hands.

"Oh, wow." Lyric turned back to the computer so she could hide her lack of enthusiasm. Kyra wanted her to spend an entire weekend in a romantic cabin with Thatch? That hadn't been in the plan. "Sounds fun and all, but that's kind of short notice for a weekend trip."

"I took the liberty of moving all your Saturday appointments." Her friend did tend to think through everything. "And Tess has already found places for the girls to spend the weekend with friends. So you and Thatch have to come. You can't say no." She moved into Lyric's personal space, grinning. "I have no idea why you would even want to say no when you have the chance to spend two nights in a romantic little cabin alone. Not to mention a weekend with your besties."

"I don't want to say no. Of course we'd be thrilled to go." What choice did they have? Other than breaking up, and Thatch hadn't wanted to do that. Truthfully, the thought had made her a little sad too. "But I'm not sure Thatch will be available." *Please let him not be available.* "I can go talk to him about it right now."

"Perfect! This will be so great." Kyra started to spin circles in the chair. "We can do some hiking during the day. Maybe some horseback riding too. And she's got a hot springs pool up there so we can lie out in the sun and relax."

"That sounds really nice." Like the perfect getaway weekend for a couple.

"Nice?" Kyra stood up. "It's going to be a blast. I promise. It'll be the little mini vacay we all need right now."

Lyric typed the Ladies' new chair session into the online calendar and then stood too. "I'll text you after I talk to Thatch."

"I'll be waiting." Her friend sent her out the door with a pat.

But Lyric took her time walking to her car. They could easily get out of this trip. There had to be a way. By the time she'd pulled up in front of Thatch's house, she still hadn't thought of any good excuses that would satisfy Kyra. She knocked on the door, almost hoping he wasn't home.

But Thatch answered right away.

"Hey." He greeted her with an alluring, simmering smile. "You want to come in?"

"Sure." Parts of her were simmering too. He always had to look so damn appealing. What was it about a cowboy in a flannel shirt and fitted jeans anyway? Steering her gaze away from him, she stepped inside.

"Want to sit?" He gestured to the couch. "I can get you a drink. No kombucha, but I do have some iced tea."

"Iced tea would be great." God, why was she so nervous? This was Thatch. Her friend. Her kissing friend nowadays. And over the last few weeks, he'd gotten to know her better than most people. Lyric perched on the very edge of the couch.

"So what's up?" He sauntered to the kitchen and opened the refrigerator, doing some digging before coming up with a pitcher.

"Kyra is forcing us to go on a couples' getaway this weekend with her and Aiden and Silas and Tess." She hadn't quite meant to blurt out the news that way, but the nerves were taking over. Even being here alone with him in the middle of the afternoon had her craving another kiss.

"She wants us to go on a couples' getaway?" He set a full glass on the coffee table in front of her.

"Yes." Typical Thatch. He made it sound like they were simply going to the café for a beer. "One of her patients offered her three cabins at her romantic bed-and-breakfast for free this weekend."

He kicked back in one of the chairs across from her. "Sounds great."

"So you think we should go?" Lyric picked up the glass and took a sip of the fragrant black tea blend.

"I don't see why not." He leaned forward, resting his forearms on his knees. "What're you worried about?"

"That's a lot of time to spend together." And she couldn't lose her heart to him.

"Are you afraid you won't be able to resist me?" he teased.

But she wasn't laughing. She did find it hard to resist him now. "This isn't funny. We have to spend a whole weekend with our best friends pretending to be a couple."

"We don't have to be a couple." One shoulder rose in a half shrug. "We can be good friends if you want."

Oh, sure. Neutrality would be that simple. She already knew she couldn't maintain any boundaries when it came to this man.

"So you're fine with this?" She studied him searching for a chink in his armor, but there didn't seem to be one. Thatch was all confidence.

"Sure. But if you're not fine with going, tell them I can't make it."

Aiden and Silas would know better. "No, I'm fine with going too," she said. Because if he was fine with going and she wasn't, that might indicate she had a reason for *not* being fine, which he might attribute to his sex appeal. "I wanted to make sure you were fine. Maybe *you* can't resist *me*."

"We've already proven that, haven't we?" The shadows in his eyes deepened, and she knew he was thinking about kissing her again. She knew because she was thinking about kissing him again too. "Okay. Good. It's settled then. We're going." She and a sexy cowboy would spend the entire weekend holed up in a romantic cabin with lines blurring and boundaries fading.

In that case, she'd best bring along her man-repelling flannel pajamas.

CHAPTER FOURTEEN

Thatch handed Franco a section of the plank flooring and supervised while he snapped it into place.
"You're really getting the hang of this construction thing."
When he'd agreed to hire the kid, he hadn't anticipated
that Franco would actually become an asset to the team.
But they were knocking out this floor faster than any of
them had thought they would.

"At this rate, we'll finish up ahead of schedule." Aiden
ripped open another box of floor planks and stacked them
next to the completed section.

Franco pushed to a standing position. "This sure beats
sitting at a computer all day like my dad does selling
insurance."

Thatch had to laugh. After growing up on a farm, he'd
never had any interest in that kind of job either. "You
go into construction, you'll never be bored at work." He
knew that for a fact.

"So you're a senior, right?" Aiden hauled over another

stack of planks he'd already cut. "You have any idea what you want to do after high school?"

"I've been thinking about the navy." The kid snapped in the floorboard and tapped it into place with a rubber mallet. "Like you guys. Maybe I could even be a SEAL someday."

Thatch exchanged a look with Aiden. "It's not an easy life." Yet he wouldn't trade it for anything. His service had made him a better person. "But being in the military is very rewarding."

"I want to do something that matters." Franco continued to work, paying attention to the details as he went. "I don't want to get stuck in this town forever." He paused and glanced up at Thatch. "Then, after I serve for a few years, maybe I could even be a bronc rider like you when I'm done."

Uh-oh.

"Bronc rider?" Aiden dropped the box he was holding. "What the hell is he talking about? You're not a bronc rider."

Franco lurched to his feet. "Was I not supposed to say anything? Sorry, dude. I didn't know your riding was some big secret."

"Not a secret so much," Thatch corrected. "More like a surprise." Even though Aiden had never liked surprises.

"You're not seriously riding broncs." Aiden didn't wait for him to answer. "Because that would be stupid. I've known some bronc riders. They can get pretty messed up."

Thatch grinned at his friend. There wasn't much Aiden didn't know. He had strong opinions about nearly everything. "I started up last year. Trained at a place outside of Jackson and then started working on Kirby Leatherman's house so he'd take me on as a student."

"Why?" Aiden abandoned the boxes he'd been unpacking. "Getting shot wasn't enough for you? You want to get yourself killed in an arena?"

Franco kept his head down and got back to work. Thatch didn't blame him for not wanting to be a part of this conversation.

"I want to challenge myself." He said the words in a pointed tone. Aiden was the same way. That was why his friend had been working on bringing Kyra's ranch back— for the challenge. "I want to do something new instead of staying in the same place." They'd both done that their entire lives. It was what he knew—moving on to the next step. Learning something. Growing.

"He's awesome at it too." Franco stood up again. "I've seen him ride. He'll probably win at the Rodeo Days coming up."

"You're competing?"

He could read the healthy skepticism in his friend's stare. That was fine. Let him doubt. Thatch would prove something to everyone. "It'll be my first pro-rodeo competition."

"He's got a real shot at winning," Franco added. "Even Kirby said so."

"That's not exactly what Kirby said." But he appreciated the kid's vote of confidence. Franco was his first fan.

An alarm went off from the kid's phone in his pocket. "Uh-oh. I've gotta jet. I've got a marathon basketball practice tonight."

Now was as good a time as any to be done working for the day anyway. They'd gotten far more done than he'd anticipated. Thatch sent the kid off with a handshake. "Thanks for your help today. You're doing good work."

"It's actually been fun. I like it way better than when

I flipped burgers at the café." He unbuckled his tool belt and left it on the table. "Minnie always kisses me on the cheek and leaves a lipstick mark."

Aiden laughed. "She does that to all of us."

"I'll see ya next week." Franco took off and left Thatch and Aiden staring each other down. It was something they'd done many times.

"Bronc riding, huh?" His friend crossed his arms. "I'm guessing the rib injury didn't really happen on a hike, then."

"Nope." He shook his head in mock disbelief. "Come on. You know me better than that. Falling on a hike? I'm surprised you didn't get suspicious then."

"I should've known." Aiden unplugged the table saw. "Why haven't you said anything? We don't keep stuff like this from each other."

"I guess I wanted to wait and see if I was any good at it." When he'd first signed up for the lessons, he'd thought it would be for fun. Something to do for entertainment. He hadn't expected to get hooked. "Silas found out not long after I started, but I asked him not to say anything. You two have been so busy with your wives anyway. I figured I'd tell you right before the Rodeo Days." Or he would've just let everyone find out when they announced his name at the arena.

"You know we'll all be there to cheer you on." Aiden swept up the debris around the saw. "Lyric is okay with you riding?"

His shoulders turned to lead. He'd almost forgotten he was supposed to be dating someone. He turned his back and started to reorganize the tool chest on the table. Thatch really didn't want to have to explain another lie right now. "She seems to be."

"Wasn't her ex a rider or something?" Aiden sounded closer.

"Uh, yeah." That reminded him. "I've been meaning to ask what you think about the break-in at the clinic." The more he'd thought about that incident, the more he'd wondered if it had something to do with Luke Copeland coming to town.

"Kyra said it was no big deal." Aiden brought the rubber mallets to the table. He'd always been a stickler for organization on a job. "Seems weird that someone came in but didn't take anything."

"They didn't have the chance to take anything," Thatch reminded him. "Lyric and I were in her studio and scared them away."

Aiden's eyes narrowed. "So you think we have something to worry about?"

"I'm not sure. I don't like it, though." He'd been lying awake at night wondering if he should be doing more to figure out who broke in. What if Luke had come to town early and was hoping to find Lyric alone at the clinic? That possibility made his gut clench. "I've wondered if Lyric's ex has already arrived for Rodeo Days. I mean, the competition is only a week away." Luke could be in the area somewhere. That was his biggest concern. "Kirby told me he's a violent type. So I don't like not knowing who walked into their clinic uninvited."

"I don't either." Aiden gave Thatch his full attention. "Natalie hasn't been able to find anything?"

"Not yet. Last I knew, she was going to try to talk to the neighbors." He'd have to follow up with her again later. "Maybe someone saw something."

"I've already started to price out security systems."

His friend showed him a screenshot of a spreadsheet. "But it'll take a while to get one installed."

"In the meantime, I guess we'll have to keep an eye on the place ourselves." He'd already started to drive by the clinic more regularly, going out of his way to make sure nothing looked suspicious. "I think I'll head over there now. Lyric teaches those high school girls tonight." He didn't want some random potentially dangerous person walking in during their session.

Aiden laughed. "You gonna join a yoga class?"

"Nah." He wasn't about to fess up to his new yoga hobby. "I think I'll sit in the truck and keep an eye on things until Lyric leaves." Otherwise, he'd only sit at home and worry anyway.

Aiden looked confused. "Won't she be going home to you?"

"Oh. Yeah." Everyone likely assumed they spent most of their nights together being in a relationship and all. "I mean, probably."

"I'll head out with you." Aiden pulled on his sweat-shirt, and they walked down the hall together. "I'm looking forward to the trip this weekend. Between the rec center and Kyra's schedule at the clinic, we've hardly seen each other lately. Hopefully, there'll be some early nights and late mornings, if you know what I mean."

Oh, he knew. What he didn't know was how he and Lyric would be spending those late mornings and early nights. On opposite sides of their cabin? He had other ideas about how they could spend those hours together, but he didn't know if she was on board.

Aiden led the way out the door, looking at him funny. "What's wrong?"

"Nothing." Thatch quickly hoofed it to his truck. "I should head to the clinic. See you tomorrow."

As he drove away, Aiden still stood there staring at him. For the first time, Thatch started to sweat going on a trip with their friends over the weekend. Silas and Aiden would see right through him.

He parked his truck along the curb two houses down from the clinic and cut the engine. Dusk had started to settle, dragging shadows across the lawns of the small bungalows and Craftsman-style homes on the west side of the street. Thatch leaned his seat back slightly and did a few of the stretches Lyric had shown him for his ribs. They were still cranky, but he'd been able to move better the last few days, so that was something. Still, he didn't want to overdo anything, and since Lyric wasn't here to supervise, he pulled out his phone to play on his Battleship game with Silas instead. Next, he sorted through his email, deleting almost everything in his inbox. He was about to pocket his phone again when it rang.

He answered on the Bluetooth before the first ring had even finished. "Hey, Mom."

"Thatcher!" His mother sounded delighted. "I thought I was going to have to leave you *another* message."

"You caught me at a good time." Most of her messages as of late had been asking how Lyric was doing, and he hadn't exactly known what to say. He didn't want to get his mother's hopes up for a future with a woman who mostly held him at arm's length.

"How are you? How's Lyric?" she asked in her sing-songy tone.

"I'm doing fine, but I'm not sure how Lyric is." He couldn't full-on lie to her.

"You're not taking her out tonight?" his mom pressed.

"Not that I know of—"

The clinic's door opened, and the girls from Lyric's class hurried out to waiting cars. Lyric followed them down the pathway across the lawn and then turned in his direction.

Uh-oh. He'd been spotted. "Hey, Mom. Actually, I need to get—"

"What's the weather going to be like when we're there?" she interrupted. "I'm seeing conflicting reports."

"This time of year, the weather is always conflicting." He waved at Lyric, who was now only a few paces away from his truck. "Plan for anything. Okay? I need to—"

"Do you think I should bring my winter coat?" She paused, clicking her tongue. "Or will my mid-weight be enough?"

"Uh, I really don't know." Lyric was standing outside his window. He held up a finger to tell her just a second, but then she apparently got impatient and traipsed around to the passenger's side, climbing in next to him before he could hang up.

"Hey, what're you doing here?" Lyric asked.

"Lyric?" There was some shuffling on the line. His mother had likely almost dropped the phone in her excitement. "Is that you, honey?"

The woman shot him an apologetic glance. "Yeah. Hey, Mrs. Hearst."

"I thought you said you weren't taking Lyric out tonight." No matter how old he got, his mom still scolded him.

"We hadn't made specific plans," he told her.

"I just kind of showed up," Lyric added.

"Well, I'm so glad you did."

Here we go.

"I was asking Thatcher what to pack for our trip out there, and he was no help at all."

Lyric looked like she was trying not to laugh. "Bring your winter coat. Always bring your winter coat in May."

"Thank you, hon."

"All right, Mom." Thatch intended to end this call before it turned into an inquest to find out if they were dating. "We have to run. I'll call you later. Love you." He hung up.

"Sorry." Lyric gave him a sheepish smile. "I didn't realize you were talking to your mom."

"It's fine." She was probably going to call Silas or Aiden right now to get the scoop anyway. So much for keeping his parents out of this.

"I wondered what you were doing sitting out here." The woman's hands were nervously knotting together in her lap. "You could come in and say hi, you know. You don't have to stay in your truck."

She'd wanted him to come in and say hi? "I was keeping watch." Thatch clicked his seat back into place so he wasn't reclining anymore. "To make sure some random person didn't try to sneak into the studio again while you were teaching."

"Awww." Even in the dark, he could see her shining smile. "You're doing a stakeout for me."

"I guess you could call it that." It was supposed to be a covert op, but he'd blown his cover. Not that he was complaining.

Lyric scanned the street. "So you haven't seen anything yet?"

"No. Whoever it was probably won't come back." But he wasn't willing to risk that knowing Luke Copeland might already be in the area.

The woman angled her body toward his. "You're very chivalrous."

"Old habits die hard, I guess. I'm used to keeping watch." Even though he didn't wear the uniform anymore, he still believed it was his job to protect everyone.

"I'm sure you had to sacrifice a lot doing what you did all those years," Lyric said quietly. "I can't figure out why some lucky woman hasn't already snatched you up."

He looked out at the dark street. Conversations like this were always a decision point. When a woman said something like that, most of the time he laughed it off or made a joke, but he wanted Lyric to know the truth. "I almost got married. Before I became a SEAL."

"Really?" It was half word, half gasp. "I had no idea. What happened?"

He forced himself to look at her. This was the hard part. The part he didn't talk about with anyone else. "I left on a deployment with the navy, and my fiancée fell in love with my younger brother and they ended up getting married."

"No!" Her eyes got wide and fierce. "She cheated on you with your brother while you were off serving your country?"

"Afraid so." He should've known. He should've picked up on something in their sparse phone calls. "She'd said it was too hard. That she worried about me constantly." As if that made the news any easier to take. "And my brother was there. He didn't have to take off for months at a time."

Lyric seemed to let the words sink in. "Are they still married?" she finally asked.

"Yeah. I haven't seen them much since the wedding." They hadn't talked much either. There'd been the occasional awkward holiday dinner that his mom had guilted him into attending, but for the most part, he'd steered clear.

She stared at him in disbelief. "You went to the wedding?"

"I had to." Showing up that day was one of the most difficult things he'd ever done. "He was my best friend at one time." And Liam had begged him to be there. "Being in the military, I had it ingrained into me that you never want to have any regrets. Life is too short." He'd always hoped he and Liam could get past the awkwardness that had plagued their relationship after Thatch found out, but so far that hadn't happened. Not that he'd made as much of an effort as he could've. Holding on to bitterness had been easier than letting go.

"Are the two of you in touch now?" Lyric asked, still intently focused on him.

"Not really." He was tempted to look away but continued to stare into the woman's eyes, holding on to the compassion he saw there. "I think he feels guilty. It's hard for him to talk to me, and I was pretty angry with him. I didn't go easy on him." He'd been humiliated. Everyone knew—all of their friends and family—before Thatch had found out because they hadn't wanted to tell him while he was gone. "I keep thinking maybe someday we'll get past it all."

Lyric rested her hand over his. "That kind of a betrayal is hard to leave behind."

"Any kind of a betrayal is hard to leave behind." He turned his hand and fit their palms together. "But I guess you can't let the past hold you back forever."

"No. You can't." Lyric moved closer to him. "At some point you have to move on. Move forward," she whispered. Her fingers weaved between his, holding his hand tighter.

Thatch wanted to lean forward and kiss her. He could've. She was right there. But he held his ground. She had to *want* him to kiss her. She had to be the one in control here. He wouldn't take any initiative without her consent.

"You're a good man," she murmured, shifting to her knees on the seat so their faces were level. "I've known some pretty bad ones."

"I'm sorry you had to know any bad ones." He would erase all of those memories for her if he could.

She said nothing more, only smiled while she brought her face to his, grazing his lips with hers, unlocking his chest. Something must've unlocked in her too, since she melted against him, kissing him with the same sudden urgency that flooded him.

"Ugh, this stupid console," Lyric muttered, climbing over the barrier between them and straddling his lap. "That's better." She clasped her hands together behind his neck.

"Way better," he managed before touching his lips to hers again. They were so soft and seductive. All of her was. He kissed along her jaw to her neck, her hands clawing at his back. How did her skin taste so—?

A loud knock at the window diverted his attention.

What the hell was Natalie doing standing outside of his truck?

"Well, this is awkward," Lyric whispered, her head bowed like she was embarrassed. But Thatch wasn't. No.

He was annoyed. Reaching around Lyric, he turned the key so he could roll down the window. "Do you mind?"

The police officer draped her arms over the window frame and leaned in. "So you decided to make out in the truck instead of in the studio this time?" she teased. "You could've at least taken her to one of the secluded mountain make-out spots, Hearst."

"Trust me. If I'd known you were going to interrupt, I would've." Or he would've taken Lyric home to his house. Yes, his house, so they could be alone with no interruptions at all. Frustration rumbled through him. "Since you're spying on my truck, I assume you have some news about the break-in."

"Um...let me just..." Lyric shifted and squirmed to climb back over the console and into her own seat.

What a shame.

Natalie's expression evened out into her official *police business* look. "One of the neighbors down the block said they were out with the dog that night and a car sped by. She thought it might've been a dark-colored older-model Dodge Charger, but she couldn't be sure because it all happened so fast."

Well, shit. That wasn't what he wanted to hear. Thatch rubbed at the headache starting in his temples.

"An older-model Dodge?" Lyric elbowed him. "Isn't that what Franco drives?"

"Yeah." He'd become pretty familiar with the kid's car at the job site. "It's a navy-blue color."

"Franco?" Natalie straightened as though surprised. "You think he'd break into the clinic?"

"I can't see him doing that." In the time he'd spent with the kid, Thatch hadn't seen any red flags. "He's been working with us for almost a month now. I don't think he's that reckless."

"Teenagers aren't exactly known for thinking before they act," Natalie said. "You want me to find him and question him?"

"No." If Franco did break in, he wouldn't have stolen anything. Thatch was almost sure. Eighty-five percent at least. There had to be another reason the kid had shown up at the clinic that night. "I want to talk to him before you do."

And he knew exactly where to find him.

CHAPTER FIFTEEN

I t had been a long time since Lyric had seen that expression on Thatch's face. Dark, contemplative. When he'd first moved to town in the aftermath of Jace's death, she remembered seeing that look often. But these days he smiled, or at least appeared more relaxed, most of the time.

When Natalie had told them about the car, Thatch's whole demeanor shifted. Every part of the man had tensed, and he hadn't said much since they'd started driving to the school to find Franco.

"You okay?" Her voice was still a little trembly from that kiss they'd shared. So were her hands, for that matter. And her knees.

"I don't want to be wrong about him." Thatch sighed deeply. "Franco just said earlier today how he wanted to make something out of himself and join the navy. He has goals and plans. Why would he pull something like this?"

She couldn't answer that question. But there would

only be one reason the kid had talked about joining the navy. "You've really had an impact on him."

"I don't know about that."

As long as she'd been acquainted with him, Thatch had always downplayed his value. "I do." She waited until he looked at her. "It's obvious he looks up to you, Thatch. He has every reason to. You're dedicated and loyal. You protect the people you care about." How many men in their late twenties would've permanently moved to a Podunk town in the middle of the mountains to help watch out for their friend's widow? How many men would go to the trouble of hiring a kid—and building a rapport with him—simply because she'd asked him to?

Not many.

Thatch paused longer than he needed to at the stop sign. "He's a good kid. He shows up on time, lets me know if he can't make it. And he's a hard worker. Everything I've seen tells me he's trustworthy." He seemed to be trying to work out the truth in his head.

"Maybe he's not the one who broke in." They didn't have any evidence Franco was to blame yet. "Maybe the car driving past is a coincidence."

"Not likely in a town this size." He started to drive again, under the speed limit, she noticed, as if procrastinating.

That was fine with her. She wasn't looking forward to this conversation either. "What're you going to say to him?"

"I don't know yet." He turned into the high school parking lot, driving toward the cluster of cars parked outside of the gym doors. "I think he gets out of practice soon." Thatch parked next to Franco's car and cut the engine, his mouth still grim. "Maybe I was wrong about him. He could've fooled me, I guess."

"Sometimes people only let you see what they want you to see." Lyric had learned that lesson a long time ago. She held her breath for a beat to ward off the residual panic that gripped her anytime she thought about Luke. She didn't have to explain to Thatch. She didn't have to tell him anything. But the vulnerability he'd shown earlier when he'd told her about his brother had touched her. Hearing about his pain had made her feel safer somehow, less alone with her own wounds. "My ex-husband was like that. A different person in front of most people."

Thatch's expression immediately softened, the tension on his face replaced with an openness. He turned fully to her on his seat, gazing into her eyes, waiting.

"Luke was funny and charismatic and everyone's friend." She swallowed hard. Every time she started to talk about her experience, the shame that haunted her rose from the ashes, threatening to silence her. But she couldn't stop now. "He never met a stranger. When we first got together, I used to wonder how I'd found such a wonderful man." Luke had been a contrast with her quieter timidity. At first, she'd thought he brought out the best in her. But it had only taken one month into their marriage to see who he really was. "The first time he pushed me, I was shocked." Somehow, even after she'd fallen to the floor, she'd convinced herself it hadn't happened. She told herself she'd stumbled and had fallen backward. Yes, his hand had been on her, but he hadn't meant to push. "Then it started to happen more."

Thatch held his eyes closed for a few silent seconds, his chest rising and falling in slow, even breaths.

"I didn't know what to do." She refused to let her voice crumble the way her heart always did when she relived those moments. "Everyone liked him. Everyone thought he was such a wonderful guy. And in a weird way, he convinced me the fights were my fault."

Thatch reached for her then, taking both of her hands into his. "No. *No.*" He was angry for her. She saw the ferocity in his eyes, but he was holding it back. For her. He was protecting her. She could see it in the hard flex of his jaw.

His restraint gave her the courage to continue. "The abuse..." That might've been the first time she'd ever called Luke's behavior what it truly had been out loud. "Became this secret I had to hide. And I was good at hiding it. I tried harder to make everything work, but I was so isolated from everyone else that I had no one to talk to." The tears she'd staved off started to burn.

Thatch rested his palm against her cheek, his steady gaze a lifeline of hope and healing. "He should've cherished you. Protected you. You're worth cherishing and protecting."

But Luke had convinced her she wasn't worth anything. "In hiding and pretending, I got lost." She let a few tears slip out. It was too hard to hold them back. "I didn't even recognize myself when I looked in the mirror." Little by little, the secret she was keeping had hollowed her. "Then when he broke my arm, I couldn't hide anymore." Her mom and stepdad had known something was going on long before she'd called them that day. No matter how often she told them everything was great, they'd had their suspicions. "So my mom and Kenny picked me up at the hospital, and I never went back."

"You're so brave, Lyric." Thatch's rough and calloused hand smoothed her hair. "So beautiful and brave."

"I want to be brave." This man made her want to be brave enough to lose herself in someone again, knowing she would be safe. But she'd never been able to fully give herself to anyone else since then. She didn't know if she ever could.

Voices rose outside, drawing her attention. Basketball players had started spilling out of the gym doors. Franco noticed them and trotted to Thatch's truck.

Thatch faced forward in his seat again and got out to meet him. Lyric got out, too, though she kept her distance to give them some measure of privacy.

"Hey, man." The kid looked surprised to see them. "What're you doing here?"

"I have a question for you, and I need you to answer it honestly," Thatch said.

Lyric watched Franco carefully under the streetlight. The kid suddenly looked pale.

Thatch didn't give him too much time to squirm. "Have you ever snuck into the clinic after hours?"

Silence droned between them for what felt like an hour.

"Yeah. I have," Franco finally said. "Only because Elina asked me to. She asked me to go in when no one was around and borrow money from the safe."

"*Borrow* money?" Lyric hadn't meant to intrude on the conversation, but sneaking money from the safe was not *borrowing*.

"She needed groceries." Franco mostly looked at Thatch. To his credit, he wasn't cowering. "Her mom hasn't been working much, and they were low on food. Elina wasn't going to get paid until this week, so she asked if I would take some money from the safe. Only until she could pay it back."

"So you were going to *steal* money from the clinic." Lyric heard the restraint in Thatch's voice again. His tone was firm but also carefully controlled.

"No." The kid raised his hands. "Not steal. I told her I wouldn't steal it. She was going to pay it all back. I swear." Franco nervously ran a hand through his hair. "I'm sorry. I didn't know what else to do. I just spent my paycheck on my new summer league basketball uniform, or I would've given her my money."

The ache in Lyric's heart forced tears into her eyes. God, poor Elina. She was only a kid. She shouldn't have to be the one worried about feeding her family. "It's okay, Franco." She walked to him and rested her hand on his shoulder. "Thanks for telling us the truth."

"If anything like this ever happens again, you come to me first," Thatch added. "You come to me with the truth. You got that?"

The kid stared at the ground, nodding.

"You can get in real trouble pulling shit like this," Thatch informed him sternly. "The police were going to find you and interview you."

That news made Franco's head rise. "I told her it was a bad idea, but she was so upset. I didn't even think anyone was around, and then I heard you two. So I took off. Are you gonna tell her I told you? She'll be so mad at me."

"We won't tell her," Lyric assured him. Thatch looked like he wanted to argue, but she squeezed his hand. "I don't want her to be embarrassed. We'll forget it happened. Okay?" They were only kids, and Franco looked scared enough that he'd probably never do anything like this again.

"I'm not fired, am I?" the kid asked. "'Cause I love the job. I don't want to lose it."

"You're not fired," Thatch muttered, though he wasn't making this conversation easy on the kid either. "But this won't happen again."

"Hell no. I swear." Franco unlocked his car like he couldn't wait to get out of there. "Next time, I'll come to you."

"All right. I'll see you next week then." Thatch waved him away. After he'd gotten into his car, they climbed back into the truck.

"I think maybe I was the one who was wrong about Franco." As much as she hated to admit it, her previous experience made her suspicious of people. She tended to see the worst. "He's a good kid. I let my own memories cloud what I saw between them."

Thatch started the engine but let it idle. "I hope you can make new memories." He found her hand and brought it to his lips, kissing her knuckles. "Maybe they won't be enough to fully erase the bad ones, but they might help you move forward."

"I think I'm ready for new memories." Or at least she was ready to try building some. Maybe this weekend would be the perfect time to start. With Thatch. In a romantic cabin.

But right now, she couldn't breathe past the ache in her chest. "I wish I knew how to help Elina. It breaks my heart to think she's the one who has to worry about food for her siblings when she's only fifteen years old."

Thatch released her hand. "Do you want to go talk to her about what Franco told us?"

She didn't know what to do. "I don't have that kind of relationship with her yet. She's still pretty standoffish with me." With everyone, really, from what Lyric had seen. Elina hadn't taken to her the way Franco had taken to Thatch. "I don't want to humiliate her or make a big deal about what happened." Especially knowing the break-in had been out of sheer desperation.

Thatch nodded, his eyes narrowed in a thoughtful expression. "Why don't we go to the store to get her some groceries and drop them off on her doorstep anonymously?" he finally asked. "That will at least solve her problem in the short term, and then you can figure out how you want to deal with this moving forward."

And just when she'd thought the man couldn't prove himself to be more compassionate. "I love that idea. But the grocery store is already closed, and we're supposed to leave for the big friend-cation in the morning." There'd be no time for shopping.

"Give me a minute." He grabbed his phone off the dash and dialed. "Hey, Craig. You think you could open up the store for Lyric and me? All we'd need is half an hour. We know of a family who's down on their luck and could use a secret grocery delivery." He paused. "Yeah. That'd be great. Thank you so much." Thatch pocketed his phone. "Craig'll open back up for us, but we'd better get over there now." He started the engine.

Lyric couldn't stop staring at him as he drove through town. "You're kind of amazing."

In typical Thatch fashion, he didn't acknowledge the comment. "Our market here doesn't have a huge selection. So maybe next week we could run to one of those bulk megastores and really stock up on some food for them. I'm sure others would be willing to donate too."

"That might be a good idea." But they had to keep this quiet. She didn't want Elina to be publicly humiliated.

"I'm concerned, too, about her mom not working. I mean, helping with food in the short term is great, but I wonder how we can help Elina's mom change their situation long-term."

"We can think on it." Thatch pulled into a parking spot at the town's only small market and rubbed her shoulder for a second. "We'll quietly talk to a few people around town. Maybe someone will have an idea of how to help. That's one thing about Star Valley—we take care of our own."

"Yes, we do." Lyric leaned into his caress, procrastinating getting out of the truck. How long had it been since anyone had given her a massage?

Thatch pulled his hand away. "You ready?"

No. But she got out of the truck, and he ushered her into the market. Craig, the owner, locked the door behind them. "Make it quick, okay? I promised Mary I'd be home soon."

"It'll be like an episode of *Supermarket Sweep*," Thatch promised, selecting a cart.

Lyric laughed. "*Supermarket Sweep*?"

"You know, that game show." He grinned as they set off down the produce aisle. "Or maybe it was only on in Iowa."

"I've heard of it. I just don't think I've ever watched it." She stopped at the selection of bananas.

"This one's good." Thatch put a bunch in the cart. "See, in *Supermarket Sweep*, you have to move fast. You can't spend fifteen minutes inspecting produce."

"Why don't you show me how it's done?" She gestured for him to lead the way. If she was in charge, she would take fifteen minutes to inspect the bananas alone.

Thatch pushed the cart onward. "Follow my lead."

They made record time through the aisles grabbing everything from fruits and veggies to simple dinner staples to snacks.

"Oh, how about Oreos?" Thatch tossed four packages into the cart. "I used to love Oreos."

She eyed all those packages. "*Used* to?" He might have been projecting his own likes on Elina's family.

"Okay, I still keep them stockpiled at home." He added one more package. "You haven't lived until you've dipped them in milk."

"I'll have to try that sometime." In the last twenty minutes, she'd learned so much about this man. And she liked it all.

"You two about done?" Craig called from a checkout station.

"Almost." Thatch turned to her. "Anything else you want to add?"

She eyed the cart. They had a good mix of healthy meal-type foods and some fun snacks. "I think you've pretty much covered it."

"Sweet. Then let's roll." He swept an arm around her and pushed the cart with the other hand all the way to where Craig stood. He started to scan the items.

"Since you two are doing an act of charity, I'll kick in a forty percent discount."

"Thank you." Tears welled up in her eyes again. It was amazing to see how one act of generosity could lead to another. And Thatch had started all of this.

When Craig scanned the last item, Lyric dug in her bag for her wallet, but Thatch already had his credit card out.

"We should split it," she insisted. "You shouldn't have to pay for everything."

"Let me. I want to." He swiped the card in the reader. "I don't get to do things like this often enough. I'm glad I have the chance."

She was glad too. Glad that she could see more of his big heart.

They hustled out of the store, thanking Craig once more, and then loaded up the groceries.

Lyric gave Thatch directions to Elina's house and told him about the conversation she'd had with the girl in the driveway. When they pulled up, her heart started to pound. Beyond the curtains, the lights were on, so they'd have to make the secret delivery quietly and quickly.

Thatch parked on the street instead of turning into the driveway, and they stealthily made a few trips, depositing the bags onto the porch.

"I'll go start up the truck and get ready to drive," he instructed like this was an official op. "You knock and then run fast."

"Got it." Lyric waited on the porch until he'd backed the truck into the driveway and then knocked as loudly as she could before sprinting to the passenger's side.

She jumped in, and Thatch peeled out of the driveway with a squeal of the tires. Lyric squealed too. "Covert ops are so fun!"

"Hopefully, our mission was accomplished." Thatch drove the truck around the block and hit the brakes. "Nice job on the sprint." He raised his hand for a high five.

"And your driving was top notch. Minus the squealing tires," she teased.

"What can I say? I like to make a dramatic exit."

That sexy grin of his brought her insides to a simmer. Between his magnetism and his compassion, she was finding him harder and harder to resist. "Should we drive around and make sure they brought everything inside?"

"Good idea." He eased the truck along at a crawling pace, and when they passed by, the stoop was empty. "I guess we can call it a night, then."

"I guess so." And what a night. The kissing, the sharing, the mission. "Actually, this might be the best night I've had in a long time."

"Me too." Thatch reached over to rub her shoulder while he drove. It felt so natural, sitting next to him in his truck, feeling his caress.

She didn't want the night to end, but she didn't know where else she was ready to take it either.

Thatch parked the truck next to her car in front of the clinic and put it in park. "So I'll see you bright and early tomorrow morning?"

"Bright and early."

They were going on a trip together, and now she couldn't wait.

CHAPTER SIXTEEN

Thatch had been trained to withstand torture. But even BUD/S couldn't have prepared him for the special kind of torment he'd endured on day one of pretending to be in love with Lyric during a romantic weekend getaway.

They'd spent the entire first day of their trip doing what a normal couple would do: after taking their bags into their cabin, they met up with their friends—except for Tess, who was napping—for a long hike into the higher terrain complete with a picnic lunch, and played volleyball with some of the other guests. Then they'd all enjoyed an early dinner together.

The whole time, he and Lyric had bantered back and forth. He'd helped her up a rocky section on the hike and hadn't let go of her hand for half an hour after. The smile she'd aimed in his direction had been different—for him alone. The connection between them had seemed so real. At least to him. But he had no idea what would happen tonight.

Now, as Thatch walked out of the changing room and

onto the lavish deck surrounding the steaming waters of a natural hot spring, he had to be honest: He wasn't pretending to be in love. He'd fallen. Spending the day with her had only confirmed how hard he'd fallen. After spreading out his towel on a lounge chair, he sat next to Silas. Aiden had already claimed the spot with the best exposure to the setting sun.

"That was some hike today." Silas pulled off his shirt and jumped into the pool.

"Quite the scenery," Aiden agreed.

Thatch stayed quiet. He'd been too distracted watching Lyric all day to notice much of the scenery. A dip in the pool was the last item on Kyra's agenda for the day. And then what? Back to the cabin with a woman he wanted more with each passing hour but couldn't have.

"Okay, I'm coming out," Tess called from the doorway of the women's changing room. "No one look at me in my maternity bathing suit."

"You're gorgeous, babe." Silas hurried out of the water to meet her, offering his hand to help her walk down the steps into the pool.

"This is amazing." Kyra walked out next, followed by Lyric.

Damn.

Thatch had been good all day. He'd been attentive but distant, making sure she had the space she needed even while they were supposed to be acting like a couple. But that bikini she was wearing would make it ten times harder for him to keep his hands off her.

"How's the water?" She sat next to him on the lounge chair and pulled her long silky hair up onto her head, securing it with a rubber band.

Think. Speak. "Uh…I haven't been in yet."

"Good. We can go together." She took his hand and led him to the pool steps.

"This is the life." Tess bobbed on a floatie a few feet away.

"Perfection after that hike earlier," Lyric agreed, wading into the water with him. She still hadn't let go of his hand.

The pool was warm and soothing on his skin, but it was the woman next to him who heated his body.

"I can't believe you two kept your relationship a secret." Kyra sat on the edge of the pool not far away. "I mean, now that I'm looking at you, it's so obvious how crazy you are about each other."

"I'd say they're both smitten," Tess agreed from her floatie.

"Yep. I'm not sure how we managed to hide it either." Lyric gazed up at him like an adoring girlfriend would. Was she telling the truth, or was it part of their act? Hell, he didn't know anymore.

"Our buddy Thatch here is good at keeping secrets." Leave it to Aiden to bring up his bronc riding right now. "Who all knows that we get to watch him compete during Rodeo Days?"

"Compete?" Kyra slid into the pool. "What does that mean?"

"Our boy here is now a bronc rider." Aiden slung his arm around his wife. "If you can believe that."

"Seriously?" Tess paddled closer to them. "Well, that'll be something to see."

"He's really good." Lyric edged closer to him, almost protectively, her bare skin brushing his. "I've seen him ride."

"Thanks," he murmured, brushing his lips close to her ear. The urge to kiss the soft skin of her earlobe almost overpowered him.

"Boy, am I glad that secret's out," Silas mumbled. "Too many secrets. Can we all just agree to tell each other everything? I'm not good at keeping things on the down low."

Thatch wasn't either. But this thing between him and Lyric was starting to feel more real by the hour.

"I'm not telling you people all my secrets," Tess sassed. She reached for the beach ball bobbling nearby. "How about we play keep-away instead? Guys versus girls."

"I don't know if that's a good idea, babe—" Silas started.

But Tess interrupted. "Losers have to make dinner for our next triple date!"

She fired the ball in Lyric's direction, and Thatch had to admit that the woman had some good reflexes. Lyric caught the ball and darted away from him before he could grab it from her.

"Kyra!" She lobbed the ball up, but Aiden dove to intercept it.

"She was throwing it to me!" Kyra tried to swat the ball, but Aiden hit it over to Silas.

"I'm pretty sure you don't want to take us on." Silas taunted his wife with the ball, keeping it just out of her reach. "Don't forget, we have some seriously good evasive skills." He tossed the ball to Thatch.

"We have skills too." Lyric's tone had a naughty ring to it. The woman sashayed over to him, dripping wet, and then launched her body at him. Thatch instantly dropped the ball so he could catch her in his arms, bringing her close. Their eyes met and his heart clicked back into place, and he kissed her because she was right there in his arms, and he could.

Lyric's arms came around his shoulders, and she wrapped her legs around his waist, kissing him back every bit as intensely as he was kissing her, and good God if his friends weren't standing right there, he would've lost control real fast.

"I've got it!" Tess yelled triumphantly. "I got the ball! And you can't steal it from a pregnant lady. We win!"

Let them win. Thatch forced himself to set Lyric down. "That was sneaky." Albeit very effective.

"Completely unfair," Aiden declared. "Come on, man." His friend punched his arm. "Seduction is the oldest trick in the book. Show a little restraint."

"I would if I could," he said helplessly. But when it came to Lyric, he didn't even want to try.

"Personally, I'm glad that's over." Kyra pulled herself out of the pool and opened a small shed near the fence. "I came here to relax." She tossed a few more rafts onto the pool deck.

For the next hour, they all lazily floated around the pool, discussing the potential for a fall trip to Napa. When darkness smudged out the last traces of the sun, everyone started to pack up.

"Remember the days we would've gone to the lodge to play some poker?" Silas asked as they walked out of the pool area. "Times have changed."

"No offense, but I'd rather spend the evening with my wife than with you two," Aiden said as he waited for Kyra.

"I think we feel the same way." Silas elbowed him. "Right, Thatch?"

"Right." He glanced at Lyric, who was walking ahead of them with Tess. Truthfully, she looked every bit as good in that bathrobe she was now wearing over her suit as she had in the bikini. He would much rather spend the evening with her than with Silas and Aiden, but where would an evening together lead them? He didn't know what she wanted. Not really.

The walkway diverged to lead them to their separate cabins. They all said a quick good night, and then he and Lyric walked the rest of the way alone.

She caught him in a shy sideways gaze. "Today was nice."

"Until you tricked me," he teased.

They climbed the porch steps together, and Lyric waited for him to unlock the door. "You didn't like my tactics?"

He'd never seen her so coy, and he liked it. "I didn't say that." He pushed open the door and gestured for her to go in first. Inside the cabin, the soft lamps on two end tables glowed, and a fire crackled in the small stone hearth. A chilling bottle of champagne had been left on the counter of the kitchenette on the far side of the room during turn-down service. And the luxurious linens on the canopied king bed had been folded over and fluffed, rose petals sprinkled on the pillows.

Damn. Someone had really set the mood for them.

"I think I'm going to rinse off in the shower." Lyric reached up and pulled the rubber band out of her hair, letting the tresses cascade down her shoulders.

"Sounds great." She would be in the shower, and he would be out here, minding his own business. "I need to, uh, catch up on some email." Email? As if that would keep his mind off Lyric wet and naked only one room away.

Without another word, the woman disappeared into the bathroom. The sound of running water made him pace for a while. Thankfully, his phone rang, though when he pulled it out of his bag, he hesitated. But his mother would only keep calling if he didn't answer.

"Hey, Mom. What's up?" Thatch sank into the leather couch in front of the fire.

"Not too much." She sounded as chipper as always. "I was trying to get our schedule set for next weekend while we're in town, and I wondered if Friday or Saturday would be a good night for us to all take Lyric out to dinner."

"Oh." And just when he distracted himself from thinking about her. "I'm not sure. I'll have to get back to you about that."

"Well, I know the rodeo awards ceremony and party are Sunday, so we can't do it then." Her voice was unrelenting. "That leaves Friday or Saturday."

"Right." But he couldn't take their charade that far. He couldn't involve his family when he didn't even know what was going on between him and Lyric. "Um, I can ask her about dinner. She's usually pretty busy teaching yoga on Fridays and Saturdays, though, so it might not work out this time."

"She's teaching yoga at *night*?" His mother didn't give him a chance to answer. "She has to eat dinner, right? We can be flexible on the time to accommodate her schedule."

"I guess—"

Lyric exited the bathroom in a cloud of steam, dressed in gray pajama pants and a long-sleeved T-shirt. "Hey, have you seen my—?"

Thatch held up a finger against his lips, but it was too late. His mom gasped.

"Did I hear Lyric? Are you two on a date right now?"

After this, there'd be no getting out of dinner for sure. "Yeah. I guess you could say we're on a date."

"I knew it!" his mom sang. "How long have you been dating her? And why haven't you just told us about it instead of all the avoiding?"

Because he hadn't wanted to get her hopes up any more than he wanted to get his hopes up. "The dating is pretty new still."

"Really new," Lyric called, shoving some clothes into her suitcase.

"Still. I'm your mom. I need to know these things." She was too excited to sound stern. "Tell her I said hello."

"Will do." Thatch covered the speaker part of his phone with his hand. "My mom says hi."

"Maybe I should tell her myself."

"That's not necessary." His mom would likely chat with Lyric for half an hour, given the opportunity.

"Hi, Mrs. Hearst!" Well, the woman certainly didn't sound like a fake girlfriend. She made it sound like she was his mother's best friend.

"Oh, tell her I can't wait to see her," his mom pestered.

Sheesh. He should just give Lyric the phone.

"I'm looking forward to seeing you too, Mrs. Hearst!"

Thatch shot her a look. She really should tone down the enthusiasm, or his mom would start asking about wedding dates.

"Okay, Mom. I should go. This phone conversation is violating all kinds of dating protocols." Not to mention digging them deeper into this fake-relationship black hole.

"Yes, of course, of course." His mom clucked. "Let me know about dinner. And call me later, sweetie."

"Will do. Love you. Say hi to Dad." He hit the end button and tossed his phone onto the coffee table. "Her timing is impeccable, as usual."

Lyric padded to the couch barefoot and sat next to him, her wet hair loosely braided. "Your mom seems like a wonderful person."

"She is. She's the best." Thatch kicked his feet up onto the coffee table and leaned back against the cushion. "She sacrificed a lot, too, when I went into the navy. I know she worried constantly. But she never tried to stop me from doing anything I felt called to do. She never wanted to hold me back." He couldn't imagine how difficult that had been for her.

Lyric turned sideways to face him, pulling her legs up onto the couch. "That's a gift."

"It was." The significance of his parents' selflessness in letting him pursue his dreams was never lost on him. He appreciated them more than he could ever express.

Even when his mother was meddling in his love life.

"She's serious about wanting to take you out to dinner when they're out here. Friday or Saturday night."

"I could make that work." There was that shy look again. "If you want me to."

He wanted her to. He wanted all kinds of things. But what he wanted didn't matter unless she wanted him too.

"How about Saturday night?" Lyric hugged her knees to her chest. "We can all go to the café, and I can meet your brother and sister-in-law too."

"Sure. Saturday works." A years-old insecurity flickered back to life. What would he tell Liam and Sienna when things fell apart with Lyric? They'd all think he'd finally found the one, and then their breakup would be one more epic relationship failure.

"Whew." Lyric let her head rest on the cushion behind her. "I'm exhausted. It was kind of a busy day for being on vacation, huh?"

"Definitely." He glanced at the clock. Almost ten, which meant they should wade through the awkwardness of figuring out sleeping arrangements. "Hey, I can sleep right here on the couch tonight. I don't want this to be weird for you."

"Actually, today hasn't felt weird." Lyric lifted her head, her dark eyes focused on his. "At least for me. We can sleep in the same bed. I'm not going to make you sleep on the lumpy couch."

There went that unlocking of his chest again. He couldn't identify the emotion that flooded him. Relief? Want? "It doesn't feel that weird to me either. But we don't have to force anything. I don't want you to feel pressure." As tempting as she was, he didn't even want to touch her until he knew she was ready for something more. He'd waited this long. He could keep waiting until she wanted to take another step.

"I appreciate you giving me space." She covered his hand with hers. "And I'm starting to feel ready for more, Thatch. Really. I'm still figuring out what. But I like you. I'm attracted to you. And I'm glad I'm here. With you."

For now, that was enough. He didn't need to know anything else tonight. "I'm glad I'm here with you too. And I think it goes without saying that I'm attracted to you too." He'd made that obvious in the pool, at dinner, during the hike. He hadn't bothered to hide his long, lingering looks from her. But he was also determined to prove that his interest wasn't only about sex. "Hey, do you want to watch a movie?" He pushed off the couch. "We could get comfortable in bed and turn on the TV, relax, and fall asleep when we're ready."

"That actually sounds perfect." Lyric stood up and crossed the room, brushing the rose petals off the pillows of the bed before climbing in. "I don't know how long I'll be able to keep my eyes open."

"You don't have to try too hard on my account." He was pretty tired himself. It took a lot of energy pretending to be her boyfriend for everyone else while also hiding from Lyric that he was in love with her. But he really was.

"What should we watch?" He grabbed the remote off the bedside table and climbed into the bed next to her.

"You choose." She scooted closer and nestled against him, her head already on the pillow.

Thatch flicked through the guide until he found *Top Gun*. "A classic."

Lyric murmured a sleepy sigh, and he eased his arm around her, holding her against him. In less than half an hour, her head rested heavily on his arm and her breathing grew rhythmic.

Trying not to move too much, Thatch reached for the remote and flicked off the TV. His arm was starting to fall asleep from the way Lyric was lying on him, but he didn't even care. He wouldn't move.

He would hold her for as long as he had the chance.

CHAPTER SEVENTEEN

Lyric woke up in a warm, contented, lazy haze that had everything to do with the man still nestled against her underneath the quilt. When she opened her eyes, two things hit her. One: Thatch had kept his arm around her all night as they'd slept, and two: she had this gorgeous, loyal, caring heartthrob of a man in bed with her and they'd spent the whole night sleeping.

Only sleeping.

She glanced at the clock on the bedside table. It wasn't even eight yet, so they still had plenty of time before meeting their friends for breakfast.

Plenty of time for *not* sleeping.

Without moving her head, she checked out Thatch, desire spilling through her. His head was tilted on the pillow, face toward hers, his broad jaw relaxed, those magnetic eyes still closed. With his chest positioned against her shoulder, she could feel his strength, his warmth, and his heartbeat, slow and steady.

Her pulse wasn't slow. Not anymore. Not in this beautiful bed with this remarkable man who'd shown her so much care. But she couldn't exactly kiss him and wake him up in her current state.

Lyric carefully shimmied off his arm, pausing while he grunted and turned over.

Don't wake up. Don't wake up. She wasn't quite ready for him to see her yet.

When his breathing evened out again, she rolled out of the bed and crept into the bathroom. *Whoa.* Her hair. Most of it had escaped the braid she'd fashioned last night and was now sticking out at random angles. Good thing she'd looked in the mirror before seducing the man again!

Turning on the water, she wet her hands and then smoothed her hair into another braid down her back. Next, she brushed her teeth and washed her face, applying a citrus-scented moisturizer to plump her cheeks.

Now on to her attire.

Her frumpiest pajamas had seemed like a good idea—a safeguard—when she'd packed for this trip, but they didn't reflect all the sexy thoughts she now had about Thatch and her in bed. She snuck back into the bedroom and started to carefully and quietly dig through her suitcase.

Hmmm. She could go with the button-down Henley and unbutton enough of the buttons to show her black lacy bra. That would probably be her best bet—

"I hope you're not sneaking out on me," Thatch said in a groggy voice.

Lyric whirled to the bed, her heart all lit up. "Um, no. I just need…" *You.* But she wasn't quite ready to say that yet. "Um, I need a minute. But you stay right there." She raced back into the bathroom and quickly changed into the Henley, undoing the buttons until a glimpse of her bra peeked through the neckline.

"Okay," she whispered, taking one last look in the mirror. The pajama pants weren't great, but hopefully they wouldn't be on too long anyway. At least her unbuttoned shirt should give the man a clue about her intentions.

Before she could second-guess herself, she stepped back into the bedroom. Thatch had sat up, his upper body propped against the many fluffy pillows on the bed. Both his T-shirt and hair were all askew, which only made him sexier.

"Sorry if I woke you up." Her voice had gone sultry without her even trying. Every part of her was warm and melty and ready. She was so ready for this.

"I'm not sorry." Thatch's gaze zeroed in on the V-neck of her shirt. "Do you always look this good when you wake up?"

"Totally." She crawled back into bed and turned on her side to face him. "I woke up with a lot of energy this morning." Good energy. Humming energy. "And we have some time before we're supposed to meet everyone for breakfast."

"That's true." He turned on his side, too, facing her. "So what'd you want to do?"

"How about a little bit of this...?" She let the whisper trail off into a kiss, touching her lips to his for the briefest second before pulling back.

"I could be persuaded." The words were a low growl.

"And maybe a little bit of that?" Lyric sat up and tugged at his shirt, pulling it off over his head.

"What about a little bit of this?" Thatch sat up also,

taking her in his arms and kissing her mouth hard and decisively, exactly the way she wanted him to.

Lyric opened her mouth to moan, and his tongue grazed hers, charging her with a renewed burst of desire. "Yes. That too," she said between gasps and kisses, edging up to her knees on the mattress. "And this." She pulled her shirt up and over her head, then tossed it to the floor.

Thatch took his time looking at her, his gaze slowly moving down her body. "I want all of this," he murmured, drawing a line with his finger from the spot between her breasts down to her belly button. "I want all of you. But the most important thing to me is that you always feel safe with me, Lyric."

"I do." She straddled his lap, her thighs hugging his waist. "You make me feel safe and valued." She kissed her way over to his ear to add, "And hot. You also make me very, very hot, Thatch Hearst." She licked his earlobe and felt a shiver run through him.

"Just wait." Thatch directed her mouth back to his. "I'll make you feel so much more." His mouth covered hers, taking their kiss deeper while he laid her down on the bed and started to push her pajama pants down her hips. Yes, they needed to get rid of those pesky pajamas. And his sweats too.

Lyric clawed at the waistband of his pants, pushing and tugging while refusing to stop kissing him because the man made her feel so much with only a kiss and she liked it all—the energy and the passion and the pure lust for more.

Thatch wriggled the rest of the way out of his pants and then was at her side, breaking their kiss and focusing on her underwear. "God, you look good in lace."

"I look good without it too." She pulled his body over hers and straddled him again, this time feeling his desire for her through their underwear. Lyric moved against him, breathless and aching, arching her back.

Kissing her again, Thatch reached one arm behind her back and unclipped her bra, peeling it away before tracing his lips down her neck and then over her breasts. His tongue moved over her skin, warm and wet, teasing and tantalizing.

"Oh, oh," was all she managed between pants.

"What?" the man whispered against her skin. "What was that?"

"Oh, Thatch." She ran her hands through his hair. "I'm just...God this is so good. You're so good." Why had she kept him out for so long? They could've been doing this months ago.

His fingers trailed over her hip, snagging the strap of her underwear and pulling it down. Lyric kicked off the undergarment and then impatiently pushed his boxers down so she could touch him.

Thatch paused then, letting out a long, slow exhale.

Seeing the control she had over him, Lyric stroked and caressed, but he shifted out of her reach and ran his hand up her inner thigh, pushing her legs apart. "Tell me what you like," he murmured over her, his gaze shifting from where his fingers touched back up to her eyes.

Lyric opened her mouth to respond but moaned instead. He did *not* need her to tell him what to do. He knew where to touch her, how to make her back arch and her hips writhe and her breaths go ragged. "Please. Now," she begged helplessly. She wanted him to be closer, inside of her, part of her when she let herself go.

Thatch sat back on the bed, hastily swiping his wallet off the bedside table and putting on a condom before he lifted her to him, pulling her thighs around his waist again. "I need to look at you." His breathing had gotten heavier, too, though he wasn't as breathless. "I want to look into your eyes, Lyric."

"I want to see you too." His steady gaze transfixed her.

Hands on her hips, Thatch guided her to move, to lift her hips and push to fit their bodies together. Lyric's mouth opened when he moved fully inside of her, but she couldn't speak. She could hardly even breathe. He made her body feel good, but there was some deeper connection binding her to him. Whenever she'd been intimate with anyone in the past, she'd always held back a part of herself, but now she was losing herself totally, completely to him.

Thatch smiled at her, a slow, dangerous smile, and reached up his hand to hold her jaw. "What's on your mind, beautiful?"

"You," she whispered. That was all. With him, the rest of the world faded away, and all that mattered to her right now was this moment. "I'm only thinking about you. And me. And us." And this safe space he'd brought her to, where she could fully abandon everything that had held her back.

"That's all I'm thinking about too." He touched a kiss to her neck and then to her jaw and then his lips covered hers again, saying so much with their tenderness and intensity. Lyric kissed him back, holding on to him, and she couldn't stay still anymore. She had to feel their bodies moving together, finding this new rhythm that had already changed her life. Draping her arms over his shoulders, she lifted and thrusted her hips, creating a fiery momentum that spiraled low and deep inside of her.

Thatch met her movements, his hands pressing into her low back while he drove deeper into her, bringing those exhilarating sensations to a breaking point. His eyes found hers again, and she tried to tell him she was done, that she couldn't hold on anymore, but the force that rocked through her stole her voice. All she could do was let go of herself and hold him tighter, murmuring his name between enraptured gasps.

Thatch thrust into her again, and then shattered beneath her, his body rocking with the same power hers had.

With a weakness spreading over her, Lyric let her forehead rest on his shoulder while he stroked her hair. She didn't want to move. She could lie here for hours with him like this, still linked together in their own world.

But if they were late for breakfast, their friends would be on their doorstep, and she didn't want that.

Thatch lay down with a loud contented sigh, gently bringing her with him. "I'm thinking we call in sick for today." He snaked his arms around her. "We can hang out in bed all day."

"I wish." Lyric flipped over to face him. His hair was still all mussed, and his eyes drooped lazily. She loved this look on him. "But you know how Kyra is with her agenda." Today, her friend had booked the men a tee time in Jackson, and Lyric, Kyra, and Tess were supposed to go shopping for little Baby Beck.

"I think you gave me a fever." Thatch's imploring eyes were adorable. "Don't make me go golfing today. I'd rather be with you."

"We'll be together tonight." They'd only finished

having sex like three minutes ago, and she already burned with the desire to do it again. But anticipation was a good thing too.

"Tonight is twelve hours away," he complained, hugging her tighter.

Lyric released her own contented, lusty sigh. She hadn't anticipated how good it would feel for him to hold her. So she let herself stay there as long as she could. But they couldn't ignore the glowing clock forever. "All right, cowboy. It's time for a shower."

He kissed her once more, and then they lingered in the shower much too long, making out while they got clean. By the time they made it to the lodge for breakfast, all of their friends had almost finished their coffee.

"Well, look who decided to show up." Aiden glanced at his watch. "Twenty minutes late."

"Leave them alone." Kyra swatted him playfully. "They're still newly dating. It used to take us a while to get out of bed too."

Exactly. And Lyric wouldn't even apologize. Instead, she poured both her and Thatch a mug of coffee from the carafe and then helped herself to some of the pastries and fruit already on the table. Morning sex made a person hungry.

All during breakfast, Thatch rested his hand high on her thigh, a delicious reminder of the morning they'd spent together. When the time came to part ways, he pulled her close, even with all their friends standing right there. "Don't have too much fun without me."

"I won't have any fun," she whispered in his ear. "Because all I'm going to think about is being in bed with you."

"Good." He kissed her for all to see, with tongue action and everything.

"Okay. Let's get going," Kyra sang. "We don't want the boys to be late for their tee time."

When Thatch finally released her and turned away, Lyric squeezed his butt and then waved playfully.

Before she climbed into Kyra's car, Tess gave her a funny look. Right. Her friend knew she and Thatch weren't really together.

"You two seemed to have a good night." Kyra turned down her radio and headed for the highway that would take them to Jackson.

"We did," Lyric said evasively. "What about you both? Did you sleep well?"

"Besides getting up to pee three times?" Tess seemed a little cranky this morning. "We slept great." She craned her neck to look over her shoulder at Lyric in the back seat. "I'm guessing you got the least amount of sleep out of all of us." Her friend caught her in an interrogating gaze.

"Actually, we got more than eight hours." Until morning time. That was when the magic had happened. But what had taken place between her and Thatch was so intimate, those moments were theirs alone. "So what stores are we going to?"

The diversion worked. Kyra started to rattle off the names of some boutiques, talking about couture baby clothes.

"But we don't want to get too much stuff since we don't know the gender," Tess insisted.

"I still can't believe you're not finding out." Kyra turned into the parking lot of a cute boutique just off the main road. "I will be finding out the minute I can."

"I think it's fun to have it be a surprise." Lyric climbed out of the car and followed her friends into the boutique. "There're so few surprises these days."

"That's how we feel." Tess held up a miniature snowsuit with teddy bear ears on the hood.

"What about you and Thatch?" Kyra eyed Lyric. "Have you talked about the future? Marriage? Babies?"

"No." The response shot out too quickly. "I mean, not yet. We're kind of just enjoying the dating thing." She did her best not to look too spooked, but she'd never pictured herself having children. That hadn't even seemed like an option for so many years. The first time she'd gotten married, she'd wanted a family. But then when she saw past Luke's facade, she knew she couldn't have children with him. She wouldn't.

"You have plenty of time." Tess smiled and patted her shoulder, bailing her out. "No reason to rush into a bunch of responsibilities when you can simply enjoy being together for a while."

"Right. Exactly." She eased out a shaky breath.

"Oh, man. Now I'm the one who has to run to the restroom again." Kyra frantically scanned the boutique.

"Wait a minute." Lyric studied Kyra's face. "Why are you running to the bathroom so much?" Her friend had to make an emergency pit stop on the way here. Only an hour ago. And she'd also been munching on saltines during the drive. "Oh, my God," she said before Kyra could respond. "You're pregnant too!" She'd been so preoccupied with Thatch, she'd missed the signs.

"Totally!" Tess agreed.

That shining smile on Kyra's face confirmed the news. "I wasn't going to say anything until after Baby Beck was born."

"Why not?" Tess hugged her and pulled Lyric in too. "This is amazing news!"

"We're thrilled for you!" Happy tears gathered in Lyric's eyes. "How're you feeling? When are you due?"

"Not until December." Kyra laughed. "Which seems like forever. But I'm feeling pretty good. A little nauseous every once in a while. And I already have to pee a lot! Sorry. I'll be right back and then we can shop and celebrate some more." She rushed off toward the back of the store.

"This is so fun." Lyric looked around the store. "Now we have two babies to spoil with all the cute things." She and Tess started to browse at a rack of onesies.

"Mm-hmm," her friend murmured. "I have to say, you and Thatch are pretty convincing as a couple." Her friend wasn't wasting any time. "Or should I assume you're really a couple after what happened between you two last night?"

"Keep your voice down." Kyra didn't need to hear this. "We're not a couple. I don't think. I don't know." Oh, how she'd like to go back to this morning when she hadn't had to define anything. "Being with him felt right. I care about him. Deeply." More deeply than she wanted to admit.

"That's a good thing, honey." Tess slung her arm around her shoulders in a half hug. "I'm not trying to give you a hard time. I've actually always thought you two would make a good couple. You complement each other well."

"He makes me feel safe." And protected. And cherished. And it was the best feeling in the world.

But she still didn't know if she'd ever want to get married again. Even to someone as wonderful as Thatch.

CHAPTER EIGHTEEN

T hree over par again." Thatch shoved his putter back
into the rented golf club bag and smirked at Aiden.
"But at least I wasn't *five* over." Like someone else he
knew.

His friend flipped him off.

"I'm taking a picture of the scorecard so everyone
will know I beat you both with two over par on this
one." Silas snapped an annoying selfie holding up their
scorecard.

They walked back to the cart together, and Thatch
hoisted his bag onto the back seat, sitting down next to
it. "What the hell are we doing out here again?" Sure,
the scenery at this course was something else—rolling,
manicured green grass juxtaposed against the backdrop
of rugged mountain peaks. But they didn't golf. Not a
one of them. He, Silas, and Aiden had all fumbled their
way through a course a few times, but they sucked at
golfing, and now here they were tromping around the

greens, taking mulligan after mulligan, when he could be hanging out with Lyric. "Why'd Kyra make us go golfing anyway?"

"Hell if I know." Aiden slid into the cart's driver's seat. "She was so excited about this golf course. And she said she needed a day with the girls." He shrugged. "I didn't have the heart to tell her that we all suck at golf."

Silas stabbed his finger into Aiden's shoulder. "You mean you didn't want her to *know* you suck at something."

Thatch laughed. Accurate. Aiden had a hard time admitting he wasn't good at everything.

"We were SEALs." His friend turned the key and steered the cart toward the next hole, bouncing them over the grass. "Everyone thinks we're good at everything. Why burst their bubbles?"

"We don't have to burst their bubbles, but we also don't have to play golf." Thatch leaned over the seat. "Hear me out. We go sit in the clubhouse, grab a beer or two, and make fun of people at the driving range." In his estimation, that would be far more enjoyable and less frustrating than playing through the eight additional holes they had in front of them.

"I'm in." Silas elbowed Aiden. "We'll even tell Kyra that you won at golf today."

"By a lot." Aiden flipped a U-turn. "Tell her I won by a lot."

"Deal." Thatch sat back and watched the people who actually knew what they were doing all the way back to the clubhouse, wondering how many of them had made fun of him out there on the course today.

They parked the cart and turned in their rented golf clubs, and then claimed a table outside on the deck overlooking the driving range. Once the beer orders were in, Thatch positioned himself in the sun. Thank God summer was almost there.

"So how're those bruised ribs treating you lately?" Silas asked, slipping on his sunglasses.

"His ribs have to be fine if he was twenty minutes late to breakfast because he and his girlfriend couldn't get out of bed," Aiden muttered before Thatch could answer.

"The ribs are better." And yes, being with Lyric hadn't hurt him one bit. "I've actually been doing some yoga with Lyric lately to get more flexible." And stronger, but he wouldn't admit he needed the strength part.

"Now, that I gotta see." Aiden tipped his beer bottle in Thatch's direction. "Can you put your foot behind your head yet?"

"Hell no." He'd never accomplish that feat. "But yoga is a lot harder than I thought. You two should try it sometime."

"No thanks." Silas squeezed a lime into his beer. "I'm totally fine not being able to touch my toes. Tess has shown me a few yoga poses, and there's no way I'd be good at moving like that."

"I didn't say I was good at it." So he sucked at two things: golf and yoga. But he wouldn't give up on the second one. Not when Lyric loved it so much.

"So things appear to be going well with you two." Aiden seemed to watch him carefully. "Do you see a future with her?"

A few days ago, he would've said no. Because it had been clear then that Lyric didn't want a future with him. But over the last few days, everything had shifted. And this morning, well, being with her had felt natural and right. At least for him. Still, he'd best play this conversation safe in front of his friends. "I think we're taking things one day at a time right now."

"That's an answer you'd give your mom," Silas complained. "Come on. This is us." His friend stared at him for a few silent seconds. "You're in love with her. Aren't you?"

He nodded. They'd see through a lie anyway. Nothing fulfilled him like seeing her happy. Nothing mattered more than making sure she always felt as safe and as cared for as she had that morning. "I could see a future with Lyric." But he didn't know if she could see a future with him. That was the risk he was taking right now. Spending time with her. Getting close to her. She might not love him back. "I'm not sure where she is right now." But they had one more night alone, away from reality, and he was going to give her a convincing argument. "I'm going to surprise her tonight. Do you think we could stop by the camping store on the way back?"

"Camping?" Aiden finished off his beer and pushed the bottle to the center of the table. "You're taking her camping?" He shook his head. "Bro, I'm not sure that'll be a *good* surprise."

"If you want to surprise her, I'd go with something more traditional," Silas agreed. "A candlelit dinner or maybe a present. We could always stop by a jewelry store."

"I'm not taking her camping, dumbasses." Seriously. They knew he wasn't *that* clueless when it came to women. Thatch stood and pushed in his chair, tossing some cash on the table. He was ready to get back to Lyric. "I only need a two-person sleeping bag and one of those outdoor mattresses. For tonight."

"Ah." Silas graced him with an impressed smirk. "A little romance under the stars."

"Exactly." They wouldn't spend the whole night outside, but their cabin sat in a clearing and had a deck that would make the perfect stargazing spot.

"Maybe I should pick up a sleeping bag and mattress too." Aiden collected all their cash from the table and secured it under one of the empty bottles. "That's actually a pretty good idea. To change things up. Throw in some creativity."

"You're welcome." See? He knew more about women than they gave him credit for. Thatch dug his keys out of his pocket and led the charge to his truck.

When they arrived back at the lodge an hour later, Lyric, Tess, and Kyra still weren't back from their shopping excursion. So the three of them shot some pool in the game room and then ate burgers for dinner when Kyra texted they were grabbing something to eat on the way back.

After one more game of contentious pool, Thatch bade his friends good night and headed back to the cabin so he could set the mood for the surprise. He blew up the outdoor mattress, laid out the sleeping bag, and placed the flameless candles he'd picked up—so they didn't unintentionally ignite any forest fires—all around the deck.

He'd just made it back inside when Lyric came through the door. "Wow. What a day." She dropped her purse on the couch and moved swiftly to hug him. "I thought we'd never get back here. Kyra kept saying she had just one more store she wanted to check out, and then they were both so hungry we had to stop for dinner."

"It was a long day." Thatch hugged her back and even

brushed a kiss across her lips. "But it all worked out. You being gone so long gave me time to put together a little surprise."

"Ohhhh." She had her hands clasped behind his neck again, like she had this morning when she'd kissed him. "I like surprises."

And he liked seeing her smile this way at him. "First things first." He went to the mini fridge and retrieved the champagne they hadn't opened last night. "We shouldn't let this go to waste." After pouring two generous glasses, he handed one to her and then took her hand to lead her outside to the deck, where a flickering glow filled the whole space.

Lyric gasped and stopped when she saw the candles. "This is beautiful." She tugged on his hand, pulling him back to her. "I love this surprise, Thatch. I love it so much."

"I'm glad." He stole her glass of champagne and set both down next to the makeshift bed he'd constructed. "I thought it would be a good night for stargazing." Taking a knee, he folded a corner of the sleeping bag over.

"Every night is a good night for stargazing in the mountains." Lyric kicked off her shoes and climbed in, fluffing up the pillows before lying down. Thatch slipped in beside her and wrapped her up in his arms. Finally.

"It's the perfect night," Lyric murmured. "Look at that clear sky."

"Beautiful." But he was looking at her. "Did you have a good time with Kyra and Tess today?"

"It was a lot of shopping." She nestled her head in the crook of his arm. "What about you? How was golfing?"

He laughed. "None of us like to golf."

She lifted her head to peek into his eyes. "Seriously?"

"We're terrible at it. All of us." He had no problem with Lyric knowing he wasn't good at everything. "We can't hit the ball to save our lives."

"That's surprising." She settled her head next to his again. "Then why did you go?"

That was the question of the day. "Kyra planned it, I guess, and Aiden didn't want to tell her he's a terrible golfer."

Now Lyric laughed softly, as though she wasn't surprised. "But you're telling me."

He hugged her tighter. "I feel like I can tell you anything."

"Me too." She gasped. "Oh! Did you see that one? A shooting star just went right over our heads."

"I missed it." He'd rather look at her anyway.

"When I was a teenager, I used to sneak out on my roof in the middle of the night with a pillow and a blanket to count shooting stars," Lyric murmured. "One night, I counted twenty-eight in two hours."

"That must've been incredible." He could picture her younger, lying on the roof and staring up at the sky. As long as he'd known her, Lyric had seemed observant, curious, and perceptive, taking time to notice things most people didn't. It was one of the things he admired about her.

"It was incredible," she continued. "I started stargazing not long after we moved to Wyoming. I was so sad. I missed Kyra and Florida, and I was so mad at my mom and Kenny for everything that had happened."

"I can't imagine what that was like." He'd heard the stories about how Kyra and Lyric had grown up together—best friends until Lyric's mom and Kyra's dad had an affair and ran away to Wyoming. Then, when Kyra's dad had passed away a few years back, Kyra had come to Star Valley to settle his estate and she'd ended up engaged to Aiden within six months. "I know that had to be a real hard time in your life." He couldn't imagine an upheaval like finding out your parent was marrying your friend's parent and moving you across the country. "But I'm glad you ended up here."

Lyric cupped her hand around his jaw. "I'm glad *we* ended up here. Right here together. Have you ever seen a view of the sky like this?" She gently turned his head to make him look up.

"I saw that one." It was quite a sight—a flash of bright light that suddenly disappeared into the darkness.

Lyric pointed to their right. "There's another one."

Thatch did his best to watch the sky, but his gaze kept falling back to her face, to the light in her eyes, to the soft smile that kept tempting him to kiss her.

She angled her body to his and draped her arm over his shoulder. "Did you ever see shooting stars in Iowa?"

"I never looked." He'd been too busy with sports and friends and school and farmwork to ever sit still long enough to watch the night sky. In fact, he'd never liked being still. But this woman was opening him up to a whole new world of possibilities.

"I wasn't much of a romantic," he admitted. Even his relationship with Sienna had been more about checking things off his life's to-do list. Find a great girl. Get married. But he hadn't spent enough time showing her how he felt. He hadn't put his heart out there for her to see. If he was being honest with himself, he hadn't even loved Sienna the way he should've loved a woman he was going to marry. Back then, he hadn't known how. But he was beginning to see now, to understand that a relationship wasn't about meeting his own needs. That alone was freeing him from the bitterness he'd held on to.

"I find it hard to believe you weren't a romantic," Lyric whispered, her face drawing closer to his. "I mean, this..." Her arm gestured to the space around them. "Is the stuff fantasies are made of."

"I'm learning." She was teaching him. Hell, he still had so much to learn, but Lyric made him want to try, to get this right.

"I'm learning too," she murmured, her lips now grazing his. "And there's no one else I'd rather learn with." She kissed him fully, lighting an internal fuse that scorched a path all through him.

Her mouth had already become so familiar to him, and yet the feel of her lips moving with his filled him with a new energy every time. She lightly bit into his bottom lip, and that was new, too, the urgency and desperation and boldness he sensed in her.

Still kissing him, Lyric pushed his shoulder down to the mattress and shimmied her body on top of his, her knees pinning either side of his hips. "You make me very impatient." She caught his hands in hers and pushed them up over his head, now pinning his hands too. "I don't know what's come over me, Thatch, but I want you. Now."

Just when he thought he couldn't get harder. "I want you too." Now. In another hour. Tomorrow morning. Next week.

Always.

Lyric lowered her face to his, a seductive smile shimmering on her lips, and kissed her way from his mouth down his jaw to the spot under his ear that made him writhe with need. She slid her tongue down his neck and released his hands, using hers to pull his shirt over his head. "I should probably check on those bruised ribs." She trailed her tongue down his chest, kissing and licking, making him grip the sleeping bag in his fists.

"They're looking much better." Her voice was a low hum against him. Then there were more kisses moving lower down his abs.

Lyric ripped open the button fly of his jeans and shoved the denim down impatiently along with his boxer briefs, exposing him; if he wasn't careful, he was going to lose himself real quick.

"Time out." He patted around for his jeans and found a condom in his pocket, turning slightly to get it on in record time. "Now come here." He urged her to sit upright on him, so he could pull off her sweatshirt and then unclasp her bra and slide it off her shoulders. Then he took his time studying her in the glowing light. "You're perfection." He traced his fingers over one breast and then the other, her back arching into his touch.

"I've never done this outside." Lyric lay over him again, her forearms propping her up on either side of him. "It's freeing. All of it. Being outside under the stars. Being with you."

"It's perfect." He kissed her slower this time, savoring the feel of her skin against his, fighting the mad rush of his blood. Moving his hands along the curve of her waist, he slowly peeled her leggings down. Lyric took over then, shifting and thrashing her legs until she kicked the pants off somewhere at the bottom of the sleeping bag.

Now there was nothing between them, only the heat

of their bodies together, the silkiness of her skin on his. Thatch let his hands wander, down her hips, over her butt, his fingers light and teasing.

"God, I need you," she whimpered, shifting her hips over him until he was fully inside her. "I've never been this needy."

And he'd never had to fight so hard to maintain control. "You can have me." She could have all of him.

Thatch clasped her hands in his and thrust his hips up, earning a moan from Lyric. That sound alone was enough to edge him too close. He strained against the pull of his body and lifted his hips again. Lyric met the movement with an arch of her back, inviting him deeper. His grip on her hands tightened while they moved in sync, both of their breaths ending in gasps and controlled cries. He didn't care how he sounded. He only cared that she was as hot and turned on and close as he was.

"Yes, Thatch." Her fingertips dug into his shoulders while she rode him faster and faster. Her eyes closed, and the last words out of her mouth were unintelligible as her body broke apart on him, everything tightening and then deflating over him with a spent sigh.

Thank. God. Thatch let himself go, his arms holding her tightly against him, the control he'd held on to shattering into a blinding rush that rocked every part of him, leaving him weak and trembling under her weight.

With Lyric slumped over him, still breathing hard, he continued to hold her, tracing his fingers along her back while he looked up at the diamond-studded sky. Another shooting star streaked above them. Then another and another.

"I think all the stars are shooting now," he murmured.

Lyric shifted her position, nestling in against him while she lay on her side. "That's because this night is magic."

Yes. Right now, the magic had sealed them into their own world—just the two of them and the stars. So he held her against him, breathing her in, not knowing if this was reality or a fantasy.

Not knowing what tomorrow would bring.

That was the only problem with magic. Eventually, it ran out.

CHAPTER NINETEEN

"Wow!" Lyric applauded Skye, Cheyenne, Tallie, and Elina. "I'm so proud of you all! You're actually holding tree pose!" She snapped a photo on her phone right before Cheyenne lost her balance and stumbled, nearly collapsing to the mat in a fit of giggles.

"I can't believe we did tree pose either." Skye slapped a high five with Tallie. "We've come a long way in a month."

"Yes, you have." Lyric lowered herself to a seated position on her mat at the front of the class. "And now you've earned yourselves a few gentle stretches before we finish up for the night."

The girls all started to chat. Normally, Lyric ended her sessions with silent focus time, but these ladies had actually managed to pay attention and concentrate for most of the hour, so she'd reward them with a little socializing.

Currently, they were laughing and discussing something that happened at school earlier that day while she walked them through a series of side bend stretches.

Everyone except for Elina was engrossed in the conversation. Lyric couldn't help but notice the girl hadn't said a word since she'd slunk in through the door and set up her mat in the back row like she wanted to hide. It had been a week since they'd confronted Franco, and Elina hadn't shown up for work since. Lyric had been careful not to look at the girl too much or act any differently than she would've during any other class, but Elina had stayed quiet and distant the whole time. She likely knew Franco had confessed about the safe, and Lyric still wasn't sure how to handle the situation without embarrassing her.

"Hey, who're those flowers from?" Tallie pointed to the colorful wildflowers sitting in the vase on the shelf behind Lyric.

"Duh," Cheyenne teased. "They have to be from Thatch. Who else?"

"Wow." Skye hopped up, seemingly done with stretching, and inspected the bouquet. "Those are better than boring old roses."

"They're way better," Lyric agreed. She'd thanked him properly for them last night. After not seeing him for most of the week since they'd been back—due to him finishing up work at the rec center and her managing a full list of appointments—they'd finally managed to sync their schedules. Thatch had surprised her with the flowers, sweet man that he was. Then he'd gone home with her and spent the night. But she didn't need to share that part.

Skye plopped back down on her mat. "Are you two gonna get married or what?"

"Oh. Well. No." Lyric abandoned her stretching too. "I mean, we're only dating right now." For real. At least she assumed. But they hadn't officially defined their relationship. She wasn't ready to define anything yet. And she couldn't even think about getting married again. Talk like that made her chest tight. "Okay, everyone. Let's focus here." Before they asked any more questions about her future with Thatch. Lyric was simply trying to live in the moment right now. "How about we finish with corpse pose?" Maybe that would keep them quiet for a while.

Lyric lay down on her mat, legs out and arms angled at her sides, and stared up at the ceiling.

The distraction only worked for three minutes.

"I can't believe we only have one more class left." Cheyenne almost sounded disappointed.

Lyric sat back up. Had she done it? Had she actually encouraged them to enjoy yoga? "If anyone would like to continue, I'm happy to offer a free class for you girls throughout the summer." That way she could stay connected with them, and they could continue a journey toward a healthy lifestyle.

"I'm interested." Skye got to her knees and started to roll up her mat. "Yoga is actually fun. And I can touch my toes now."

"I'd probably come too," Cheyenne said.

"I'm in," Tallie added.

Nothing from Elina, but Lyric would ask her to stay back after class so they could talk. Based on her withdrawal, the girl was likely afraid she would get in trouble for asking Franco to borrow the money, but all Lyric wanted to do was offer the support she clearly needed.

"Perfect. We can even do movie nights sometimes too." Lyric tried to tame her smile. She had to play it cool, so they didn't roll their eyes like they did when they talked about their moms. "You let me know what day works best, and I'll get it on the schedule."

Everyone started to clean up—stashing their mats and blocks on the shelf. Elina especially seemed to be in a big hurry, but before she could sneak out the door, Lyric snagged her arm. "Hey, can you hang out for a few minutes? I'd like to talk to you."

Elina stared at her with a wide-eyed look of fear. "Uh. I guess."

"Busted," Skye joked on her way past them.

"No one's in trouble. We just need to chat about work stuff." Lyric held the door open for them and gave each one a hug goodbye. She'd really grown to love these girls. "Don't forget your homework. I want to see improvement in those warrior poses by next week." They'd all reached the point where she could challenge them more.

"Yeah, yeah, yeah," Tallie grumbled.

"I can't believe we actually have homework for *yoga* class," Cheyenne added when they were all out in the hall.

"Bye, ladies," Lyric called before closing the door.

"I'm sorry," Elina blurted out right away. "I never should've asked Franco to take money from the safe. I was too scared to do it myself. And then I went and got him in trouble—"

"No one's in trouble." With her hand on Elina's arm, she guided the girl to the bench and invited her to sit. "He explained everything and told us your family needed some food."

Elina's head continued to hang. "I know you're the one who brought all those groceries. But you didn't have to. I coulda figured out something." Tears glistened in the girl's eyes, but her jaw tightened like she was trying to hold them back. "We're not some big charity case. My mom's having a hard time right now, that's all. She has a job for a company doing data entry at home, but she hasn't been working much lately."

Lyric sat next to her. She could almost feel pain radiating from the girl. "Is she drinking a lot, honey?" She made sure her tone held no judgment. Only compassion.

"Because she's sad, okay?" The girl jerked her head up, anger flashing in her eyes. "My dad took off. She misses him." A humorless laugh slipped out. "I don't know why she misses him because he was even more of a mess than her."

Slowly inhaling, Lyric gave Elina's emotions some space. She knew how it felt to carry something on her own, keeping everyone out so they wouldn't discover the secrets you were trying to keep. But isolating herself had ended up hurting Lyric far more than admitting she needed help. "You shouldn't have to take care of your family," she finally said. "You're still a kid. You should be hanging out with your friends and going to movies and focusing on school and your homework." She should be free to simply be a teenager.

"I don't mind helping out." The girl wiped her eyes with her shirtsleeve. "My brothers and sisters need me. I can take care of them."

"I know you can." Elina obviously had a lot of strength. "But I'd like to help take away some of that burden. In fact, there're a lot of people who would help with food and reaching out to your mom so she can get back on her feet." The only way to help her would be for Lyric to lead a coordinated effort to take care of Elina's family, but she couldn't do that without her permission. "I don't want to talk to anyone until you say it's okay."

"I don't want everyone to know!" Her voice rose. "People don't need to know what our house looks like. That my mom is drunk all the time. It's so embarrassing." She covered her face with her hands.

"I know." Lyric put her arm around her. "Sometimes it feels easier to hide the problems than it does to confront them. There was a time I felt the same way."

Elina raised her head, her tearstained eyes skeptical.

Lyric hesitated. Her story was very different, but she could relate to feeling ashamed of something that wasn't her fault. Even after all these years had passed, she was still tempted to change the subject and continue guarding her own secret. But she had to start confronting the past or she'd never be able to move on. And right now, she wanted to move on more than ever.

"I was married a long time ago." Her voice started to weaken, but she continued anyway. "But my husband... he didn't treat me very good. And I hid the problem for a long time because I was embarrassed too. I didn't want anyone to know what was going on. I thought I could handle it all on my own."

Elina turned fully to her, her posture less guarded. "What happened?"

She tried to choose her words carefully so she wouldn't divulge more than the girl could handle. "Eventually, I ended up in the hospital and I *had* to confront the problem." But that wasn't even fully true, was it? She had never confronted Luke. She'd run away, back to her parents' house, and had never spoken to him again. She'd never looked the man in the eyes and told him how much he'd wounded her. Not only physically but also emotionally. She'd never found closure.

"How bad were you hurt?" Elina looked at her differently now. Almost with admiration.

"It could've been much worse." She didn't need to traumatize the girl with the details. "The point is, I should've let people in long before that happened. I had friends and family who would've helped me, but I kept them out. It was a lonely road to walk alone." Truthfully, she'd been walking that road to healing alone for a long time too. She'd never even told Tess what had happened to her, and the woman was one of her best friends.

"That's why you thought Franco was hurting me." The earlier defensiveness in the girl's tone had disappeared. "Because of what happened to you."

"Yes." Her past still colored how she saw the world. "I know now that he's a good kid. And he really seems to like you a lot." Franco had risked getting into a lot of trouble to help her. "Because of what I've been through, I misread some things when I saw you two together, and I apologize for that."

"You don't have to apologize." Elina didn't seem to have any trouble looking Lyric in the eyes now. "That's horrible what happened to you. I'm sorry you went through that. But now you have Thatch, and he seems to love you so much."

Did he love her? Or maybe the bigger question was, Could she let him love her fully? When they were alone together, separated from everything else, she thought maybe she could. But if she were being honest with herself, she would admit something still held her back from him.

Yet that obstacle wasn't something she could identify right now. "I want you to have people you can count on, too, while you're going through a tough time." She stood so Elina didn't feel like she had to stay all evening. "I want to make sure your family doesn't have to worry about food, and I know there's a whole army of people who would bring a meal once a week, so you don't have to cook for everyone every night. All you have to do is give me the okay."

"Meals would help." Elina pushed to her feet, standing a little taller than she had before. "And I've tried to get Mom to go to one of those programs at the church. For people who drink."

"I know there are some wonderful women who would reach out to help her find options." She didn't want to overstep when it came to Elina's mom, but Minnie and her friends with the Ladies Aid Society in town could gently encourage her. "But even if she's not ready for that, we at least want to help meet *your* needs, and the needs of your siblings, so you don't have to do that on your own." No one should ever have to feel alone during the hard times.

"Wow." Tears started to flow down Elina's cheeks. "You have no idea what a relief it is to hear that people would help us."

"I do know, honey. Trust me." Lyric opened her arms, and the girl stepped into her embrace, sobbing now.

"You're not alone," she murmured. "Everything'll be all right."

*   *   *

"I gotta say, I didn't think we'd finish this project in time." Thatch used his paintbrush to touch up the wall behind the reception desk.

"We didn't only finish," Silas said from where he was

fixing trim across the room. "We knocked this one out of the park. This has been our biggest project to date in this town, and look at this place. It's perfect."

"Not quite. We still have some finish work to do," Aiden reminded them. He always had to be the voice of reason.

But he was right. They'd likely be here for most of the night, which meant Thatch wouldn't get to see Lyric until dinner with his family tomorrow. "I might have to take a break to at least go greet my parents." They were scheduled to arrive in town anytime now. "But even if I have to leave for a while, I'll come back to finish up."

"We can handle it," Silas assured him. "If you need to be with the fam."

"Nah. A quick hello will be enough for tonight." His parents always got tired after traveling anyway and, well, he didn't know how things were going to go with Liam. It wasn't like they'd be palling around or anything. But he planned to have a word with his brother. Over the last month, he'd straightened some things out in his own head and had come to forgive Liam and Sienna in the process. Things between them didn't have to be this hard. Hopefully, this trip would be a new beginning for all of them.

Thatch searched the wall for more weak spots in the paint, but his touch-ups seemed to have done the trick.

"You going to introduce your family to Lyric?" Aiden started to screw in a light switch cover near the door.

"That's the plan." Even though he'd hardly seen the woman since they'd gotten back from the cabin, they'd been texting all the time and talking on the phone. And then last night, they'd managed to sneak in some romance.

Two weeks ago, he would've hesitated to introduce her

to his parents, but they were together now, and he was looking forward to the future.

"I give it one year before you two are hitched." Silas pounded a nail into the trim.

"Six months," Aiden countered.

"I'll take that bet." Silas crossed the room and his two friends shook on it.

Thatch shook his head at them. "We're not going to rush down the aisle or anything." But yeah, he could see them getting there eventually. That was what he wanted anyway.

"Technically, you wouldn't be rushing anything. You've known her for a few years now," Silas reminded him. "It's not like you just met."

"And when it's right, it's right," Aiden added wisely. "Hey, who's that?"

Thatch turned away from the wall and gazed out the front windows. A truck had parked outside. His brother got out.

"That's…uh…Liam." But no one else was with him. Not Sienna and not their parents. *This should be interesting.*

"Your brother?" Silas openly gawked in the direction of the window. His friends knew he didn't have a great relationship with Liam, but he'd never told them what had happened between them.

"Yep." Thatch watched the man who used to be his best friend open the door and step inside.

"Hey." Liam stopped right where he was, keeping a whole roomful of distance between them. "We just got into town, and Mom told me I could find you here."

Thatch simply looked at him. Liam hadn't changed

much since he'd seen him at the Christmas gathering before he'd moved here. Staring at his younger brother was still almost like looking in a mirror. They were born only two years apart, and for most of their childhood strangers mistook them for twins.

Breaking the silence in the room, Aiden pushed Silas toward the door. "Hey, we were just about to go out and grab some dinner. You want us to pick up something for you?"

"That's all right." He wasn't hungry. While his friends made a hasty exit, Thatch set the paint can and brush on the workbench and walked to where his brother stood. "Where's Mom and Dad?"

Liam shoved his hands into the pockets of his coat. "They're at the café getting a snack and a drink and chatting with your good friends Minnie and Louie."

He wasn't surprised. Minnie and Louie were the most gracious hosts. "Those two are the best."

Liam nodded stiffly. "Listen, I'm not sure how this is supposed to go. This reunion or whatever it is." His brother's gaze kept cutting through Thatch's vision, but Liam wouldn't hold eye contact. "I guess I wanted to clear things up between you and me before we're all together. Before Mom, Dad, and Sienna are around too. So things aren't hard and awkward like they have been in the past."

"Probably a good idea." But Thatch wasn't sure how this should go either. It had been so long since he'd seen Liam. He had a lot to say but wasn't exactly sure where to start.

"I know none of my apologies ever meant much. And I don't blame you for being pissed off at me for the last decade." Thatch opened his mouth to say something, but Liam didn't give him the chance. "I guess the thing I've always wanted you to know was that I didn't mean to fall for her. I swear. I didn't want to have feelings for her, and I tried to ignore them for a long time."

Liam had told him that before. In letters, emails, text messages. But his sincerity came through now. Regret and guilt seemed to weight his brother's shoulders.

This was where the conversation had stopped in the past. Liam apologized, and Thatch walked away from him, still angry. But things had to be different this time. "I believe you." Now he knew you didn't always get to choose what you felt for someone. He hadn't stopped caring for Lyric when she'd told him she didn't want to date him. He'd wanted to stop, but he couldn't. "I know things aren't as black and white as I made them out to be."

"I should've kept ignoring my feelings, I guess," Liam went on. "I mean in a way, my relationship with Sienna has always been this big rift in our family. Between you and me, but it's also affected Mom and Dad. And Sienna." His brother finally looked at him for longer than three seconds. "Things have been so messed up because of what happened."

Things *had* been so messed up. Thatch had let them stay that way for too long. Everything he'd wanted to say now finally came together in his head. "I know you didn't set out to betray me. But it hurt, man." He couldn't deny that. "I was humiliated. I mean, I went from being engaged to a woman to having to attend her wedding to my brother, and all of our friends and family knew about the whole ugly ordeal." He'd never expressed any of those feelings of humiliation. Not to Liam. Not to anyone except for Lyric. And now, somehow, talking about this was easier.

"If you want the truth, I'm tired of the past standing between us. I'm tired of holding a grudge." Avoiding Liam had been easier before, especially when Thatch was constantly going on missions. But his life was different now. He wanted a future with Lyric, and he wanted his entire family to be part of that.

"I mean, it was my fault too. I think I wanted to know someone back home was waiting for me. I guess I thought maybe that would give me more purpose out there fighting." He'd been too young to know what marriage required. "Truth is, Sienna and I were never a good fit. We didn't have what you two have." And Thatch suspected his feelings for her had always been much stronger than hers for him. Marrying her wouldn't have been fair to either one of them. He needed to be with someone who wanted him as much as he wanted her. "I guess I never realized what was missing until Lyric and I got together. Now I'm figuring out what it really takes to love someone."

At the mention of Lyric, his brother seemed to relax. "Mom told me you're seeing someone. I'm really happy for you. I can't wait to meet her."

"She's joining us for dinner tomorrow." And that time together would be a new beginning. For him and Liam. For him and Lyric. "I'm really glad you came to Star Valley."

Thatch shook his brother's hand. It was time to move forward.

CHAPTER TWENTY

Lyric turned onto Kirby Leatherman's driveway, taking the curve too fast. *Oops.* She'd better slow down or she'd end up in the ditch. And then she wouldn't get to surprise Thatch with a quick visit before she went to meet with Minnie at the café.

She parked outside the training arena and found Thatch talking to Kirby and another man near the bucking chute in the open-air corral.

"Hey." He ran to greet her, ducking under the fence before pulling her into his arms. "I wasn't expecting to see you until dinner."

Lyric leaned into him, her whole body humming at the feel of his arms around her. "I thought I'd stop by real quick on my way to meet Minnie at the café." Now, there was a lie if she'd ever told one. Kirby's ranch was nowhere near the café.

"Because this place is on your way?" Thatch teased.

"Because I wanted to see you." Alone. Tonight would

be fun, but there were going to be a lot of people around, and she was used to having Thatch all to herself. "I'm a little nervous about the big dinner," she confessed. She'd liked his parents the few times she'd met them, but now that they knew she and Thatch were together, there would be a little more pressure.

"Yo, Hearst," Kirby called in his brusque tenor. "You about done gabbing?"

"Almost." Thatch didn't even look at the man. He was too busy staring into her eyes, and she couldn't look away either. Energy always crackled between them when they were this close. That was why she had to come here. So she could clear away all the doubts that were starting to creep in.

"I might find it hard to focus if you're here," he murmured, like he didn't want his trainer to hear.

"You'd better focus." She closed her arms around his waist and grinned. "You can't get injured before your big day tomorrow."

"I'm not gonna get injured. I'm gonna ace this ride and the ride tomorrow, and I'm gonna win something." He grinned and kissed her lips. "All because you taught me how to use my core."

Lyric laughed and pulled him closer to her. She really had to get going so she wouldn't keep Minnie waiting. Or distract Thatch any more than she already had from his training. But first... "How was it seeing your family last night?"

"It was good. Really good." He cast a quick glance over his shoulder and lowered his voice. "Liam and I talked some. Before we got together with everyone else. And I think we'll be able to move forward now." His forehead leaned against hers. "Partly because of you, you know."

That made her smile. "Me?" She'd helped him with his family? After all he'd done for her, she hoped so.

"Yeah. I mean, being with you has been so different for me than being with anyone else, Lyric." He smoothed his hand over her hair. "Being with you has made me realize that I've never had the real thing with someone else. And I'm really thankful that I never married Sienna."

But he didn't want to marry her, did he? She didn't know how to tell him that she had no desire to go there again. Marriage had been like prison to her at one time. She'd spent those years feeling trapped and lonely, and now she needed freedom and independence.

Thatch gazed at her as though he was waiting for her to say something.

"I'm glad you and your brother worked things out." Her arms dropped to her sides, but he didn't seem to notice that her smile had faltered.

"I can't wait for you to meet them. Fair warning. They're pretty excited about dinner. They might be a little over the top."

What was his family so excited about? They were only dating.

"Come on, Thatch," Kirby grouched. "I got stuff to do. You don't ride now, you're gonna miss your chance."

"Sorry. Can't keep the boss waiting." He hugged her and kissed her cheek before releasing her. "I'll see you tonight."

"Yep. See you then." She walked out of the arena and got into her car, trying to submerge the panic starting to bubble up. She probably should've set some clear boundaries about the direction of their relationship. She loved hanging out with him, especially when they could escape and just be alone together. But she couldn't say what would happen in the future.

Lyric tried to shake off the sudden tension building inside her. She'd talk to him about all of that later. Thatch would understand.

By the time she made it to the café, the parking lot was full, and she had to find a spot down the block. Inside was crowded, too, but she managed to secure herself a stool all the way down at the end of the counter.

It took a few minutes, but Minnie finally made it over to her.

"Wow. You've got a crowd in here." This might not be the best time for them to discuss plans to help Elina's family.

"Everyone's here for the Rodeo Days." The woman wiped her brow with her apron. "But I can pop over as much as possible so we can discuss the family you were telling me about."

"Perfect." Lyric pulled her notebook out of her bag. "I'm thinking we'll need you to rally the Ladies Aid Society for some meals and support."

"I'm happy to." The woman glanced past her. "Oh, sorry, sweetie. I gotta run. I'll be right back."

"That's fine. I've got plenty of time." She had all afternoon free before the big family dinner debut. Maybe she'd even be able to catch Thatch alone again so they could discuss how to manage his family's expectations about their future. She wasn't even sure how to manage her own expectations. Instead of dwelling on the complications in her life, she started to list the names of people that she knew might want to help Elina's family.

After a few minutes, Minnie appeared on the other

side of the bar and set a glass of her favorite mint iced tea in front of her. "All right. Now, who is this girl you're trying to help?"

"Do you know Elina Mills's family?" She didn't know why she asked. Minnie knew every family.

"Well, sure. I know *of* them." The woman started to stack cups. She'd never learned how to sit still. "Don't think I've ever really talked to Cathy, but I've seen her around."

Working at the café every day—aka the gossip hub—she'd likely *heard* about the woman too. But that was the best thing about Minnie. She didn't judge anyone.

"I guess her husband left recently, and things have been difficult," Lyric told her, making sure no one else around them heard.

"Oh, how awful," Minnie murmured. "Those poor kiddos. Well, we absolutely have to step in and help."

Yes, but they'd have to be careful. The last thing she wanted was to get Elina in trouble with her mother. "I'm not sure how open Cathy is to help, so we'll have to ease in."

"Sure, that's no problem." She slung a towel over her shoulder and snatched a carafe off the warmer. "I'll send her a nice card to start. And then we'll get meals going and maybe some babysitting services, too, so she can have some space to work on herself."

Before Lyric could respond, Minnie was gone again, refilling coffee mugs up and down the bar.

When she came back, Lyric was ready. "I can put a meal schedule together if you want. Then you can send it out to your network for sign-ups."

"You got it." She set the carafe down. Somehow, even

with all the running around, the woman didn't seem tired. "So, how're things going with Thatch?" Her eyes twinkled.

The dullness that had blanketed her heart earlier came back. "Things are good." She hoped they'd still be good after they could talk. Before, Thatch had told her he didn't need to define their relationship, and she hoped that was still true.

"You look so happy when you're with him, darlin'." Minnie sighed dreamily. "It's a beautiful thing to see."

"I am happy when I'm with him." So why did her stomach keep tying in knots at the thought of building a real future with him?

"Oopsie." Minnie was gazing over Lyric's shoulder. "It looks like we've got some customers running low on soda. I'll do my rounds and be right back."

As she scurried away, Lyric started to write out a schedule on the page of her notepad. She'd be more than happy to contribute a meal once a week. Kyra and Tess would both pitch in too. Though she might not even ask Tess, given the whole *upcoming birth of a baby* thing. But all in all, it shouldn't be difficult to get at least most of the week covered on a regular basis.

Lyric lifted her head to look around for Minnie, but her gaze landed on a figure standing inside the doorway. That looked just like—

Luke.

The man turned enough that she could see him now. Fully. The black hair, the sturdy build, the beard. An icy panic slid through her veins, making her shudder. She was suddenly freezing.

He was talking to another man, and then Minnie

hustled to greet them and led them to an open table by the windows.

Lyric turned her head and ducked toward the wall, her lungs shriveling. She couldn't breathe. God, how was she going to get out of here without him seeing her?

"You want some more iced tea?" Minnie approached her from behind, but Lyric didn't turn around. She couldn't. Luke might see her. And then what? What would he do to her?

"Um. No." Her throat ached like there was an ice cube lodged there. "Thanks, though."

"Are you okay, darlin'?" The woman leaned in, studying her face.

"I'm fine," she squeaked. Her stomach roiled. "Just really...focused."

"All right. Well, I have some more orders to get into the kitchen, but then I'll be back to help you with that schedule."

Lyric cranked her head into a nod, the writing on the notepad blurring. While one minute ago she'd been frozen in her chair, now the fire of adrenaline burned her up. She had to get out of here.

Without fully turning her head, she glanced sideways. Luke still sat in the booth by the window, his seat facing her direction. In full view of the exit. As long as he sat there, she'd be trapped.

Trapped like she'd been when she'd married him.

Lyric's breaths started to echo in her ears. They were too shallow and too fast. She had to get control.

"Hey, Lyric!" Doris called from a few seats down. "I didn't even see you sitting there."

"Hey." She kept her head ducked and cocked to the left slightly.

"How're you doing?" The woman slid off her stool and approached her, blocking her view of Luke.

"I'm good." Nausea churned her stomach, making her dizzy.

"Are you sure?" Doris adjusted her glasses and leaned closer to her face. "You look like you might be a little under the weather today." In a motherly gesture, she pressed the back of her hand to Lyric's forehead. "Oh, my. You're very warm. I think you might have a fever." Before Lyric could stop her, the woman flagged down Minnie. "We should get this poor girl home. She's not feeling well."

"You're not?" Minnie inspected her face again. "I knew something was wrong. Ten minutes ago, you looked fine, but you're awfully pale now."

Lyric slid a look in Luke's direction. He was engaged in a conversation with the man sitting across from him. "You know, I'm actually feeling pretty awful." She could throw up any minute. "But I don't want to make a scene. Can you two just help me go out the back?"

"I'll call Thatch." Minnie pulled her phone out of her apron pocket. "He can come and pick you up—"

"No!" She didn't need Thatch here. That would only make this situation worse. She needed to get away. "I'll be fine. Really. If you could each stay on one side of me?"

Keeping her back toward Luke, she eased out of the chair and along the bar with Minnie and Doris fussing over her until she could skirt the opening. They cleared the counter and then rushed her through the kitchen.

"I really think we should call Thatch," Minnie insisted. "Or Kyra or Tess. You shouldn't drive when you're sick."

"It's not safe," Doris agreed.

"I'm feeling better now." Lyric stumbled out the back door and into the alley. "Yes. That's much better. I think I only needed some fresh air. I ate some eggs this morning, and they must not be agreeing with me." She hurried away from the two ladies before they could try calling anyone. "We'll work on the schedule for Elina another time," she called over her shoulder.

Staying out of view of the windows, Lyric ran to her car and got in, heaving like she'd just crossed the finish line of a marathon. Her hands shook all the way to her house.

No matter how many times she told herself to breathe deeply, dread crammed her lungs, leaving no room for air. After clawing her way in through her front door, she staggered down the hall and found her suitcase. Amos whined, trotting along right on her heels.

"It's okay," she whispered over and over. "We're going to get away for a while, boy." She blindly snatched articles of clothing out of her drawers and shoved them into the bag. "We can't stay here this weekend." God, how long would Luke be in town? She'd known she could run into him anytime, but she hadn't been prepared for the emotional assault seeing him had brought. One look and she'd become that terrified woman she'd tried to leave behind. "We'll just stay away." She'd leave for a week and not look back. That was her only option. She couldn't face him. She couldn't even look at that man without her blood running cold and her skin burning hot.

Amos whined again, and Lyric turned and knelt, hugging her arms around his soft fur. "Oh, puppy. How can it still be so hard? How can it still hurt so much?" She was supposed to be over this, stronger now. "I just want to go." She didn't want to think. "Come on." She latched up her suitcase and rolled it down the hallway. Outside on the stoop, she locked her door and then rushed her dog to her car.

While they pulled away from the curb, Amos howled for joy at the prospect of a car ride while the molten tears in her eyes spilled over. Damn Luke for coming to Star Valley right now.

Damn him for still having so much power over her.

CHAPTER TWENTY-ONE

"All right, Wild Bill. Give me hell." Thatch climbed up onto the fence for his final training run. He'd taken two already, and, while they hadn't been perfect, they were enough to be competitive. At least he thought so.

"Don't go easy." For some reason, talking to the bronc before he slid onto its back made him feel better, like he had some semblance of control over what would happen out there.

"Just get on with it already," Kirby muttered from the gate. His trainer wasn't big on pre-game rituals.

"Okay. Here goes."

Thatch wrapped the rein around his hand and slid onto the bronc's back, finding his posture—limbs loose, core engaged the way Lyric had taught him. There was no rush like that first jump out of the gate when the bronc lunged and bucked. But Thatch had learned how to move with the animal instead of against the momentum. Even the breathing techniques Lyric had taught him steadied him, slowing down his mind while the rest of the world passed by in a whirl of chaos.

Wild Bill gave a couple of strong bucks and then did a spin-turn to the right. The momentum rocked Thatch, but he managed to stay on and even keep his arm above his head. The ribs were vaguely sore, but overall he felt strong.

Another lurch and spin, and Wild Bill kicked his hind legs high into the air, arching Thatch forward. He compensated by tightening his legs around the animal and resisting the urge to hunch his shoulders. During another turn, he caught sight of the time board. He'd made it. Now he just had to get off before things went south.

He unwound his hand from the rein. The bronc jack-knifed, and Thatch used the momentum this time to launch himself off the side, hitting the ground running and not stopping until he'd made it to the fence.

Kirby's assistant lured Wild Bill through the gate, and Thatch hunched over the fence, out of breath.

"That was some ride, kid." Kirby handed him a water bottle. "You ride like that tomorrow, you'll place no problem."

"You think so?" Thatch eyed him to make sure Kirby wasn't being sarcastic.

"Whatever yoga crap you've been doing has fixed your form." The man started to walk away. "You're ready."

"Sweet. Thanks." It had only taken the man eight months to compliment him. "Will I see you tomorrow?"

"I'll be there." Kirby was almost out the door now, so it appeared their heart-to-heart was over.

Thatch checked the time clock. Yikes. He had to get going too. He couldn't be late for his own family dinner.

He'd asked Louie and Minnie to set up some tables at the back of the café where things were quieter, and Lyric had texted him earlier to ask if they could invite Aiden, Kyra, Silas, and Tess to stop by too. The more the merrier, he always said. But he also couldn't help but wonder if she didn't want to be with his family alone.

After shedding his gear and stuffing everything into his bag, he trotted to his truck and headed straight home for a shower. By the time he'd made it to the café, his family was already there, waiting outside the restaurant.

"There you are!" His mother threw her arms around him for one of her signature hugs. "Where's Lyric?"

"She should be here anytime." He'd texted her to tell her he'd be a little late, so she'd probably delayed herself too. She'd seemed nervous earlier, but he had no doubt everything would be fine once she got here.

"Hey, son." His dad pulled him in for a hug too. "I'm looking forward to Minnie's pot roast."

"You should be. Trust me, you won't be disappointed." Thatch ordered the dish at least once a week. He stepped away from his dad and moved along to where Liam stood with Sienna. She still wore her hair short, but she was a little blonder these days. "Good to see you." His ex had made herself scarce last night when he'd dropped by to greet his parents. After their history, he had to take the lead on making sure she didn't feel awkward.

Sienna looked at him with a hopeful smile. "It's good to see you, too, Thatch. Really."

"I'm glad you're all here." He waved them into the café. "I'm sure Minnie and Louie have everything set up for us."

There was a crowd inside, but their two tables in the

back had already been reserved. They all took their seats, leaving the spot next to him open for Lyric and the other half of the table for his friends whenever they could make it.

"Welcome, welcome." Minnie cruised around the table with a pitcher, filling their water glasses. Thatch had already asked them to serve up her pot roast family-style, so she took drink orders and then disappeared.

"I'm telling you, there are such nice people in this town." His mother turned to his father. "Maybe we should move here if you ever retire."

"That'd be fun." Thatch would love to have his parents close, though he couldn't see his dad living away from the farm full-time. "Or you could even have a summer home here and a winter home somewhere else."

"Now you're talkin'." His dad clapped Liam's shoulder. "This one's about ready to take over the whole farm anyway. Soon he won't need me around at all."

"That's awesome," Thatch said. His brother and he could not be more different if they tried. Ever since they were young, Liam had always been more of a homebody. He'd never even liked going on vacations. And from the sound of things, Sienna was the same way. They were good together.

They all chatted about the farm for a while, with Liam giving an update on future plans, and then Thatch checked his watch. Lyric was almost half an hour late.

While his family continued to talk, he pulled out his phone and sent her a text. *Hey, are you on your way?* He left his phone sitting screen-up on the table, but she didn't reply. That was weird. Not like her at all.

His mom seemed to sense his concern. "Have you heard anything from Lyric?"

"Not yet." He checked his signal to make sure his service was good. "She probably just got held up with her last session or something." But then why wouldn't she have texted him to let him know?

"You all are going to love this wine." Minnie brought out two bottles of Cabernet Sauvignon and started to fill their glasses.

"Hey, have you heard from Lyric?" he asked when she got to him. "She was supposed to be here half an hour ago."

"No, I haven't heard from her at all." She set down his glass. "Not since this afternoon when she was here anyway. But she got sick."

"What?" He stood. "What do you mean she got sick?"

"One minute she was sitting at the bar chatting, and the next she was pale and not feeling well." Minnie moved on to pour the wine into his mom's glass. "I almost called you to come and pick her up, but she wouldn't let me."

"Oh, no." His mother clucked. "I'm sorry to hear she's not feeling well. Thatch, you should probably check on her."

"Doris and I helped her outside, and then she all but ran away from us," Minnie explained. "I think she was embarrassed, poor girl."

Thatch glanced at his phone again. Something *had* seemed a little off when she'd visited him at the arena earlier. "Did she say what was wrong?"

"It was her stomach, I think." The woman continued to move around the table. "When we got her outside, she said she felt better."

"Thanks. I'll try calling her." He stepped away from the table and found a quiet corner. After six rings, her voicemail picked up. "Hey. Minnie said you weren't feeling well. I'm at dinner, but I can come over if you need me to. Just call me and let me know you're okay."

He hung up right as Aiden and Kyra made their way to the table. Everyone erupted into chaos, greeting them as though they really were members of their family. Which his comrades were, based on the care packages his mom had always sent to Silas and Aiden and Jace too.

Before they could sit back down, Thatch snagged Kyra. "Have you talked to Lyric? She's not here yet, and Minnie said she was feeling sick earlier."

"No." She rifled through her purse and pulled out her phone. "She hasn't texted me or anything, but that's weird." Kyra swiped around her phone's screen. "There are notifications from our computer system that say she canceled the two yoga sessions she was supposed to teach this afternoon."

Damn it. Something was wrong. He knew it. Lyric wasn't like this. She wouldn't ignore him when they had plans. "I think I'll drive to her house and check on her."

"I'll come with." His friend jammed her phone back into her purse. "If she's really not feeling well, maybe I can help."

"That'd be great." He offered a quick explanation to his family, and then he and Kyra took off, racing for his truck.

"Maybe she's taking a nap," the woman suggested when they were buckled in. "She could've easily overslept, especially if she's not feeling well."

"That's true." But his gut didn't settle. Lyric knew how important this dinner was to him. She knew he would be waiting for her. She would've texted him to cancel if she was sick.

"I'll call her too. See if I can wake her up." Kyra brought the phone to her ear. "Hey, just wanted to check on you. It sounds like you might be sick or something? Thatch and I are headed over to check on you. Be there in a minute." She lowered the phone with a worried frown. "Have you seen her today? Did she look okay to you?"

"I only saw her for a few minutes when she stopped by Kirby's." He thought back. "She did seem a little subdued, I guess. I mean, not her normal happy self." So maybe she really had gotten sick. He parked the truck in front of her house and noticed her empty driveway. "Her car's not here."

Kyra got out and checked the front door. "It's locked," she said when she came back.

"She has to be at the clinic then. Right?" Where else would she have gone?

"We can check." Kyra climbed back into the truck. "I'm sure everything's all right." Her tone sounded as hollow as he felt.

"This isn't like her." He'd known Lyric for a few years, and she'd always been one of the most dependable people he'd ever met. "She wouldn't ignore us. Not unless something bad happened." Not unless... "You don't think Luke came looking for her, do you?" The man must be in town by now. And he easily could've found out where she lived.

"God, I hope not." Kyra checked her phone again and then brought it to her ear. "Hey, Lyric. We're really worried about you. We just stopped by your house and are headed to the clinic. Can you please call us as soon as you get this message?" She continued to hold the phone in her hand as though waiting for it to ring.

What could he do? Helplessness gouged him. He didn't know where she was. Had her ex taken her somewhere? He tried to shut out the nightmare scenarios playing in his brain.

Thatch sped around the corner and took the left turn too fast.

"She's there!" Kyra pointed up ahead of them to where Lyric's car was parked along the curb in front of the clinic. Amos had his head out the window, tail wagging as though all was well.

Relief whooshed out of him. "She must've gotten held up at the clinic then." Maybe there'd been some kind of emergency with one of her clients. He parked behind her, and both he and Kyra got out of the truck.

The front door opened, and Lyric hurried outside, a bag slung over her shoulder, but she stopped suddenly when she saw them.

"Hey." The closer Thatch got to her, the more warily she looked at him. Something was definitely wrong. "Are you okay?"

"I'm fine." Her voice sounded different—sharper— and he'd never seen that tight expression on her face.

"Why haven't you called us back?" Kyra marched up to Lyric, seeming to disregard the obvious tension. "We've been worried about you. You're really late for dinner."

"Can you give Thatch and me a minute?" Lyric spoke to Kyra in that same harsh manner.

"Oh." Kyra started to back away. "Sure. Yeah. Um, if you need me, I'll just be in Thatch's truck."

While their friend walked away, Thatch waited for Lyric to take the lead on this conversation, although he already had a pretty good idea where it would lead. She was running from him.

"I'm sorry. I have to go," she finally said, keeping her distance from him. "I forgot I have to teach in Jackson tonight. So I won't be able to come to dinner."

"Oh." There was more she wasn't saying. Her eyes wouldn't meet his, and tension still gripped her face. "You're sure nothing's wrong?"

"I'm sure," she almost snapped. "I said I was sorry."

"It's okay." Why did she sound mad at him? "I'm just glad you're all right." He couldn't remember the last time he'd been so terrified. Not since his retirement anyway.

"Besides, it's probably best that I don't hang out with your family." Now Lyric had a robotic tone, devoid of any emotion. "I mean, we don't want to create any expectations about the future or anything. Things between us have moved a little too fast, and I think it's best if we take a step back." She didn't give him a chance to speak. "I have to go. Maybe we can talk another time."

Another time? No. Something had upset her. "What happened? I know something happened." He stepped to her, studying her eyes, searching for the openness that had been there just the other night. "I don't have any expectations, Lyric. I don't want more than what you can give. But I care about you. Hell, I'm falling in love with you, and whatever has happened we can work through it together. I want to be here for you."

"I don't want you." The words would've been more convincing if tears weren't streaking her cheeks. "I can't do this. So leave me alone, Thatch. Please. Just leave me alone." She sidestepped him and got into her car, driving away before he could even turn around.

After a few stunned seconds, he got back into the truck, his head still clouded with shock.

"What in the world happened?" Kyra clicked in her seat belt. "Where's she going?"

"To Jackson." He just sat there letting the truck idle. "She said she has to teach at the spa, and she doesn't know if she'll be back tomorrow." She'd also said she didn't want him. Just like that, kicking him out of her life.

"She didn't mention anything to me about teaching at the spa this week." Kyra rolled down her window. "Usually, she tells me if they ask her to come. No, she *always* tells me. This is just off."

"Tell me about it." He slipped the truck into gear but drove slowly in the direction of the café. What was he supposed to tell his family? "She basically broke up with me."

"Are you serious?" Kyra shook her head. "She was just telling me how much she liked you. How you'd changed everything for her. Something is not right."

"Maybe she changed her mind." Maybe the prospect of having dinner with his family had sent her running. Or maybe she'd never had deep feelings for him in the first place. "Our entire relationship was fake at first anyway. It was a lie." He should've known things would end this way.

"What're you talking about?" Kyra demanded. "You two are great together."

He parked the truck outside the café and spilled the whole story to Lyric's best friend. How he'd asked Lyric out at Christmas, and she'd turned him down; how she'd accidentally let her yoga class believe they were dating; how the cover made sense for him to keep his yoga sessions a secret.

"But you love her," Kyra said when he'd finished. "And she loves you. I know she does. You can't fake real love."

"I wasn't faking anything." Forget trying to save face. He'd gone all-in with Lyric. He'd laid all his cards on the table. And it wasn't enough. He wasn't enough.

"She feels the same way you do." His friend grunted in frustration. "Something happened. Something had to have happened."

"I don't know. Maybe this was all too much for her. My family coming and wanting to spend time with her." In any case, Lyric had made up her mind, and he refused to force anything. He'd already told her that. He wouldn't track her down and beg. She knew how he felt about her. That was all he could do. "We'd better get back inside." Once again, he'd get to endure humiliation in front of his family. He shouldn't have played up their relationship so much with his mom. He'd gotten her hopes up and had likely driven Lyric away in the process.

Thatch got out of the truck and trudged into the restaurant behind Kyra. Silas and Tess were now seated across from Aiden.

"Where's Lyric?" His mom stood. "Is she all right?"

"She's fine." He deflated into his chair and looked right through everyone. "She's not coming. And I think she broke up with me." He might as well just put it all out there and stanch the flow of questions right now. "I'd rather not talk about it. We can just eat, if that's okay." And they could all sit there and feel sorry for him. It wouldn't be the first time.

"Sure." His dad cleared his throat. "Yes, let's eat." He signaled a passing server. "We're ready for our food now."

"And wine," his mom added. "We'll need more wine."

A hushed conversation was going on down at the end of the table where his friends sat. Kyra was likely filling them in on everything he'd told her.

Great. All he wanted to do was get in his truck, go home, and be alone. He'd fooled himself in this relationship with Lyric as much as he'd fooled everyone else.

"Tess and I have to run an errand." Kyra stood up abruptly. "So sorry we won't be able to stay for dinner."

An errand? Thatch shook his head at them. They were obviously going to track down Lyric. Not that it would do any good. She didn't want him. The words wouldn't stop echoing around his brain.

"Yes, so sorry." Tess staggered to her feet. "But it was lovely to see you all again. Hopefully we can chat more tomorrow at the party after the rodeo."

"Are you sure you can't stay for some food?" his mom asked. If there was one thing she loved, it was a good party, and this one was quickly dying.

"Unfortunately, this can't wait." Kyra winked at Thatch. "We have something very important to take care of."

Thatch didn't try to stop them. He appreciated their effort, but he also didn't expect Lyric to change her mind after a pep talk from her friends. He'd meant what he said. He loved her. He'd been falling in love with her for a while now. But he also wanted to be with someone who could love him back. He wanted to be with someone who would choose him, even when things were hard. He wanted to be with someone who would give him the same loyalty he would offer them.

But Lyric had walked away.

CHAPTER TWENTY-TWO

Lyric woke up with a serious crick in her neck and a debilitating ache in her heart. She shifted in the chair she must've fallen asleep in, the bright sunshine pouring down on her through the glass door that looked out onto the deck of the cabin she'd shared with Thatch.

She hadn't thought it would be so hard to come back here. When the owner had told her this was the only cabin she had left, Lyric didn't hesitate to take it, hoping for refuge. But all evening, memories of Thatch had closed in on her, reminding her of what she'd walked away from.

A heartsick sigh slipped out, and Amos nudged her leg with his nose from where he lay sprawled at her feet. Yes, she was a mess. She hadn't eaten dinner. She hadn't even changed into pajamas. She'd simply sat in this chair staring out at the deck, remembering the magical night under the stars.

Amos let out a low rumbling bark, prompting her to move. "You're probably hungry, aren't you, boy?" In her haste to leave, she'd forgotten his food but had stopped at a grocery store on the way here and picked up some of that gourmet canned food he loved.

She should be hungry, too, but she couldn't stomach the thought of eating one of the granola bars she'd bought. How had dinner gone last night after she'd disappeared? She could only imagine how disappointed Mrs. Hearst had been. The dullness in Thatch's voice during their confrontation still haunted her. She'd never heard him sound like that. Hollow. Like she was now.

Tears spilled down her cheeks again as she found a bowl and a can opener in the kitchenette. "Here, buddy." She set the food in front of her dog, but he simply gazed up at her, whining.

"I'll be all right." She lowered herself to the floor next to his food dish so he'd eat something.

Lying on the floor, Lyric tried to do some of her yoga breathing. It always worked when she found herself worried or anxious. But even deep, cleansing inhales and exhales weren't enough to soothe her heart.

Amos took a few tentative bites of the food, but her dog had always sensed her emotions. After looking back and forth between his food and her a few more times, he lay down protectively right next to her, resting his head on her leg.

"I'll eat too," she promised. "In a few minutes." She would have to eat. She didn't do this. She didn't fall apart and run away and hide. Not anymore. Yet here she was, lying on the floor of a cabin where she knew no one would find her.

Amos rumbled off another bark, this time sitting up with his ears perked. "Bwoof, bwoof." Her dog had always been a polite barker—not too loud and sharp. Now his tail started to sweep the floor.

Lyric slowly sat up too. "What?"

A knock sounded on the door, flooding her with hope and panic at the same time.

"Lyric?" Tess yelled. "We know you're in there! Your car is out here, and I heard Amos."

"So you might as well let us in right now," Kyra added. "Or I'll have to break down the door."

Amos trotted toward the voices, panting and furiously wagging his tail now.

Lyric scrambled to get up before her friends made good on their threat. Kyra had some serious lower-body strength. She could easily kick in the door.

Without bothering to make herself more presentable, she unlocked the door and pulled it open. "How'd you find me?"

"We spent all last evening doing some detective work." Tess marched past her. "First we thought you were in Jackson, so we went there."

Oh, geez. Her poor friends. They'd probably been out all night.

"Then we finally got ahold of the spa manager, and she told us you weren't teaching." Kyra stooped to pet Amos. "So we had to have a little brainstorming session about where else you might've gone. I knew you had Amos with you, and Tess remembered seeing they allow dogs here."

"But we called, and they wouldn't tell us if you were staying here." Tess dropped to the couch with an exhale, rubbing her belly.

"So naturally, we had to drive here, and then we saw your car outside." Kyra clutched her arm and dragged her to the couch, forcing her to sit between them. "What. The. Hell, Lyric?"

She had nothing. No explanation that would justify her behavior. She couldn't even begin to form an apology that would make up for sending her friends all over Wyoming to look for her. "How's Thatch?" Tears started to fall again when she said his name.

"He's awful." Kyra wasn't exactly the most subtle of the three of them. "I mean, he was worried sick about you. I don't think I've ever seen him as frantic as he was when we were looking for you." The concern on her face balanced her tone. "We were all worried sick."

"I'm sorry." That was so inadequate. "I don't know what happened." Another lie. Lyric hugged her knees into her chest, trying to hold herself together. She had to start telling the truth. These were her best friends. "I was sitting in the café yesterday, and I saw Luke come in."

The only sound was Kyra's slight intake of breath. She didn't know all the details about what Luke had done to her, but she knew enough.

"Luke?" Tess looked back and forth between them. "Who's Luke?"

Lyric forced herself to keep her head up, to look at her friends. "My ex-husband."

"Oh." Tess's posture immediately softened. "Did you talk to him?"

"No. I couldn't." A familiar panic punched her in the stomach again—the same way it had when she'd seen him. "I totally shut down. I got sick and terrified, and I was desperate to get away."

Tess's eyes were growing wider and wider. "What happened between you two? I mean, I knew the divorce wasn't a great time in your life, but you've never said much."

"He was abusive." That was the simple truth. "For our whole marriage." Though the behaviors had started when they were dating; she recognized the signs now. The controlling and the isolating and the belittling. "He was mean and angry, and he pushed me around."

"Oh, my God. Lyric." Tess slipped her arm around her while Kyra held her hand.

"I thought I'd left that all in my past, that I was over it." A sob slipped out. She'd wanted to be over the pain, but she'd never fully confronted the damage he'd done. She'd simply stuffed it down deep. "And then I saw him, and it brought me right back to that helpless, frantic place." And then she'd walked away from the one man who'd shown her care, compassion, and tenderness.

"I didn't know." Now Tess was crying too. "I'm sorry. How awful. That's so awful."

"No wonder you ran." Kyra squeezed her hand harder. "Any of us would've done the same thing. You can't blame yourself for having a reaction to seeing someone who mistreated you."

"But I wasn't thinking. I didn't want to hurt Thatch." Yet she had hurt him. Deeply. She'd heard the wound in his voice. She'd seen his expression fall. "Things with us were moving fast, and then his parents wanted to hang out with me, and then I saw Luke and remembered how horrible my marriage was, how I had felt so trapped. I panicked."

"Of course you did." Tess pulled some Kleenex out of her purse. "Why haven't you ever talked to us about this? It's so much to carry on your own."

"I didn't want anyone to know how weak I was. That I stayed with a man who hurt me for so long." She'd never fully been able to accept that their problems weren't her fault. Until now. She had to accept her past in order to have a future. She had to forgive herself and let go. "I got out and got away, and I never wanted to think about him again." But that method of moving on hadn't worked. She'd never dealt with the scars he'd left on her heart. For the last week, she'd been telling Elina not to keep secrets—to let people in and let them help—and she wasn't following her own advice.

"Does Thatch know about Luke?" Kyra asked.

"Some. But he doesn't know I saw him. I didn't tell him." She'd run away instead.

"He'll understand," Tess insisted. "Everyone will. We could've helped you. We could've protected you from him, especially knowing he was in town for the rodeo."

"I should've told you everything." These friends were her family. They would fight for her anytime she needed them to. But she needed to start fighting for herself too. She'd never gotten closure. She'd never taken a stand, and she had a right to tell him how much he'd hurt her. God, she was still hiding from Luke after all these years. "I want to confront him." She needed him to know that she wasn't going to be afraid anymore.

"I don't know, honey." Tess shared a look with Kyra.

"That doesn't seem like a good idea," Kyra agreed.

"But I'm ready." She was stronger now. With her friends. And with Thatch. He'd made her stronger, and she had to fight for a future with him. "I want to see Luke again on my terms. I want to face him so I can be done with this."

Kyra was still shaking her head. "But what if he loses his temper and comes after you?"

"You two will be there." Heck, the whole town would be around. They'd make this confrontation public. "I'm sure Natalie will be hanging around the rodeo grounds too. He can't hurt me now. Not when I have everyone standing with me."

Both of her friends fell silent.

"You're sure you want to do this?" Tess finally asked.

"I'm sure." If Thatch was going to be a bronc rider, they might run into Luke occasionally, and she didn't want to worry every time she went to a competition. "I'm falling in love with Thatch." She'd known that when they shared this cabin. Even before that, she'd felt the beginnings of something special when she'd danced with him at Kyra's wedding. And when she'd told him she didn't want to date him at the Christmas party. Her heart had ached then too. "I'm afraid, but that doesn't change my feelings for him. I want to be with Thatch, but first I need freedom from my past." So they could start anew together.

"Okay." Worry still gripped Kyra's features. "So what's the plan?"

Lyric checked the clock. They had two and a half hours before the bronc riding would start. "We'll go to the rodeo grounds and find Luke." Beyond that, she didn't know what would happen. "You two will go with me?" She wouldn't be able to do this by herself.

"You don't even have to ask." Kyra was already on her feet. "And I'm going to call Natalie and explain the situation and make sure she's right there with us too."

"That asshole will not lay a hand on you," Tess added.

"If he tries *anything*, Aiden, Silas, and Thatch will be on him so fast he won't know what hit him."

"Thank you." Lyric helped her pregnant friend to her feet. She couldn't show up at the rodeo grounds looking like this. "I'm going to shower really quick. You two call in the troops and get them mobilized."

"You've got it." Kyra had her phone to her ear.

Despite the lack of sleep, energy buzzed through Lyric while she showered and got dressed. Years ago she hadn't known how to fight back, how to stand up for herself, but now she wouldn't have to do this alone.

"Okay." She hurried out of the bathroom and got her stuff packed up. "Are we ready?"

"Ready," her friends said at the same time.

"Tess will ride with you," Kyra told her as they walked out the door.

"Sounds good." She got Amos settled in the back seat and made sure Tess could comfortably buckle in.

"I called Silas," her friend informed her. "He's talking with Aiden. Thatch is already at the rodeo grounds, and he wasn't sure if they'd be able to catch up with him before he rides. But they're ready to stand watch while you talk to Luke."

"That's good." She was ready too. The panic she'd felt yesterday had simmered into a far more powerful anger. She had a life to live, damn it, and she wouldn't let Luke take that away from her now.

"Do you know what you're going to say?" Tess asked.

"Not yet." She didn't need to know. The words would come based on her feelings, based on the truth of what she'd been through. She didn't need to script anything out.

"I knew you and Thatch were really in love." Her

friend's tone had a triumphant tenor. "I just didn't want to tell *you* that."

Deep down, Lyric had known too. That was why she'd tried to keep distance between them. "I've been in denial for a long time." Because pretending was easier. She'd known what loving someone had cost her before. "I hope he'll forgive me for telling him I don't want him."

"He'll understand," Tess assured her. "And he'll support you too. In whatever ways you have to process everything you've been through so you can move on." She suddenly grimaced and rubbed at her belly.

"Are you okay?" Lyric slowed the car and eyed her. "You're a little pale."

"I'm fine." Her friend shifted in her seat. "Not feeling spectacular, but that's normal when you're eight months' pregnant."

"I can't believe you're so close." Lyric turned up the air conditioner in an attempt to keep Tess comfortable.

The rest of the way to Star Valley, Tess helped her keep her mind off the confrontation by talking about the baby. Lyric even got to feel a couple of kicks on her belly.

After dropping off Amos at home and leaving him with a bone, Lyric drove them to the venue and parked the car.

"Neither one of the girls was this active during my pregnancies," her friend said as they made their way across the parking lot. "So Silas is convinced this one's a boy."

"I love that you're keeping it a surprise though." Lyric made sure to walk close by her friend in case she needed some support. There was still over an hour before the bronc riding competition was set to start, but crowds were already streaming into the arena's stands.

After they'd gotten through the gate, Lyric steered Tess down the corridor to the right. "We should head to the staging area." The riders usually gathered there.

"Lead the way," Tess said dramatically, linking their arms together. At the entrance, they ran into Kyra, Natalie, Aiden, and Silas.

"Where is this guy?" Silas had that dangerous SEAL look in his eyes.

Aiden nudged Lyric. "You just point him out, and we'll take care of the rest."

"No, you won't." Kyra marched to her husband. "This is about what Lyric needs to say to him. You two will only get involved if he gets out of hand."

"We'll get involved if he even takes one step toward you," Aiden confirmed.

"I've got my cuffs too," Natalie added, patting her hip. "So there'll be no need for assault and battery today. Not on my watch."

"Thank you." Lyric gave each of them a hug. "I appreciate you all being here. And yes, I want to handle this myself."

Natalie nodded. "Just know you have backup if you need it."

"*A lot* of backup," Kyra added.

Lyric looked around them, hoping to see Thatch.

"We haven't found him yet," Silas said. "But we'll keep looking."

"Okay." She steeled herself with a deep inhale. "I'm ready. Let's go."

The group of them all moved together through the gates to the staging area where the riders milled around between livestock trailers. Lyric employed her yoga breathing technique, which helped settle her. She scanned the cowboys they walked past, and then she saw his name plastered on the side of a truck.

"There." She pointed to where Luke stood near the tailgate talking to another man.

"You've got this." Tess side-hugged her.

"We're right here." Kyra squeezed her hand.

Lyric left them standing there and went straight up to him, a strange calm coming over her. "Luke."

He turned, eyeing her coolly for a second before his jaw dropped. "Lyric?"

"Why do you look so surprised? You know this is where I'm from, where I live." He'd visited Star Valley with her a few times when they were married. "And yet you still had the audacity to come here. To my hometown."

Her friends—and her friendly neighborhood police officer—gathered behind her, and the other man he'd been talking to started to back away.

Luke glared at them all, taking on a defensive stance. "What the hell is this?"

"This is my chance to call you what you are in front of everyone." Lyric made sure she spoke loudly enough that those who happened to be standing around them could hear. "A man who victimizes women."

Shock registered on his face, and he swiveled his head, looking around them. "What the hell are you doing? Shut up." He took two steps toward her.

"I think you'd better stop right there and let her finish," Natalie called somewhere behind her.

Oh, yes. She would finish this. "For two years, you preyed on me, pushing me around, hitting me, and I covered up everything. I hid behind that secret." Somehow, she felt taller standing there facing off with him. Taller and stronger than she ever had. "Well, I'm not hiding anymore. I'm going to make sure everyone in this world knows what you are." Plenty of people standing around them had already heard. This was a small community, these riders and cowboys. Word would spread. Hopefully, his reputation would precede him, and she would prevent another woman from enduring what he'd put her through.

"I never touched you."

She recognized that angry tone, but it wouldn't silence her anymore. She was free. She didn't have to walk around on eggshells. "You broke my arm when you pushed me down six years ago." She wouldn't let him deny that. "You gave me countless bruises before that. And you know what?" *She* stepped closer to *him*. "For a long time, I thought that mistreatment was my fault. But the truth is, you have a major anger problem. And now everyone knows it." She turned away from him, lighter and freer. Full of a shining new energy.

Then she saw Thatch standing there, Aiden and Silas on either side of him, their hands on his shoulders as though holding him back.

But nothing could hold them back now. She ran and he ran, and they collided in a hard and powerful hug right in the center of everything.

CHAPTER TWENTY-THREE

I'm sorry." Lyric sobbed on his shoulder. "Thatch, I'm sorry I didn't show up for you—"

"That doesn't matter." He held her close, shuffling his feet to move them behind one of the cargo trailers and out of everyone's line of sight. This moment was theirs. Between them only. They didn't need to share it with the thirty or so strangers who were standing around.

"I saw Luke at the café. Before dinner with your family. And I ran. I couldn't face him." Lyric peered up at him, tears flowing, but her eyes were wide and bright and hopeful.

That look right there told him everything he needed to know—that he hadn't imagined their connection, that she felt this strong pull to him too. "You shouldn't have had to face him alone." When he'd first seen Lyric talking to Luke, he'd been ready to go over there and deck the guy, but that wouldn't have made him any better a man than the one she'd left behind, as Silas and Aiden had reminded him. "I should've been there with you. I knew he was in town. I should've been watching out for you."

"It's not your fault." Lyric loosened her hold on him but didn't let go. "I kept you out. I acted like it wasn't a big deal that he was in town." One single tear still clung to her eyelash. "I didn't know how big a deal it was until I saw him. I just panicked."

"I get that." He ached for her, that she had to fear someone because of what had happened to her, that someone so good and sweet and warm had ever been touched by violence.

A smile crept onto her lips, and she moved her hands to his chest. "I didn't mean what I said to you. That I don't want you. That's not true at all. I just wanted to get away. So I took off, not really sure where I would go, but then I ended up at the same cabin we stayed in."

"Really?" He smiled too. "The same one?"

"That was the only one available." She laughed a little. "Fate, I guess. All night, I kept thinking about how I made the biggest mistake of my life when I walked away from you. But I didn't know what to do. That fear was so debilitating. And then Tess and Kyra showed up and reminded me that I'm not powerless."

"You were brave, Lyric." It had been difficult for him to stand back simply watching while she confronted Luke. But she hadn't needed his help. "You're so brave."

"All of you make me braver." She backed him up against the trailer, pressing her body to his. "I should've run *to* you instead of running *away* from you. I won't make that mistake again."

"You can come to me about anything." Even her concerns about his family's expectations. "I know it was probably a lot for you to think about having dinner with my family." Especially given everything she'd been dealing with. "We don't have to hang out with them if you're not comfortable. I told you that we didn't have to define our relationship right now, that we could take this at your pace, and that's still true."

"I appreciate that." A smirk replaced her earlier smile. "It would seem that my pace might be picking up speed. I haven't stopped thinking about you, Thatch. Not even for an hour when we're apart."

"Then we're in the same boat." He went to kiss her, but she started talking again.

"All I can think about is when I can be with you again. I love being with you. You make me laugh and you make me feel safe and you bring out the absolute best parts of me." She kissed his lips softly, her lips clinging to his for a few extra seconds. "And I'm sure I'll love your family too. It'll be fun to spend some time with them. If we can still make that work?"

"They'd love that." He tightened his hold around her, lifting her feet off the ground while he kissed her. "And so would I."

Her arms went around his neck and her legs around his waist so he was holding her up, holding her against him, kissing her like he might never have the opportunity again.

Lyric pulled back, her expression suddenly stricken. "What'd you tell your family when I didn't show up?"

He set her feet back on the ground but still didn't let go. "That you broke up with me. That's what I thought. That I'd driven you away."

"No," she whispered an inch from his lips. "No. You made me believe again. That love was possible. That—"

The obnoxious loudspeaker crackled. "Bronc riders, please move to the arena."

"Aw." Lyric's perfectly kissable lips pouted. "I guess we'll have to finish this later."

"We'll have plenty of time." He couldn't resist the temptation to lay one more kiss on her before he climbed onto the back of a bronc with a whole new motivation. "We can finish this at the big barn party tonight. And then at my place or your place after."

"Yes and yes." She stepped away from him, giving him a pat on the butt. "Now go win yourself a new purse."

Thatch laughed. "I'll do my best." They'd taken two steps when he saw their friends had quietly gathered around them, watching everything. "All right. Show's over." He waved them away.

"Sorry, but, oh, my God, that was like watching a scene from a movie." Tess was actually weepy.

Kyra had a hand over her heart. "So beautiful."

"Glad you all approve." Lyric winked at him. "Don't worry. We'll have plenty of alone time later."

How was he supposed to go ride a bronc now? Somehow, he'd have to get his focus back because he had to go in there and kick Luke's ass in front of this whole town. With his score, of course.

Silas shook his hand on his way past. "Good luck."

Aiden clapped him on the back. "Give 'em hell."

He'd give 'em hell all right. One person in particular.

"We'll be watching from the stands," Lyric reminded him. She brushed one more kiss across his lips and then backed away.

"I'll look for you up there." This ride would mean something entirely different from all the others he'd ever taken.

Thatch gave his friends one more wave and then met up with Kirby at the back entrance where the riders were gathering.

"Where have you been?" his trainer demanded. "I should probably give you a pep talk or something."

"I won't need a pep talk today." He had all the motivation he'd need gathering like a storm inside of him. "This will be my best ride to date. I can promise you that." He wouldn't accept anything less.

"Okay, then." Kirby nudged him into the tunnel. "You're up last."

Thatch didn't know if that was a good or a bad thing. "Fine." It didn't matter where he fell in the lineup or who went before him. He would give this everything he had.

They found a place at the fence where they could watch. The first two riders were bucked off short of eight seconds. "Damn. Those are some angry broncs today."

"Wild Bill can hold his own against these guys," Kirby assured him. "Trust me. You've been training on one of the best. They won't throw anything at you that you haven't seen before."

For the most part, Thatch trusted him, but there were some good riders out today. At least three of the guys in the lineup had scored over eighty.

When the announcer introduced Luke Copeland, some cheered in the crowd. Thatch watched the man climb up onto the fence, full of swagger and confidence. Right out of the gate, Luke was in control, boots at the mark out position, free hand high over his head. He had strength and good spurring action, but, in Thatch's estimation, Luke hadn't been doing any yoga.

"He's good," Kirby muttered. "That's your competition, kid."

"I can beat him." He wanted to beat him for Lyric, and Thatch always rose to the occasion.

Luke held on the full eight seconds and then let the bronc throw him, landing on his knees with his arms raised in showmanship. The crowd really went for that, hooting and whistling, and the judge rewarded the performance with a score of eighty-five.

"Damn. That's a good score. Remember, this is your first competition," Kirby said gruffly. "So even a score above eighty would be good."

"A score above eighty isn't good enough." He needed a score above eighty-five. Thatch walked to the bench where he'd stashed his gear earlier that day and started to dress. Chaps, protective vest. Cowboy hat, of course. White today, which seemed fitting in contrast with Luke's black one. While the second-to-last rider was finishing up, Thatch made his way to the chute.

He climbed up onto the fence and scanned the crowds. He had a lot of support today. *There.* Lyric waved at him from about twenty rows up and to his left. All his friends waved, and then his family, too, who were seated ten rows below them. His mom proudly pumped a sign she'd made into the air. THAT'S MY BRONC RIDER! He had to laugh. It didn't matter if he was playing football or lacrosse or bronc riding, she was always his biggest supporter.

His eyes found Lyric again. She'd been through so much to be here. For him. With him. He couldn't let her down.

"Rider ready?" The handler waited for him to slide into the saddle.

With a nod, Thatch took the rope and found his balance with the horse shifting underneath him.

"On your signal." The man looked at him, waiting.

This was it. For one second, Thatch closed his eyes and found the breathing technique Lyric had taught him, and then, without another thought, he gave another nod.

They threw open the gate.

Crowd noise droned around him as he got his boots on the mark. *Forward, easy*. He found the bronc's rhythm, keeping his arm raised, working the spurs for points. Everything blurred into a surreal haze, faces passing by him in a fog. Feeling the animal's movements, he anticipated every buck and lurch and turn, staying fluid and loose, and he even managed to remove his hat and wave it to the crowd.

Cheers rose around him, but he blocked them out, placing his hat back on his head and staying focused and centered. Two more seconds. That was all he needed.

The bronc kicked and spun, lurching Thatch's body left.

No, not left. He fought to stay on, to keep himself upright, his equilibrium intact. *Hold on, hold on…*

That was it. Eight seconds. He had it. And it was a damn good thing because the bronc had had enough. It arched and sent him catapulting off to the side, face-planting him into the dirt. But that didn't matter, because he'd done it. He'd racked up points for style and technique. He was sure of it.

The crowd seemed to agree, the noise rising into a deafening cheer for the hometown rider. Thatch got to his feet looking for Lyric in the stands again. She was moving now, rushing down the steps to the fence. He met her there and kissed her to a collective *awww* from everyone around them.

"Eighty-six."

Thatch almost didn't hear them announce his score, but Lyric squealed. "Eighty-six! You did it! You won!"

He ducked the fence, then, so he could lift her up and into his arms. They laughed together, hugging and kissing, and then they were surrounded by everyone else. Everyone who mattered. His mom and dad. Liam and Sienna. Silas and Tess. Aiden and Kyra.

His family. Their family.

"I knew you could do it," Lyric whispered in his ear. "I'm so proud of you."

"I did it for you." Who cared about the money?

"That's my son!" his mom called from somewhere nearby.

Thatch released Lyric but not before his mother saw them together.

"Oh, my God! Lyric!" His mom hugged her before she even looked at him. "I'm so happy to see you here."

"I'm very happy to be here." She took his hand, and his mom's eyes got even bigger. "Oh, you two!" She slung an arm around both of them. "Does this mean we can do that family dinner again?"

"Yes, please." His girlfriend—girlfriend!—smiled. "You just let me know the time, and I promise I won't miss it."

"Perfect." His mom gasped with excitement. "Maybe we could do a family yoga class too!"

"That'd be fun." Thatch found Lyric's hand and towed her back to him. "Yoga is one of my new favorite things."

CHAPTER TWENTY-FOUR

What do you think about this dress?" Elina cautiously crept out of Lyric's walk-in closet, turning to look at herself in the mirror.

"I think you look fabulous!" She admired the girl in the flowy robin's-egg-blue baby-doll dress, marveling at how far they'd come since that first yoga class. When she and Elina had started to chat after Thatch's award-winning ride earlier that morning, Lyric had asked if she planned to go to the barn dance, and Elina told her she didn't have anything to wear.

Well, *she* had a whole closet of things to wear—dresses she'd worn more often in her old life. So she'd invited the girl to get ready at her house and take her pick of clothes.

"Or should I wear this one?" Elina disappeared back into the closet and emerged holding the hanger of a flowery faux wrap number Lyric had worn to several barn dances back in the day. "You have such amazing clothes. It's impossible to pick my favorite."

"I hardly ever wear dresses anymore." But she might have to start putting some effort into her appearance now that she had a certain cowboy to impress. It would be fun to go on dates again, to dress up occasionally. "That dress you're wearing now really brings out your eyes." She hurried to her bureau and rifled through the jewelry box in search of the perfect complementing necklace. *Aha.*

"Are you sure you don't mind if I wear it?" Elina smoothed her hands down her sides, looking at herself from all angles with a small smile that didn't hide how much she loved the dress.

"I don't mind at all." Lyric clasped the necklace on her. "You can even take the dress home if you want. I don't think I've worn it in years."

"Thank you!" She threw her arms around Lyric in an exuberant hug. "Maybe I could wear it to homecoming next year too."

"I think that'd be perfect." Now for earrings. She started to search through her collection. "Will Franco come back to town for homecoming?"

"I think so," the girl said through a dreamy sigh. Lyric could relate to that tone.

"He's such a great guy. Really supportive." Lyric handed Elina a pair of dangly earrings the same color as the dress as the girl sat on the bed. She ducked into her closet in search of some fun shoes. "But you don't only have to rely on him. You're going to have a lot of support moving forward." Yes, the silver cowgirl boots would look perfect. She handed them to Elina to complete the ensemble.

"Minnie stopped by to talk to Mom." Elina put on the boots and then stood and went back to the mirror, turning and grinning. "I think it went well. She's so nice."

"Minnie is nice." And generous and nurturing. There would be no better person to walk alongside her mom so Elina could simply be a kid. "And we're working on a schedule for meals, so your family should be covered for a while." While the whole town had mingled outside the arena after Thatch's victory, she'd talked to at least twenty people who wanted to help. Minnie had started to spread word at the café as soon as Lyric had run out.

"Mom has always said we don't need anyone's charity." The girl was smiling down at the cowgirl boots on her feet.

"This isn't charity." Lyric found earrings and a necklace for herself. "This is kindness. This is friends coming alongside friends. And, someday, when you come across someone who needs a kind gesture, you'll return the favor."

"I will." Elina abandoned the mirror and hugged her again. "You look really pretty too. Thatch is going to lose his mind when he sees you."

She couldn't wait to see him either. "It's been a while since anyone has seen me dressed up." And getting ready was even more fun knowing she had someone who would be looking at her in an extra-special way tonight. "I guess we should get moving." They were already what could be considered fashionably late.

Elina grabbed the jean jacket Lyric had set out for her. "I'm ready. Thanks to you."

"Perfect." Lyric gave Amos treats and kisses, and then she and Elina walked out the door and got into her car.

"I'd like to keep working at the clinic," the girl said as they pulled away from the curb.

"We'd like that too," Lyric assured her. "You can have complete flexibility. We know school always comes first."

"Yeah. I actually really want to work on getting my grades up. I think it'd be kind of cool to do what Kyra does. Be a nurse practitioner."

"You'd be great at that." Truthfully, the girl would be successful in whatever she tried. She had a lot of grit. "I'm sure Kyra would be happy to help you get there." Lyric would support her on the journey too.

During the rest of the ride to the rodeo grounds, they chatted about what kind of colleges Elina might be interested in attending. By the time she parked, anticipation simmered, warming her through. She looked for Thatch the second she climbed out of her car.

A crowd had already gathered on the patio of the big red barn where they held all the town celebrations. White lights had been strung from light post to light post, shimmering above the dance floor and clusters of tables where people chatted over drinks.

"We'll never find Franco and Thatch," Elina murmured, walking next to her.

"I think they'll find us." Thatch had only texted her three times in the last half hour asking where she was.

"Hey, gorgeous."

Thatch's low vibrato came from behind her. She turned slowly—for added effect. "Look at you, cowboy." She checked him out, letting her gaze move from his crisp button-down shirt and vest to his snug jeans. "Winning awards really agrees with you."

"That was nothing." He pulled her into his arms. "This is what I've been looking forward to all day."

"Oh, there's Franco!" Elina headed off toward the ice cream stand. "See you two later!"

Lyric waved and then went back to admiring her man.

"I'm just warning you: my parents are already here, and they've been waiting for you." Thatch nodded toward the barn. "We could still run."

Lyric laughed. "No, we can't. I'm looking forward to seeing them again."

"Well, that's good." He sighed playfully. "Because here they come."

"Lyric!" Mrs. Hearst waved both arms. "You're here! And oh, my, do you look lovely."

"Thank you." She stepped away from Thatch to greet his mom with a hug. "So do you."

"Have you met Liam and Sienna?" She waved the couple standing behind her forward.

"Not officially, no." They hadn't been in the center of the crowd at Thatch's award ceremony. "It's nice to meet you both."

"Nice to meet you too." Thatch's brother could've been his twin except his hair was a little darker and shorter. "This is some party."

"Everyone comes out for the Star Valley Rodeo Days." She snuck her arm around Thatch's waist. "And this year is extra special because now we have a local celebrity in our midst."

He planted a kiss on her cheek. "I wouldn't have won if you hadn't been there."

"I don't know about that." Thatch had been training hard, and he'd come a long way with his yoga practice too. But she appreciated the sentiment.

"Let's go get some tables." Mrs. Hearst linked one of her arms through Lyric's and the other through Sienna's. "Thatch, you can help your dad and brother get us some drinks."

"Yes, ma'am." He walked away with his dad and brother, discussing the beer choices.

"It's good to see Thatch so happy." His mom steered them to a table next to the dance floor. "I haven't seen him smile this much in a long time."

"I'm not sure he's ever smiled this much," Sienna added. "I'm so happy for you two." The words came across as warm and genuine.

"I've been smiling a lot lately too," Lyric admitted. "And I'm really sorry I didn't make it to dinner yesterday." She wasn't exactly sure how to explain her behavior. "I was dealing with some things."

"Don't you worry about that for one minute." Mrs. Hearst waved off the apology. "You don't owe us an explanation."

"Auntie Lyric!" Tess's daughter, Willow, ran up to her from the dance floor. "We were dancing, but Mommy's tired."

"I'll bet she is." Lyric pulled out a chair for her friend. Poor Tess looked even more pale than she had earlier. "I'm sure dancing isn't easy in your third trimester."

"Nothing's easy in your third trimester." Tess eased herself down into the chair. "I haven't been feeling so hot today."

Silas approached with Morgan. "We should've stayed home."

"No way," Tess grumbled. "I'm not missing the biggest party of the year for a little stomachache. The girls have been looking forward to this for months."

"Auntie Lyric, we only have one more month until the baby's born," Morgan reported.

"I know. It's so exciting." Lyric eyed her friend again. Was she breathing harder than normal? "Are you sure you're okay?"

"I'm great!" Tess smiled a little too brightly for her pallid complexion.

"Drinks." Thatch carted a tray of pitchers and empty glasses to the table. "Beer, margaritas." He winked at Tess. "Soda. Something for everyone."

"Come on, Daddy." Willow tugged on Silas's hand. "Let's dance again!" Silas and his daughters walked away.

Thatch sidled up next to Lyric. "Will you dance with me?"

"You don't even have to ask." She let him lead her away in a two-step while she clung to him, staring into his vivid eyes.

"It's been quite a day," he murmured, his gaze lowering greedily to her lips.

"It has," she agreed, fitting her body to his.

"I kind of can't wait for it to end." The man took her and twirled her away and then back to him.

"Really?" Lyric slowed her movements. "But it's your big day. You won." All his hard work had paid off. "Why would you want the day to end now?"

His hands moved from her hips to her lower back. "All I can think about is going home with you."

"That's all I can think about too," she whispered against his neck.

He spun her again. "Maybe we should go now."

"But it's only seven thirty," she teased. "What would we tell your family?"

"We'll sneak away." He trailed kisses along her neck. "They'll never notice."

Lyric glanced in the direction of their table, and Mrs. Hearst waved at them before snapping a picture. "I'm pretty sure they'd notice." She laughed.

"All right." He played up a sigh. "Fine."

"Uncle Thatch!" Willow pulled on his sleeve. "Can you come and dance with me?"

He hesitated, but Lyric stepped away from him. "Go." No one could resist sweet Willow.

After snapping a few of her own pictures on her phone, she went back to the table and sat next to Tess.

Her friend seemed to be staring off into space. Something wasn't right. "Are you okay?"

"I don't know." Tess shifted in the chair. "I feel like I have indigestion or something. I'm drinking a ginger ale, but it's not helping." She patted her belly.

Uhh . . . maybe she was wrong, but a stomachache this close to her due date couldn't be a good sign. "You haven't felt good all day. Maybe you should get checked out."

"Nah. I might've eaten too much earlier." She sipped the ginger ale. "It was probably the pizza I had yesterday. I've felt off since I woke up."

"Hopefully, you're not in labor." Tess would know, right? Lyric had never had babies, and Tess had already had two.

"No. There's no way." She shook her head, grimacing. "I can't be in labor. We still have three and a half weeks!"

"But due dates aren't always accurate, right?" Her friend liked everything scheduled and planned, but babies didn't follow an agenda.

"I can't be in labor." Tess turned to Lyric, her eyes wide. "We're not ready. The nursery's not even done!" She began breathing harder. "I haven't washed all the clothes and put them away. I was going to do that this week!"

"Don't panic." Lyric put an arm around her shoulders.

"I'm sure you're not in labor." But was she sure? She couldn't be. She wasn't a doctor.

"There are pains, though." Her friend poked at her belly. "And they seem to be getting worse."

"Pains?" Lyric shot up out of her chair, kneeling in front of Tess. "Do they feel like labor pains?"

"I don't know." Her lips formed an O, and she exhaled loudly. "I mean, it's been so long since I had Willow. But I don't remember labor feeling like this."

The tremors in her voice were enough to kindle Lyric's panic. Labor didn't always feel the same, did it? From what Lyric had heard, every experience was so different. "Maybe we should get Kyra, just in case."

"But my suitcase isn't even packed." Tess staggered to a standing position. "We're supposed to have plenty of time to get to Jackson."

Oh, dear. Her friend was about to have a meltdown. "I'm sure everything's fine, but Kyra could at least check." Because God knew Lyric couldn't deliver a baby.

"Oh." Tess clutched her belly. "Oh, dear God. Now, *that* felt like a contraction."

"Kyra!" Lyric sprinted out onto the dance floor. She found her friend and Aiden chatting with Minnie. "I think Tess is in labor." She yanked on Kyra's arm. "You have to come. Now."

"Right behind you." They raced back to the tables where Tess was doubled over again.

"Silas!" Lyric waved both of her arms to get his attention across the dance floor. "We have a situation."

He scooped up both Morgan and Willow and jogged to the table. "What's happening?"

"I'm pretty sure she's in labor." Lyric stared at Tess.

No, she was more than sure. "And the contractions seem really close together."

"Oh, God! Oh, God!" He set down his daughters. "This isn't supposed to be happening yet."

By now everyone had gathered around them. Willow hugged her mom's waist.

"Are you okay, Mommy?"

"I'll be fine, honey," she grunted out.

"I don't think we'll make it an hour to the hospital. We need to go to the clinic." Kyra supported Tess with an arm around her waist. "Now."

Thatch grabbed Aiden. "We'll go get your truck."

Silas moved to the other side of Tess, holding her up. "It's okay, hon. You're doing great. We'll—"

Tess stopped moving. "My water just broke."

"Oh, boy." Now Silas started to breathe harder. "Okay. Everything's gonna be fine. We can do this."

"Can we?" his wife screeched. "Because we're supposed to be at one of the nicest hospitals in Jackson right about now. This is *not* part of my birth plan!"

"Honey..." Kyra took her arm, leading her toward the parking lot. "I don't think you have time to get to Jackson. I'm not even sure an ambulance would make it here in time. You've probably been in labor all day."

Lyric stepped in line with them. "This is so exciting, Tess!" She might not be able to deliver a baby, but she could be the cheerleader and remind her friend this would be one of the best nights of her life. "The baby is coming! You'll get to meet the little one soon."

Tess breathed and nodded, even smiled a little.

Aiden and Thatch drove up in their trucks and both hopped out. It took a group effort to get Tess settled in the back seat, and then Silas, Aiden, and Kyra climbed in with her.

"We've got the girls." Thatch scooped up Willow and set her on his shoulders.

Morgan peered up at Lyric, holding tightly to her hand. "Is Mom going to be okay?"

"She's going to be great!" She kept hold of the girl's hand, and they all made their way to Thatch's truck. "And you're going to have a new baby in your family very soon."

"I can't wait to be a big sister!" Willow clapped. "This is the best day ever!"

All the way to the clinic, the girls started to brainstorm names for their new sibling.

"I like Charlie for a boy and Amanda for a girl," Morgan announced.

"No." Willow scrunched up her face. "Brady for a boy, and Jenny for a girl."

Her older sister rolled her eyes. "Those are your friends' names at school."

"You both have some great ideas." Thatch smiled at Lyric and took her hand in his. "But sometimes you have to wait to see the baby before you know what to name it." He parked the truck in front of the clinic.

Both girls scrambled to take off their seat belts and tore into the old house ahead of them.

"How're things going?" Lyric asked Aiden, who was pacing around the waiting room.

"Sounds like this is moving pretty fast." He nudged her toward the hallway that led to the exam rooms. "Kyra might need an extra set of hands, and believe me, I'm not qualified."

"I've got it." Before moving down the hallway, she

directed Thatch to the paper and markers in a drawer. "You guys can draw some pictures for the new baby." That might make the waiting easier.

Lyric ran down the hall and into the first exam room. Tess was on the table, and Silas was holding her hand, trying to help her breathe.

"Oh, good." Kyra pulled her to the end of the table and handed her gloves. "She's going to start pushing. Ambulance is still ten minutes out for a transport to Jackson. We're going to have this baby soon."

"Got it." Lyric pulled on the gloves.

"Everything's going great so far," Kyra said soothingly. "Baby's heartbeat sounds perfect, so now I'm just going to have you start pushing, okay, Tess?"

Their friend grunted a response.

"I'll let you know what I need," Kyra whispered to Lyric. "But I'm fully anticipating everything will go smoothly."

She didn't doubt that at all with her friend in charge.

While Kyra directed Tess through the pushing, Lyric offered encouragement every now and then. She got teary watching Silas lean over his wife, kissing her head and murmuring softly to her. Such a beautiful moment.

"Okay, head is crowning, so we need one more push." Kyra handed Lyric some towels and then grabbed an aspirator. "Ready? Let's go, Tess. Give me everything you've got."

Lyric was crying now, watching this precious new life unfold. Kyra delivered the baby and then secured him in the blanket. A him!

"It's a boy," Kyra announced, handing the bundle to Lyric and then suctioning his mouth.

Lyric used the towel to carefully clean the little sweetheart.

"A boy?" Silas let out a cheer, and Tess sobbed joyfully, her head now resting back on the pillows.

"Meet your new sweet boy." Lyric moved the baby to Tess's chest, and he started to wail. She stepped back and pulled off her gloves so she could take pictures while Kyra walked Silas through cutting the cord.

The paramedics rushed in with a gurney and started tending to Tess while Kyra gave them an update.

Lyric stepped to the bed and helped Tess swaddle the baby.

"The girls." Her friend was still out of breath from her heroic efforts. "I want the girls to see him before we go. Aiden and Thatch too."

"On it." Lyric covered her friend's lower half with a sheet and then ran out to get them all. She brought in Morgan and Willow by the hands, and they rushed to their mom's side. One by one, Silas lifted them onto the bed, and their little family all huddled together.

Thatch came up behind Lyric and wrapped his arms around her.

"What's his name, Mommy?" Willow asked.

"Jace." Silas took the baby into his arms, still leaning over his girls. "His name is Jace."

They all lost it then. Lyric glanced around the room, and she wasn't the only one bawling.

Thatch rested his chin on her shoulder, sniffling. "What an incredible moment."

"Beautiful." For the first time ever, she wondered if she could have a moment like this someday too.

CHAPTER TWENTY-FIVE

Liam stopped in the middle of the trail and patted the backpack he wore until he found his water bottle. "I'm not sure a hike was a great idea before yoga."

Thatch laughed. "Feeling the altitude, are we?" After living here for the past few years, he forgot there was a little adjustment when you weren't used to the elevation.

"We're higher than Iowa, that's for sure." His brother took a long drink. When Thatch had suggested a morning hike before their big family yoga session, his brother had been all about it, but they hadn't made it very far. Distance wasn't the point of this outing, though. After everything that had happened between them, they were forging a new relationship.

Thatch parked it on a rock and let his brother rest. "We can quit now, if you want." Hell, they could hang out here in the sunshine and the fresh air among the aspen trees. There were worse places to sit and talk.

"But you said there're some good views in the meadow

up ahead." Liam wiped his forehead with the end of his shirt. "I'm not going to wimp out now."

"Suit yourself." Thatch waited until his brother got going so Liam could set the pace.

His brother trudged up the trail in front of him. "You've built quite the life for yourself here."

"Star Valley has become home." He hadn't expected to put down roots, but now he wouldn't want to live anywhere else. "There're good people here." His best friends. Really, they were more like his family now.

"I've gotta say, I didn't think you'd stay." The slope grew steeper, and Liam paused. "I mean, I know you came to help Tess after Jace passed away, but then I thought you'd be off traveling the world again."

"I'll still do some traveling." He had a whole list of places he'd like to take Lyric. "But it's nice to have a place you feel like you belong. The way you do on the farm." It was strange to realize he and his brother didn't really know each other at all anymore, and that had to change.

"I'm glad you found your place." Liam started hiking again. "And I'm glad we can spend time together again. I hope we can make this a more regular thing."

"Me too." Thatch passed him by, his old habits dying hard. "The meadow I was telling you about is right up here." He took the last switchback quickly, knowing Liam wouldn't be able to resist staying with him.

They crested the hill out of breath and laughing, but then Liam stopped abruptly. "Wow. You weren't kidding. These are some views."

"Never gets old." Thatch gazed at the glacial pond set in front of cragged mountain peaks. Who needed public trails when he could hike on Silas and Tess's land and witness vistas like this? "Those are the wildies over there." He pointed to the pasture he'd helped them section off to house the herd of wild horses Tess cared for through her sanctuary.

"Incredible." Liam snapped a few pictures on his phone. "Sienna's gonna be bummed she missed this." His brother seemed to hesitate before speaking again. "I didn't want her to come because she's pregnant."

"What?" Thatch went in for a hug. "Seriously? That's amazing."

"I don't know why I was afraid to tell you." Liam shot him a guilty look. "I don't want to worry about telling you things anymore."

"You shouldn't." He hoped his brother could sense the sincerity in the words. "I'm not sure I was ever as angry at you as I was with myself, Liam." Because he'd pushed so hard for this future he thought he wanted. He'd pushed too hard, and it had all fallen apart. "You two are great together. And you're going to be great parents too."

"Thanks." His brother took a drink of water, hesitating again. "I know we're not as close as we used to be, but we were hoping you'd be the baby's godfather."

"Sign me up." As far as he was concerned, from this moment on, they were close. "You're my brother. I'd do anything for you." He'd do anything for his family.

They hugged it out once more, and then Liam studied him. "Think you and Lyric will get married?"

"I don't have an agenda this time." And that was freeing. "I love her, and I want to give her the kind of life *she* wants. Whatever that looks like." He wouldn't push Lyric into marriage. He wouldn't envision their future for them alone. He wanted them to build their future together. At their own pace.

"I'm just warning you that Mom has all kinds of ideas about the grandkids and cousins visiting the farm together."

"That sounds like her," he said with a laugh. "And I'm not saying it's impossible." Something had clicked in him when he'd seen Silas holding his baby boy for the first time. "But we won't be rushing into anything."

Liam pushed his shoulder. "You're a lot wiser than you used to be."

"I'm a lot faster too." Thatch took off down the trail, leaving his brother to chase him. "Last one down there has to be front and center in the yoga class."

Liam's voice was growing more distant. "Oh, hell no!"

But about halfway down, he let his brother catch up. Thatch could be front and center at yoga. He'd actually gotten pretty good.

The rest of the way down the trail, they talked about the farm and reminisced, getting to the studio ten minutes late.

"I thought you boys were going to skip," their mom scolded.

"Not a chance." Thatch went to steal a quick kiss from Lyric while she messed with a Bluetooth speaker.

"Did you two have a nice time?" She fully faced him, setting her hands on his hips.

"We had a great time." But he would have an even better time here. With her.

"Until he wanted to race me down the trail," Liam threw in. "You'll have to go easy on us, Lyric. I'm already exhausted."

"I can do that." She started to hand out mats.

"What are you boys, five years old still?" Their mother chastised them with a good shake of her head while she rolled out her mat.

"It's always gotta be a competition with you two," their dad said fondly while he set out his mat at the back of the studio.

"That's what brothers do." Sienna was smiling bigger than Thatch had seen her smile the whole time she'd been in Star Valley.

He positioned his mat next to Lyric's. "I just had to remind him who's faster." He and Liam used to race everywhere—down the stairs for dinner, home from school, out to the tree house their had dad built for them.

"He didn't win," his brother informed everyone. "It ended up being a tie."

"Oh, for Pete's sake," their mother mumbled, but happiness shimmered in her eyes.

"All right, everyone. Let's go ahead and get started." Lyric used a remote control to turn on calming music, but you really couldn't hear it between his dad and brother discussing what kind of flooring the studio had and his mom and Sienna commenting on how nice and cushy the mats were.

"Good luck," Thatch mouthed to Lyric. She was going to have her work cut out for her with this crew.

The extra chattiness didn't seem to bother her. She directed them all to start with a breathing warm-up, and then they went through seated side bends.

His brother groaned. "I'm not even bending."

"I can't sit up straight," their dad added, still hiding in the back of the group.

"Thatch couldn't either, when he first started," Lyric told them. "Do what you can do. Flexibility is a process."

Ha. He seemed to remember her "helping" him get into poses during his first few sessions. Not that he'd minded her touching him.

"Let's move into some cat/cow spinal stretching," she suggested.

Then his father proceeded to moo every time he moved into the cow stretch, which made everyone crack up, including Lyric. His father had always nailed the whole dad humor thing.

"Next time, we're only doing a girls' yoga session," his mother announced, following all the rules and movements perfectly, as per usual. "Poor Lyric, having to put up with all this silliness."

His dad shrugged, still in a cow stretch. "What can I say? I'm much better at humor than I am at yoga."

"That's debatable," Thatch muttered, making everyone laugh again.

They were never going to get through this class.

"I'm actually having a wonderful time with you all. I want this to be fun." Lyric raised an eyebrow. "Tell me the truth, though, how bad are things going to get if we go into a downward dog pose?"

"You don't want to know," Liam said.

"Downward dog is one of my favorites." Sienna smirked. "At least when no one is cracking jokes."

"That settles it." Lyric assumed the position. "Everyone, curl your toes under and push your hips up toward the sky." She lifted her head and aimed a playfully stern frown at their father. "But no barking please."

"I wouldn't dream of it," he said solemnly.

But then the man started to sing John Denver songs when they were in mountain pose, and his family continued to talk the entire time too. They'd never known how to be quiet.

After they'd ended with a few sun salutations, everyone started to roll up their mats.

His father brought his to the shelf first. "I didn't believe yoga would fix my posture." He paused dramatically. "But I *stand* corrected."

Thatch shared a wince with his brother. "Yikes."

Lyric seemed to think the joke was hilarious, though.

"Don't encourage him." His mom nudged his dad away from Lyric. "What a fabulous class. Thank you, honey. You absolutely have to come and visit us on the farm sometime."

Whoa. Next thing they knew, she'd be asking about a wedding date. "Mom, Lyric's pretty busy—"

"I'd love to come and visit the farm." She put her arm around him. "Maybe in the fall."

"Oh, it's lovely in the fall." *See? Told you so*, his mom seemed to say with her eyes.

"We've got to head out." Liam put his and Sienna's mats away. "We're doing a Jeep tour this afternoon."

"But thank you for the class. I feel wonderful." Sienna squeezed Lyric's hand warmly, and Thatch could hardly believe how comfortable all of this was, his family together, Lyric with them. Everything seemed to fit.

"We're on our way out too," his mother informed them. "We're meeting Minnie and Louie for happy hour."

"Sounds fun." Thatch tried not to look as thrilled as he felt that he could spend the rest of the evening alone with Lyric.

"But we'll see you both for breakfast in the morning before we head out," she said on her way through the door. "Nine o'clock. Don't be late."

After the door closed, Thatch let out a long, slow, yoga cleansing breath. "I'm sorry my family's so weird."

"Are you kidding?" Lyric walked her hands up his chest. "They're hilarious. And so welcoming and friendly." Her smile brightened. "They make me feel like I fit right in."

"You do." He kissed her, leaning into her, breathing her in. "You fit perfectly."

CHAPTER TWENTY-SIX

What a place to grow up." Lyric watched out the window, taking in the rolling kelly-green hills that were sectioned into fields growing various types of crops in neat rows. Red and white barns dotted the landscape with contrasting colors, their silos bookending the squared structures. Huge oaks, white ash, and sugar maples filled in the spaces between the farms, tire swings hanging from their branches.

"It was an incredible place to grow up." Thatch slowed the truck and turned off onto a dirt road between two cornfields growing taller than them. "I pretty much lived outside from sunup to sundown, working on the farm but also swimming in the pond, fishing in the creek, climbing trees, and getting lost in the cornfields."

"I could see how that would happen." She took his hand and gazed out the window, fascinated with the tall stalks.

"I'm so glad you're here with me." He slowed the

truck again and turned onto another road where the fields ended, and trees encircled a sprawling brick ranch-style house. "Mom may be even more thrilled than me that you're coming."

"I'm thrilled too." For reasons she couldn't disclose to him quite yet. The four months they'd spent together after their initial fake relationship had flown past. In some ways, though, it seemed she'd known him her whole life. "I wouldn't have missed spending your birthday with your family. It's going to be so fun to see where you grew up. And to meet your grandma and all your aunts and uncles and cousins."

"You may want to wait to say that until you've actually met them," he teased. "Don't forget, my mom and dad each have five siblings, and most of them will be here with their kids and even a few grandkids. Thankfully, we have a couple of hours before the big bash. That way we can ease you into the Hearst crowd in small doses."

"I'm ready," she assured him. The Hearst crowd could throw anything at her, and she'd still be standing by his side. After a whole summer of dates and hikes, weekend camping trips and lazy evenings at her house or his on the couch together, she was ready for so much more.

"Okay." He drew the word out as he parked the truck.

His parents must've heard them coming because they both appeared on the home's wraparound porch, waving.

"You're here!" His mom got to them first. "Welcome to the farm!"

"I'm so happy to be here." Lyric had grown to love her hugs, warm and encompassing. She hugged Carl next before Thatch's dad insisted on getting both of their suitcases by himself.

"How was the drive?" Nancy ushered her up the porch steps, where there was a real porch swing overlooking the yard. Lyric hoped she'd get to sit there when the fireflies came out later tonight.

"The drive was fun." She'd never thought she would say that after sixteen hours in a car, but everything was fun when she and Thatch were together.

"Good, good. You must be starving." Nancy opened the creaky screen door and gestured for her and Thatch to go inside.

Everything about the great room Lyric stepped into screamed *farmhouse chic*. From weathered oak floors to the white country-style cabinets in the kitchen across the room to the fieldstone fireplace between two large picture windows. "I love your home." It was warm and cozy and a place she'd want to come back to again and again.

"It belonged to my grandparents," Carl said proudly. "We've renovated it, of course. But these are the original floors."

"I remember refinishing the floors," Thatch said with a wince.

"No one gets out of any work at the farm." His dad lumbered down a hallway, dragging the two suitcases behind him.

"I have snacks." Nancy waved her into the kitchen, where a spread of yummy-looking dips, chips, cheeses, and crackers sat. "And sun tea." She poured four glasses from a pitcher.

While they snacked, his parents told her embarrassing stories about Thatch, and he pretended to be annoyed but never stopped smiling.

Her darling boyfriend took her hand and prompted

her off the stool. "How about a little walking tour of the property?"

"Sure. I could go for that." She started to help bring dishes to the sink, but Nancy shooed her away. "You two go off and have some time alone together while you still can."

"The whole circus will be here in about an hour," his dad added. "Which reminds me, I'd better check on the smoker."

Lyric thanked them—for probably the tenth time already—and then let Thatch lead her out the back door. The deck, which already had multiple tables set up for the party, overlooked a large pond with a small dock and a canoe. To the left of the pond was an elaborate tree house with a rope ladder perched about ten feet off the ground in a weeping willow tree.

"Wow. You really did have the perfect childhood." Not that hers had been bad—growing up five minutes from the beach in Florida before moving to the mountains. But this farm had a feeling of longevity, perseverance, and resilience. That was why this would be the perfect place for her to propose. They could come back here often, and their kids could swim in that pond and play in the tree house.

"No childhood is perfect." Thatch took her hand and led her down the steps and into the thick green grass. "But it was probably as close as you could get." He pointed at the tree house. "We helped Dad build that when I was six and Liam was four. My first construction project."

"Very impressive." It wasn't your typical shack of a tree house. It had real windows and an upper lookout deck.

"I used to skinny-dip in this pond sometimes too." He peeked over his shoulder toward the house as though making sure they were alone, and then he pulled her close. "A memory I'd like to re-create with you. Maybe later tonight?"

"Maybe." Oh, who was she kidding? "Probably." Like she could resist him. "Definitely."

He laughed low, the way he did when they were in bed together and teasing each other. "I wonder how fast we'll be able to kick everyone out of here tonight."

"Won't there be, like, sixty people?" She grinned at him. "Skinny-dipping might have to wait until tomorrow night." And she would have to test the temperature of the water first. She pulled him closer to the tree house and then sat on the wooden plank swing hanging from one of the branches. "I haven't done this in years."

Thatch moved behind her and pushed her, swinging her high up in the air, her feet dangling, hair flowing. "Such a special place." Hopefully, it would be a special place for them always.

Thatch grabbed the ropes and slowed her down, bringing her to a stop. "It's even more special when you're here." He kissed her cheek and then her neck, making her body sigh with happiness. She turned her head to offer her lips too, but the sound of an engine interrupted them.

"They're early. Probably because they can't wait to meet you." Thatch kissed her once more, and then they walked around the house hand in hand to greet the masses.

Over the next half hour, Lyric was introduced to so many aunts, uncles, cousins, and nieces and nephews that there was no way she would remember everyone's names. His grandma arrived fashionably late in her newer-model

Caddy, and it was fitting how the crowds all parted for her car, the matriarch of their family.

Grandma Kay seemed to look for someone when she stood in the driveway.

"Thatch! You bring that girl right over here to me now," she called, leaning on her bedazzled cane.

He gave the elderly woman a sweet gentle hug first and then nudged Lyric in front of him. "Gran, this is my girl-friend, Lyric."

"So nice to meet you, Mrs. Hearst."

"Gran," the woman insisted. "Everyone calls me Gran. Oh, my, you are a beautiful girl." She hugged her almost the same way Nancy had. "Welcome to the family, honey."

"Thank you," Lyric said at the same time Thatch cleared his throat. He was probably still nervous that comments like that would make her uncomfortable.

Little did he know.

The next hour passed in a blur of chitchat and yard games and kids and dogs running around, and it was so beautiful how this big family all came together, function-ing in chaotic harmony.

"Grub's on," Carl called just after Lyric and Thatch had won a cornhole game.

Lyric didn't know how long it took to get everyone through the buffet line, but she didn't mind the wait as all of these people were so friendly and interested in her—where she'd come from, what she did for a living. A few of Thatch's cousins even asked if she could put on an out-door yoga class later in the week.

They took their seats at a table with Carl and Nancy and Gran, Liam, and Sienna. When the food was mostly gone and the sun hovered low over the tree line, Lyric gave Carl a wink. As they'd discussed on the phone when she'd called them last week, Thatch's dad used an air horn to quiet the crowd.

"Thank you all for coming out to celebrate Thatch's birthday." He put his arm around his wife. "There were many times we wondered if he would make it home when he was serving his country, so every birthday we get to celebrate with him is extra special."

Uh-oh. Lyric dabbed at her eyes with a napkin. She was already crying.

"Love you two." Thatch stood up and hugged them both. "And thanks for a party that is somehow more epic every year than it was the last."

Everyone started talking again, but Carl held up his hand. "Hold on, now. Our guest has something she would like to say too."

That was her cue.

Thatch gave her a funny look as he sat back down and she stood, pushing in her chair and trying to get her nerves under control. It wasn't only being in front of all these people that had her heart rate going. It was the anticipation of what would come—the future, *their* future together. These people—the family Thatch loved—would all be a part of that future. That was why she wanted them all to be a part of the moment that would mean so much to both of them.

For a second she tried to squelch the tears, but the effort proved futile. She turned to the man she loved, the man who'd helped her believe in love, and tuned out everyone else sitting around them. "Thatch, these last five months have been the absolute best of my whole life." She waited for the collective *awww*s to die down. "I love you in a way

I've never loved anyone else. I love you in a way I know I *could* never love anyone else." The rest of her speech got fuzzy, but that was okay because only one question truly mattered right now. "So I was hoping you'd marry me?"

"What?" He launched out of his chair and swept her up into his arms, laughing. "Are you serious? You're asking me to marry you?"

"Yes, Thatch Hearst." She could hardly see through the tears now. "Will you marry me?"

His smile turned serious as he gazed at her, almost like he was memorizing the details of her face. "I love you that way too, Lyric. I'll never love anyone the way I love you."

She felt that love all the way down to her toes. But she also had to tease him. "Umm...is that a yes?"

He held her face in line with his, his hands on her jaw. "Yes." He kissed her lightly and then pulled back. "*Hell yes.*"

The party really started then. While they were kissing, the hoots, hollers, and toasts started and might've kept going on all night from the sound of things.

In the middle of all that noise, Lyric stared into Thatch's eyes, only the two of them standing in the middle of a promise, a dream she never thought she would be able to claim.

But love had a healing power all its own.

ACKNOWLEDGMENTS

My biggest thanks go to all my readers who have joined me on this journey to Star Valley. I appreciate you so much, and I hope you will carry happy memories from your visit along with you.

I am forever grateful to my family for the support, encouragement, and sacrifices that allow me to continue doing what I love. Will, AJ, and Kaleb—you are truly my greatest blessings. It's simply not possible to list all of the incredible family members and friends who enrich my life on a daily basis. Words cannot express how grateful I am for all of you.

There are so many people behind the scenes who don't get nearly enough credit for the incredible work they do. A special thank-you to my editorial team—Amy Pierpont and Sam Brody, and to all of the amazing professionals I'm so blessed to work with at Forever. I appreciate your hard work and dedication more than I can say! And no acknowledgments would be complete without a shout-out to my fabulous agent and her team. Thank you, Suzie Townsend, Sophia Ramos, and Olivia Coleman. You are rock stars!

ABOUT THE AUTHOR

National bestselling author **Sara Richardson** writes uplifting stories about love, friendship, and family. In addition to authoring romance novels, she also writes women's fiction under the pen name Eliza Evans. Her books have received numerous award nominations and critical acclaim, with *Publishers Weekly* recognizing her stories as "emotionally rich, charmingly funny, and sensitive."

Completing a master's degree in journalism inspired Sara to become a storyteller, and she wrote her first novel soon after. When not writing, Sara can be found traveling to adventurous destinations, teaching Pilates, and living the lake life with her family in the Upper Midwest.

You can learn more at:
  SaraRichardson.net
  X @SaraElizaBooks
  Facebook.com/BooksbySaraandEliza
  Instagram @BooksbySaraandEliza

Enjoy the best of Western romance with these handsome, rugged cowboys from Forever!

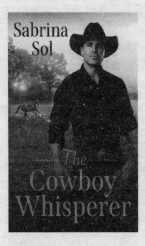

THE COWBOY WHISPERER
by Sabrina Sol

After her last disastrous competition, Olympic hopeful Veronica del Valle is finally ready for another shot. The family-run ranch where she's training lacks the amenities she's used to, but what Rancho Lindo does have is a handsome cowboy who offers Veronica unsolicited advice. Tomás cares only about his horses and the ranch—and not their unhappy boarder. But he soon realizes Veronica is nothing like he imagined, and the harder he falls, the more he worries her dreams will eventually take her away.

SECOND CHANCE AT RANCHO LINDO
by Sabrina Sol

After being wounded in the military, Gabe Ortega has returned home to Rancho Lindo. But he plans to leave again as soon as possible—despite his family's wishes—until he runs into a childhood friend. The beautiful Nora Torres is now a horticulturist in charge of the ranch's greenhouse. She's usually a ray of sunshine, so why has she been giving him the cold shoulder? As they work together and Gabe breaks down her walls, he starts to wonder if everything he'd been looking for had been here all along.

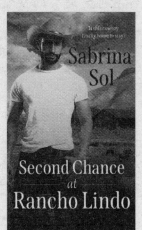

Connect with us at Facebook.com/ReadForeverPub

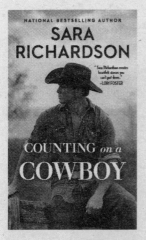
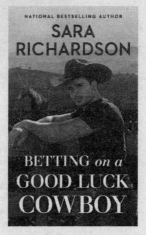

MONTANA PROUD
by R. C. Ryan

Get swept away with two cowboys in the McCords series. In *Montana Legacy*, a reserved rancher is content to live alone years after the one person he ever let in suddenly left. Now she's back, and he's determined to resist her charms. But soon he must protect their very lives—and growing chemistry—from an unseen enemy. In *Montana Destiny*, a woman who lives for trouble stumbles upon a clue to the legendary McCord gold. Now she's in a mysterious killer's sights—and the arms of an irresistible McCord playboy who claims he finally wants to settle down. Trust is the one thing she can't easily give…but when danger closes in fast, only surrendering to each other can ensure their survival.

SECOND CHANCE COWBOY
by A. J. Pine

Ten years ago, Jack Everett left his family's ranch without a backward glance. Now what was supposed to be a quick trip home for his father's funeral has suddenly become more complicated. The ranch Jack can handle—he might be a lawyer, but he still remembers how to work with his hands. But turning around the failing vineyard he's also inherited? That requires working with the one woman he never expected to see again. Includes a bonus story by Sara Richardson!